The little boy who could talk to BIGFOOT

Gigantopithecus Primates of Humboldt County, California

Dante P. Chelossi Jr.

ISBN   Softcover   978-1-950580-61-3
            eBook   978-1-950580-62-0

Printed in the United States of America.

To order additional copies of this book, contact:
Bookwhip
1-855-339-3589
https://www.bookwhip.com

I want to dedicate this book to my two newest grandsons. Harley Wyatt Osborne, and Beau Allen-Lee Christen. Harley came first in 2013, and Beau followed in 2014. I am very happy to be able to say that I now have some grandsons, and I also hope that I can live another twenty years or longer so that I can have an opportunity for them to get to know me. For now, they are young infant's that do not have a clue in the world who I am, but maybe, as they get older, they will like me as a person that they can look up too, and understand how much that I love them. Let me tell you little guy's a secret…I used both of your first names for a character in the later parts of this book. I think that is kind of cool. Love always, your Grandpa… Dante' P. Chelossi Jr.

P.S.….Maybe someday when you guys are old enough you might decide to read some of my books. That would be cool too.

Acknowledgement

I WANT TO GIVE a great big thank you to Dakota Daetwiler once again for creating a beautiful cover for this latest book that I have written. She also did a wonderful job in creating a fantastic cover for my last book. Now she has two book covers that will forever be in the Library of Congress of the United States Of America. I feel very honored to have had the opportunity to hire someone like Dakota who has such a high level of artistic talent. She now has an Art studio located in Fortuna, California… so I suggest to anyone who wants to see wonderful works of art, and maybe have thought's of hiring someone as talented as this woman, go in and meet her, look at her work, I bet that you will be amazed at what you see, and I bet you might purchase one of her works, or even hire her as I did. Dakota…you are a born artist of the highest degree…Take care…and once again…Thank you so very much from the bottom of my heart…Dante' P. Chelossi Jr.

Chapter One

A GLIMMER OF SUNLIGHT seeped through the center of the window where the light blue curtains were parted slightly a few inches. It crept up towards the top of a small bed where a little boy slept.

It grazed the side of his face, and came to rest directly on top of his right eye.

His eyelashes detected a small portion of this sunlight and caused an eye to blink a few times.

The little boy stirred a bit, and moved over out of the path of this ray of sunshine.

This little boy was named Augustus.

Everyone called him "Augy."

His father, Samuel Goodson, was well known throughout the world as a person who was obsessed with hunting the mythical species of ape called by many names, the most notable being "Bigfoot."

Samuel Goodson traveled all around the world in search of evidence that this creature was still alive in modern times.

At the present time, he and his young son were in central Malaysia following a good tip that he had received a few months ago from another Bigfoot hunter.

Shortly, they would leave the hotel to travel to a wildlife refuge that was very large in size, and had barely ever been investigated by very many humans up to this point in time.

After breakfast, they would travel for half of an hour to meet their paid guides.

They were going to be guided by two locals from a village that was located a few miles from the boundary of this wildlife refuge.

Jubine and Destra were their names.

These two guides were very nervous about this paid assignment to lead this man called Samuel Goodson, and his son, through this very dense forest.

This was a place that people avoided because of the local legend about a monster that inhabited the area.

There had been many sightings going back many generations, of this monster.

The monster was supposed to stand over eight feet tall, and have hair over it's entire body.

Nobody could ever remember an instance where this creature had harmed anyone.

But the fear was still present with the people who lived near the area.

The only reason that these two guides agreed to take this man and his young son into this area was obviously the money.

They were being paid very well for this assignment.

The money was equivalent to what they might make in half of a years work.

One condition for them before they agreed to this assignment was that they be allowed to carry high powered rifles with them.

Samuel Goodson agreed to this because he had been having a very hard time in finding anyone, that would agree to this assignment as guides.

Breakfast ended, and Samuel Goodson, along with his son "Augy," loaded up their gear in the vehicle that would take them to where their guides were waiting for them.

Half an hour later, they were at the site where their guides... "Jubine" and "Destra" stood waiting.

Both men had with them, high powered hunting rifles slung over their shoulders.

Within a few minutes, all four people departed in the direction of the dense forest that was only about a quarter of a mile away from the meeting spot.

Samuel Goodson and his son both carried with them, high powered binoculars.

Samuel Goodson's binoculars had a built in computer hard drive that had the capability to take a photograph if needed.

His son's binoculars did not have this same capability.

All four people carried backpacks with their essential items for this trip.

Both guides had machete's with them to use whenever they came across vegetation that was to thick to get through.

At first, there really was no need to use these machete's, because the jungle was not to dense in vegetation to travel through.

As they traveled through this forest, there was a wide variety of sounds coming from many different animals.

Most of these sounds were familiar.

Monkey's, and bird's made up the majority of these sounds.

As they looked around them while they walked, they could see some of these animals that were making these sounds.

Samuel Goodson was already taking some pictures with his photo-binoculars.

The terrain that they traveled on was constantly changing.

Sometimes they were walking on very flat ground, and sometimes they walked downwards and upwards through slightly rolling hills.

Within an hour, they had already traveled very deep into this beautiful, seemingly non-human occupied jungle.

As far as anyone knew, there was not, or ever had been any human occupation anywhere in this pristine jungle.

There had been attempts in the past by logging companies to try and get permission, to do some cutting of tree's in this forest, but these request's were always denied by the government agencies that had jurisdiction over this area of land.

The two men that were acting as guides for Samuel Goodson did not talk very much.

They were too busy with their eyes and ears, capturing, and analyzing all of the minute sounds and sights around them as they led the way forward.

Little "Augy" was very quiet as well because this was his normal demeanor.

Little "Augy" did not communicate very well with people.

He was severely autistic.

One would not be able to detect that he was autistic unless they tried to communicate with him.

Otherwise, he acted like any other normal little boy.

His father never sent him to a special needs school for various reasons.

He decided early on after he found out that his son had autism, that he would take it upon himself to take care of the boy, and teach him everything that he could to function as well as possible in society.

The boys mother had died during child birth due to complications that the doctors were not able to successfully take care of.

This was a devastating life event for Samuel Goodson.

His wife had also shared in his enjoyment of pursuing evidence of whether or not "Bigfoot" actually existed.

It took Samuel Goodson a little over two years to get over the pain of the loss of the love of his life… his dear wife "Tara."

He finally was able to mentally pull himself back together enough to get back to his passion of finding evidence of the existence of a large creature called by many names… where he came from… "Bigfoot."

This was also about the same time frame that he was told by doctors that his son "Augy" was autistic.

This news hurt him slightly at the time, but he quickly made decisions in regards to how he would handle this condition with his son, and quickly moved on.

They would be a team… father and son, searching for this evasive creature all throughout the world.

So now, this father and son team were in a thick jungle, somewhere in Malaysia, being led by two local guides, who quietly went about their business as guides, but harboring fear within them… every step they took through this jungle.

"Augy" did not feel any fear.

He remained silent, but curious about all of the things that he was observing as he followed his father through the jungle.

Sometimes he would stop to use his binoculars to look at something that caught his attention.

Unknown to even his own father was the fact that "Augy" had hearing and sight that was beyond what a normal human had.

His sight was far superior than normal people.

His hearing was extraordinary, and also very superior to the average person.

Because of his autism, he was not able to communicate very well with his father, or others.

He made mostly garbled sounds, mixed in with a small amount of English when he spoke.

Only his father was able to translate these sounds mixed with the English well enough to where he was able to understand what his son was trying to say.

How did other people react when they heard these garbled sounds mixed with a little English from his mouth?

Forget it, the boy was unintelligible to them.

They traveled for another hour and a half through the jungle before the guides finally had to start using their machete's at various locations to travel any farther.

For the past half of an hour, unknown to anyone accept "Augy," there was a presence in the distance that was aware of them as they traveled deeper into this jungle.

"Augy," with his superior eyesight had already seen brief glimpses of a large creature covered in dark hair.

Because of the many sounds emanating from the jungle around them as they walked, "Augy" was not able to hear this creature . . . yet.

He did not attempt to communicate with his father about what he was seeing.

He just continued to walk behind his father and the two guides.

Finally, the two guides decided that it was time to take a break, and so they found a small clearing to set up a temporary camp to rest and eat.

They would not stay here for very long though, because they wanted to get to higher ground for an over night encampment.

This could be compared to a race car pit stop, they would be here only long enough to replenish themselves for enough energy to continue their hike to where they would finally set up camp.

Meanwhile, they were being monitored without their knowledge.

There was indeed a creature that knew that they were there in the jungle where he lived in privacy from the world of humans.

He stood seven inches over eight feet tall when he stood upright.

His feet measurements were huge, compared to that of a human.

His body was completely covered by very thick dark hair that was several inches long.

This creature was absolutely massive in size if he were to stand side by side with an average human man.

His girth and weight was huge as well.

This particular creature weighed almost 1100 lbs.

He had very sharp vision, and his hearing was phenomenal.

He was approximately a hundred yards away from where this temporary encampment was.

He was looking at the little human boy out of pure curiosity.

It seemed as if this small human could detect his presence.

Several times, he had noticed that the small human boy had been looking directly at him, even from the distance that separated them.

This creature had indeed seen other humans in the past, but had always kept a safe distance from them.

He did not fear them because of their size, as compared to himself.

He could sense a danger from them that no other animal that he had ever encountered… projected towards him.

The dominant way that they carried themselves, not showing any apparent fear for any animal that they came in contact with.

This made him feel instinctively like he had to always keep a safe distance from them, and certainly never come into contact with one of them.

This was the only creature that he did not feel a dominance over as a species.

He stealthily walked through the dense forest to another spot, still at a safe distance from the people that he was tracking.

He turned his head, and looked at the little young human.

He was startled!!

This little human was looking directly at him… eye too eye!!

Their eyes were locked in a gaze… directly at one another, as if looking at each other in a mirror.

He tilted his head sideways to the right, and then in the opposite direction to the left, and then back to normal to see if there was a reaction from the little human.

To his surprise, the little human mimicked him exactly, tilting his small head back and forth.

Now he was absolutely sure that this small young human was in fact looking at him.

He thought of running, and hiding deeper into the jungle, but he knew that he was already at a safe distance from the humans, and he also knew that the other larger, and older humans could not see him as this young human was able to do at this very moment.

So he just stood there watching the small young human, to see if he would alert the older humans about his presence.

He did not in any way, alert the older humans about him.

This made him even more curious about this small young human.

Why did he not tell the older humans that they were being watched by him?

Maybe the small young human was harmless… and friendly?

It did not matter if the small young human was friendly or not, he did not like to have these humans in the jungle where he lived.

He wanted them to leave the jungle.

He decided that he would try to make them leave through intimidation, without being seen by the older humans.

He would get closer to them, and then start throwing rocks at them… try to scare them.

He would wait for the right time to start throwing rocks at them.

For now… he would just follow them from a safe distance, and wait for the right time to start throwing rocks at them.

He watched the humans for another half of an hour, and the small young human watched him as well.

Finally, the guides decided that they were ready to continue on with their hiking, and move to where they really wanted to set up camp for the night.

They quickly gathered their items, and started to move on through the jungle.

As they did this, he continued to follow them from a safe distance.

He could see that they were making their way to higher ground.

Once he figured this out, he decided that he would quicken his own pace, and travel ahead of them and get to the higher ground before they did.

He would find a place where he could set himself up with some rocks, and ambush them when the time was right.

It would have to be a safe place where he would be able to launch rocks at them, and still not be able to be seen by any of them… except maybe the small young human.

He was able to get to the higher ground in plenty enough time before they arrived, and set himself up at the area where he felt safely out of sight, and close enough to throw the rocks that he had gathered, to reach them in flight through the air.

He did not have any intentions of harming these humans.

He did not want them to retaliate against him.

He had rocks that were very small in size.

They were not large enough to really do any harm on the humans if one happened to hit them.

They were just large enough to get their attention that rocks were being thrown at them from an unknown source . . . him.

He hoped that this would scare them enough to where they decided to leave the jungle… his home.

He settled down and waited.

After waiting for almost forty five minutes, they arrived near the area that he thought they might come too.

He was right.

They stopped in a small level ground area, and started to set up camp.

Almost right away, the little human spotted him, again locking eye to eye him.

Again, this startled him.

He waited until their camp was all set up, and they were all sitting down on the ground.

He picked up a small stone and threw it in the direction of their campsite.

The men in the camp did not notice the small stone glide through the tree's a few feet from where they sat.

But… "Augy" noticed right away, and gave an obvious frown in his direction.

He ignored the gaze from the little human.

So, again he picked up a small stone, and threw it at the campsite.

This time, the stone fell directly into the camp area and skidded to a stop only a few inches from where all three men sat.

They noticed it this time.

Samuel Goodson jumped backwards a little, while still sitting on the ground.

"Augy" did not move, not slightly.

The two guides, reacted very similarly to how "Augy's" father had, but even more so.

Both men jumped to their feet and grabbed their high powered rifles, and put the guns to their shoulders.

They took aim in the direction where they thought the stone might have come from.

Both men used their sights on their rifles to get a better long distance view of what, or who, might have thrown the stone at them.

Both men were completely wrong in guessing what direction the stone came from.

The only one in the camp that knew for sure where the stone came from was little "Augy".

Little "Augy" did not say anything to any of the three men because he sensed that this creature was not trying to harm any of them.

He also sensed, by the reaction of the men, that if he did say anything to them, the creature that he had been watching, might be harmed in a bad way.

So he kept quiet, watching the creature as he relocated to another spot in the jungle, but still at a distance where he could be safe, and still throw rocks to the camp.

The creature waited for almost half of an hour before he threw another rock at the camp.

All of the men, by that time, had concluded that the rock thrown earlier was of no significance.

It was probably some "fluke."

But... this time, when the creature threw yet another small stone, this time, actually hitting the leg of one of the guides... "Jubine," it quickly became very obvious that this stone was definitely not a "fluke."

Now... both guides, and Samuel Goodson, were standing on their feet.

Each man looking with their magnified devices through the jungle in all directions.

The guides again, used the scopes of their rifles, and this time, Samuel Goodson, used his photo-binoculars, hoping that he would be able to see what had thrown the stone at them, and if he had any luck, maybe get a photo of the guilty party… a Bigfoot?

He was slightly nervous that he might finally get a good look at a real Bigfoot, but that was why he was here.

He did not have any fears that this creature, whatever it might turn out to be, would bring any harm to him or anyone else at the campsite.

This could not be said about the two guides though, they were instantly petrified for their lives.

Especially "Jubine."

The small stone that had struck his leg did not injure him at all, but it stung enough to get his complete attention, and create a fear within him that made him feel like he would shoot anything that moved in the jungle around him.

His mindset was… shoot it, and then find out what he shot.

In America, this could be compared to an old saying… "shoot first, and ask questions later."

But they were not in America right now.

They were deep in a jungle in the far away land of Malaysia.

If any of them were to become injured, they were very far from the nearest facility that could give proper aid.

After throwing this last stone, the creature blended farther into the jungle, even out of sight of little "Augy."

After a few minutes went by, and there was not any sign of anything in the jungle, and no more stones being thrown, the three men started to talk anxiously.

The two guides were now convinced that the "monster" of their jungle, heard and seen for many generations, was in fact nearby their campsite.

Samuel Goodson was also convinced that at the very least, there was some type of intelligent being nearby in the jungle that was definitely trying to get their attention.

Again he asked himself… "was this a Bigfoot?"

Little "Augy" did not engage in their conversation… because he did not have the ability, or desire.

He still sensed that this creature was harmless to any of them.

He just sat there on the ground as if it was just another ordinary day.

The three men started to argue about what they would now do.

The two guides were to scared to continue this tracking assignment for Samuel Goodson.

Samuel Goodson was adamant with the two guides that they continue doing what they were hired to do.

He explained to them that they did not know for sure who or what had actually thrown the stones.

For all anyone knew, it could be people doing this to them for whatever unknown reasons.

He also reminded them that they were being paid very well for this tracking assignment, and that they knew before hand that they had been hired to track the "monster" that supposedly has lived in their jungle for a long time.

He also told them that if he was able to get evidence of this "monster" on a photo, or if they could actually capture of kill this creature, if it did in fact exist, they would be given a few extra bonus's, one by him… monetarily, and the other by their people as heroes, and lastly, by the world, for being the first people to ever get concrete evidence that this creature did in fact actually exist… they would all be famous.

After several minutes of going back and forth with their own specific arguments, they all decided that the tracking assignment would continue.

It finally took Samuel Goodson to offer the two guides extra money to complete this assignment for them to continue.

He reminded them that they had high powered rifles for their protection, and whoever was throwing stones at them certainly did not have what they had for protection.

They agreed that if any more stones were to be thrown at them while they were camping, they would fire random shots from their rifles into the jungle where they thought the stones were being thrown from.

Little "Augy", even though he could not communicate very well, was easily able to understand anything that was said by anybody.

He could understand people when they talked, but they could not understand his special… to them, unintelligible language.

After a while, the creature crept closer to the camp again, and again "Augy" was able to quickly find him with his superior vision.

Again, he did not alert the adult men in the camp that the creature was nearby.

The creature watched as everyone in the camp except for one of the large humans, went to sleep.

The one human stayed awake watching and listening.

The creature decided that he would travel to a nearby stream to use to defecate, and urinate.

This was a custom that he was taught since he was very young by his mother, and constantly reminded to always do so by all his elders.

He would be severely punished if he defecated or urinated on any ground.

It had to 100% of the time… always be in running water.

His species wanted to always make sure that there was as little evidence as possible that would show their existence.

The use of running water for this necessary custom was also a way of cleansing oneself afterwards.

They were definitely a very secretive species with customs that would keep them hidden from others, as best as possible.

The creature went, and came back from the nearby stream in around an hour.

The one large human… the guide named "Jubine," had his rifle ready to shoot in a split second.

The creature did not know that what the human held in his arms was a deadly weapon.

He had never seen a firearm before.

But, he could detect, instinctively, that the piece of wood in the humans arms could be dangerous to him.

After a few hours had passed, the creature watched as another large human awoke from his sleep, and replaced the other one who had been awake.

This human resumed the same posture with a piece of wood cradled in his arms.

The creature watched these humans for the rest of the night without bothering them by throwing anymore small stones at them.

When light came, he decided to go to his area of safety to get some rest, and then he would resume his monitoring of the humans in his jungle.

He was now convinced that he would not be able to scare these humans into leaving the jungle area where he called home.

He decided that he would just watch them… especially the young small human, and hopefully, they would get tired of finding nothing to excite them, and decide to finally leave the jungle and go back to where ever they came from.

Certainly, where ever they came from, he would not ever dare to travel.

For the next three and a half days, this exact scenario transpired as the creature had hoped, without intimidation from him.

Very often, he and the young small human watched each other secretly from a distance.

The creature almost felt as if he had some type of strange connection with this small young human.

Finally, after not seeing, or hearing anything since the small stones incidents, Samuel Goodson decided that he would not be able to find any evidence of a large secretive creature… a "Bigfoot," anywhere in this jungle.

He asked his two guides if they would please take him and his son back to civilization as soon as possible.

The two guides were pleased to hear this request, and started back immediately.

The creature continued to follow them at a distance until he was sure that they had in fact left the jungle.

He felt a great sense of relief when they finally were gone.

The last thing that he would remember about these humans was when he saw the young small human for the very last time.

He raised his small arm upwards towards him and moved his small hand up and down several times, slowly.

The creature did not understand this hand gesture, but instinctively bowed his head up and down in return.

The little human then showed an expression on his face with his small mouth spreading out and upwards, curling on the side corners, and showed his teeth for an instant.

The creature sensed that this was a feeling of happiness.

Maybe these creatures… these humans, were not as bad as he had been taught by all of the elders of his species since he was very young.

This was only a fleeting thought for only an instant in his head.

Slowly, the creature blended back into the jungle, relaxed and happy that these humans had finally left his safe home.

Samuel Goodson, and his son "Augy," were on a flight home back to the United States, about eight hours after they had left the jungle.

The two guides were paid in full as promised, and were happy to go back to their homes as well.

It took nearly thirteen hours for Samuel Goodson, and his son to finally arrive back to their home country.

They landed in Los Angeles, California, and quickly rented a car to travel the rest of the way home to beautiful Humboldt County, one of the northern most places in the state.

Humboldt County was one of the best kept secrets in the state of California.

The population was not very large, as compared to the rest of the state.

It took almost another thirteen hours to finally get back to Humboldt County to where their actual home was located.

They had a nice beautiful two story home up in the mountains in a rural area of the county.

The nearest town was called "Rio Dell."

Home sweet home… finally.

They both went straight to their comfortable beds and quickly fell into deep slumbers.

Tomorrow, Samuel Goodson would start making new plans about where the next place would be where he and his son would travel, to hopefully find that very elusive evidence that "Bigfoot" actually did exist.

"Augy"? . . . He would probably do his normal outdoor exploring in the mountain forest near his home, as he did so often, while his father was busy doing his thing.

Would they ever find a "Bigfoot?"

Chapter Two

LITTLE "AUGY" WOKE FROM his sleep late in the morning, almost around noontime.

His father had already been awake for a few hours, and was already busy with more "Bigfoot" related things.

"Augy" went downstairs to the kitchen to eat.

He walked by his father silently, but his father noticed him and greeted him lovingly with a kind gesture… "Hey little man, finally awake?"

"Augy" ignored the gesture, and continued on to the kitchen.

The hunger in his stomach took all precedence for the moment.

He found his normal cereal that had raisins mixed in with the flakes, and put this and some milk in a bowl.

This was actually a morning ritual of his with the bowl of cereal.

He always had this type of cereal every morning.

Afterwards, he went back upstairs to his bedroom to get dressed, so he could go outside in the forest nearby and do his favorite… private thing… explore.

"Augy's" father had already taught him the trail to hike in the forest area behind their home.

It was a trail that was barely inside of the forest.

It ran along the edges, and only about twenty feet into the foliage and tree's.

If "Augy's" father wanted him home immediately, he had an old police whistle that he would blow three short blast's.

"Augy's" father had made sure his son understood that there were dangers beyond this trail, and he was not permitted to go off of the trail and into the deep forest.

The forest was awake with the sounds of life in all directions of the compass.

The weather was slightly misty, with the sun playing hide and seek behind the moisture in the air.

Typical teaser… Humboldt County weather.

"Augy's" father did not notice his son leaving the house out the back door towards the beautiful dense forest.

"Augy" wore his "Camy" pants, a short sleeved brown shirt, and his expensive hiking boots that his father had bought for him.

He also had his favorite baseball cap on his head.

A San Francisco Giants black and orange World Series Champions ball cap.

When you looked at little "Augy", you would not notice that he was a child with autism, he appeared normal in appearance.

He was a normal sized four foot five inch boy with brown hair, and eyes the same color.

He was slightly thin, but in general, very average looking.

As he made his way into the forest, "Augy" could hear all of the normal sounds that he always did on his walks with nature.

Most of the time, he would travel the exact same path through the forest, but this time, he decided to go in another direction.

This was totally against what his father had said he was allowed to do.

"Augy" was now going to break his father's main rule when it came to hiking in the forest.

So… off the trail he went.

He could sense something different as he went in this other direction.

He was careful not to step on the wild ferns as he walked because he knew that they were alive, as he was.

"Augy" really respected all of the living things in the forest… animals, and plants alike.

There was some type of strange connection between this particular little boy and all living things in nature.

He walked silently, almost stealthily, at a slow steady pace.

He stopped all of a sudden.

He could hear very faintly, a sound of another person, or animal, walking at a distance.

"Augy" did not feel any fear in his body about this faint sound in the distance.

In fact, curiosity, and excitement, were an even mixture for him at this moment.

He started to go much deeper into the forest, going in the direction of this sound that he could hear with every footstep.

Unknown to "Augy," he was not actually in any danger from this sound.

The sound was coming from another person.

This person was a Native American from the Yurok tribe here in Humboldt County.

The name of this person was… "David Sleeping Beaver Dunn."

Everyone just called him "Sleeping Beaver."

He was a very spiritual man in his late twenties.

He liked to hike all over Humboldt County, along the many rivers, and through the many mountainous forests that made up a large amount of this beautiful spot on the map.

He was not aware that there was a little autistic boy named "Augy" that was gradually tracking him from a distance, and getting closer with every second on the clock.

"Sleeping Beaver" was at total peace with himself as he slowly walked through this dense forest area.

"Augy" could now hear the sounds from "Sleeping Beaver" much better as the two of them were now only about one hundred feet from each other.

Still… "Sleeping Beaver" could not hear little "Augy" coming towards him.

Little "Augy" crept closer to "Sleeping Beaver" . . . now only about thirty feet away.

"Sleeping Beaver" stopped in his tracks.

He could sense that there was something, or someone nearby… close.

Little "Augy" noticed this, and stopped as well.

It was difficult to see the young boy because of how he was dressed.

His clothing blended in with the surrounding forest very well.

"Sleeping Beaver" smoothly, and quietly sidestepped behind a massive redwood tree.

He stood there, waiting to see if whatever he detected would show itself to him.

Little "Augy" did not see "Little Beaver" step behind the tree.

He slowly walked over in the direction of where he last seen "Sleeping Beaver."

He was now on the other side of the redwood tree where "Sleeping Beaver" quietly stood… frozen.

"Sleeping Beaver" heard the little boy walk up to the tree, but still did not know who or what was on the other side, only a few feet away from him.

He took out his hunting knife from his sheath on his waist.

He stood there with his knife, ready to strike if it turned out to be dangerous.

Little "Augy," step by step, very slowly, hugged the edge of this tree and started to circle around to the other side.

He took two more almost silent steps, and then he stood in front of "Sleeping Beaver."

As he took this final step before being seen, "Sleeping Beaver" almost swung his knife at the little boy.

He stopped himself abruptly, quickly putting the knife back into the sheath on his waist.

They both looked at each other silently for a few moments.

Finally "Sleeping Beaver" spoke to "Augy."

"Who are you?"

"Why are you in this forest?"

"There are many dangers in this forest."

"You should not be here by yourself."

"Do you have a parent with you nearby?"

After all of these initial quick questions to "Augy," "Sleeping Beaver" waited for an answer from the little boy.

"Augy" did not answer any of the questions.

He understood the questions, but knew that this man would not be able to understand his special language.

Upon seeing that "Augy" was not going to answer his questions, "Sleeping Beaver" decided to talk once again.

"Well, my name is "Sleeping Beaver.""

"I am here in this forest exploring, and enjoying the natural beauty that the Mother Earth has given us."

"So, I am going to guess that you do not have anyone with you here in this forest."

"There are dangerous animals here in this forest that could hurt you very badly."

"Bears, and mountain lions, just to name a few."

"You need to follow me out of this forest, and I will take you back to your home."

"Come now, follow me."

He motioned with his arm as he started to walk away.

Little "Augy" did not follow "Sleeping Beaver."

Instead, "Augy" started to walk away in the opposite direction from "Sleeping Beaver."

"Sleeping Beaver" called for the little boy to stop, and to come back to him.

"Augy" ignored his request, and continued to walk, now at a faster pace.

"Sleeping Beaver" did not have any choice except to follow the little autistic child.

"Sleeping Beaver" had never went in this direction in this forest.

So he was unfamiliar with what or who might lie ahead.

Little "Augy" basically backtracked the exact path that he had taken before he met "Sleeping Beaver."

It was about this same time that "Augy's" father decided that he wanted his little boy home because they were going to travel to Eureka to take care of some errands.

He stepped out into the back of his home with his police whistle, and blew three loud blast's.

The shrill of this whistle could be heard from very far away.

Upon hearing the sound of this whistle, little "Augy" started to run.

"Sleeping Beaver" heard this same whistle, and also noticed that the little boy had started to run.

He was not sure if the boy was running because the whistle scared him, or if he was scaring him, or if the little boy recognized the sound of the whistle, and maybe someone was calling him to come back home.

It did not matter, he was going to follow the boy no matter what, and find out where he was going.

If the little boy did happen to be going home, and if there was an adult there waiting for him, maybe a parent, he decided that he would certainly speak to them about where he had found "Augy," and give his opinion that the little boy should not be in that part of this massive forest because of the many possible dangers.

He started to run as well, in order to keep up with the little boy.

They both ran fore several minutes before they finally exited the forest near a small meadow.

"Sleeping Beaver" could see a two story house in the distance.

He could also see an adult man standing near the backside of the house staring directly at both him and the little boy.

The man near the house waved at both of them, and motioned them to come over to him.

"Augy" slowed down to a walk, and started towards the house.

"Sleeping Beaver" caught up to "Augy," and walked at his side.

As they walked closer to the house where the man stood waiting, both men realized that they recognized each other.

They did not actually know each other, but they had a mutual friend that knew them both.

Her name was "Shamieka Kiel."

She was a forest ranger.

She was well known in Humboldt County for her diligence in making sure that all life in the forest's were safe and well preserved.

She was "Sleeping Beaver's" girlfriend.

She was not a Native American like himself, she was an African American, very smart, and very motivated in her job.

She spent time with her boyfriend whenever time would allow.

That seemed to be not often enough.

There was certainly a very strong bond between the two, and it was very evident whenever they did happen to be in each other's company.

Samuel Goodson knew Shamieka because of the many times he had been around her when he was in any of the numerous forest's of Humboldt County.

They had run into each other on several occasions.

Personally, she thought that Samuel Goodson was a bit out there... maybe a bit crazy in his pursuit of the famed mythical creature known locally as "Bigfoot."

On the other hand, Shamieka also had the opportunity to know little "Augy" as well because he was with his father everywhere that they went.

She was aware of "Augy's" autism, and she absolutely adored the little boy.

"Augy" felt very comfortable around her as well.

In a matter a moments, upon exiting the forest area behind the "Augy's" house, "Sleeping Beaver" and "Augy" were standing before Samuel Goodson.

Samuel Goodson began to speak.

"So... I recognize you, but I do not know your name."

"Why are you with my son "Augy?"

"Sleeping Bear" introduced himself, and replied to Samuel Goodson's question.

"I was out in the forest, doing what I enjoy... exploring, and I came upon your son, very deep within this forest."

Samuel Goodson looked over at his son.

"Augy" looked back at him with absolutely no emotion upon his face whatsoever.

He asked his son if it was true that he was not on the normal path that he had instructed him to always stay on.

"Augy" started to talk in his special, garbled language back at his father.

"Sleeping Beaver" was surprised to hear how this little boy talked.

He quickly realized that the little boy was not an ordinary child, but in fact was someone with special needs, and challenges in everyday life.

It seemed to "Sleeping Beaver" that Samuel Goodson was able to understand what the little boy was saying, even though he did not have the faintest clue what "Augy" was saying.

Samuel Goodson walked over to his son and hugged him tightly, and told him that he was concerned that he could get hurt if he did not stay on the forest path that he had taught him.

Punishment was not something that Samuel Goodson ever gave to little "Augy."

It was a complete waste of time to try and administer punishment to his son.

It simply would not have any positive or substantial impact upon the boy in any way.

Plus, the guilt factor was always present as well.

He asked his son to go and get into their truck, and wait for him.

He turned his attention back to "Sleeping Beaver" as his son walked away towards the truck.

He spoke very politely to "Sleeping Beaver."

"I want to thankyou from my heart for making sure that my son made it home safely to me."

"I don't know what I would do if any harm ever came upon him."

"He likes to explore the forest area."

"I have taught him the exact trail that I want for him to travel when he does go out to explore."

"I feel that it is safe, and he always comes home when I blow this whistle."

"Sleeping Beaver" acknowledged the sincere statement from Samuel Goodson, but felt a need to speak his own opinion.

"There are many dangers within that forest."

"I have walked these forest's and seen many dangerous things that could cause harm to your son."

"Mountain lions, Bears, Coyotes, Foxes, Snakes, just to name a few."

"These animals could easily kill your son, and eat him as food, and you would never even find any trace of him anywhere, unless you were lucky."

"I do not want to disrespect you with knowledge that you are already aware of, I just want to emphasize that your son is very vulnerable when hiking through these woods… alone, or even on the outer edges."

"There should at the very least be another person with him when he wants to hike in these forests."

Samuel Goodson thought for a minute about this statement from Sleeping Beaver.

He knew that Sleeping Beaver meant well by saying what he said, and he also knew that the statement was in fact true.

He was aware of the many dangers that lurked within the nearby forest, but he had always felt that as long as his son stayed on the path at the edge of the forest that he had taught him, that he would be alright.

After thinking about what Sleeping Beaver had said for a few minutes in silence, he finally came to the conclusion that he should change his mind about his son going alone to the forest.

So he turned to Sleeping Beaver and made a proposal to him.

"Alright, you are correct in what you have said about the many dangers in this forest."

"But my son really likes to explore, and sometimes I am too busy with my work to take the time to go with him on his little explorations to the forest."

"Do you have any suggestions Sleeping Beaver?"

Right away, Sleeping Beaver had an answer for Samuel Goodson.

"Well Samuel, since I do make many treks through the many forests in the area, I would not have a problem in having your son along with me when I hike these forests."

"You would of course have to tell me ahead of time when your son is available, and if I happen to be exploring during that time, I would welcome his company."

Samuel Goodson, again took some time to think before answering this latest statement.

Finally, he decided that he felt safe with having Sleeping Beaver as a companion with his son when he wanted to explore.

So he told Sleeping Beaver that he would agree with the proposal to have his son go along with him whenever the time was convenient for both of them.

Sleeping Beaver was delighted with this decision, and stuck out his hand for a friendly shake.

The two men shook on it. Sleeping Beaver then tried to shake hands with Augy, and did not get a response.

Samuel Goodson told Sleeping Beaver all about his sons condition, and told him not to worry about Augy not wanting to shake his hand. He invited Sleeping Beaver into his home to go into complete detail about his son so that Sleeping Beaver would have a better understanding about his son, and his needs.

He did not want any misunderstandings between them.

After explaining everything there was to know about his son, even about the communication problem, he asked Sleeping Beaver once again if he still wanted to do what he offered with his son.

Sleeping Beaver did not even hesitate with an answer of yes once again when asked by Samuel Goodson.

Nobody was sure if Augy understood the new arrangement about his explorations to the forest, but both men were in agreement that from now on, Augy would be safer whenever he wanted to go and explore the forests.

Sleeping Beaver stayed for another hour before he bid farewell, and started his hiking back to the forest.

He told Samuel that he would be in touch, and if he wanted to contact him, leave a message on his phone, and he would get back to him as soon as possible.

Samuel Goodson and Augy walked back into their home as Sleeping Beaver disappeared into the forest.

Chapter Three

S HAMIEKA KIEL AWOKE FROM her slumber after staying up very late into the early morning hours past midnight.

She stretched and rolled back and forth in her very comfortable king size bed.

She needed a large bed because she was a big girl.

She stood a little over six feet tall, and had a body frame that matched her height.

She was a very attractive woman, and had men looking at her in obvious flirtation very often on a daily basis.

At first glance, one might not be able to distinguish her ethnicity because she had skin the color of hot cocoa light brown, and facial features that could be thought of as Native American, Pacific Islander, or even Hispanic.

Unless she were to tell you what her ethnic background was, you would probably be guessing what the actual truth was.

She had a very sweet personality that matched her looks.

She could be very quiet at times, and very serious about whatever she was doing.

But the bottom line was that she was a genuine good girl at heart.

She could have as any friends as she wanted… male or female.

As she climbed out of her bed, she could hear her answering machine beeping in the other room.

She casually walked over into the other room and pressed the button on the answering machine.

The voice of Sleeping Beaver… her boyfriend, started to talk in a playful sweet voice for her.

He told her about his meeting with Samuel Goodson, and the new arrangement he had about taking little Augy along on some of his treks to the forests.

He asked her to call him whenever she had time, and passed some love and kisses to her into the air of the room before his voice said goodbye and went silent.

She smiled softly and walked back to her room and flopped down back onto her large bed.

She decided to take another short nap before really getting up for the day.

Less than twenty miles away, Sleeping Beaver was already awake for the day, and getting ready to go out for more explorations in the same forest as he had hiked through the day before when he met little Augy.

His plan for the day was to go and meet one of his many friends who happened to live deep into the forest where he had found little Augy.

This particular friend of his was very well known throughout Humboldt County.

His name was Mylo Phillips.

Everyone called him… "Crazy Mylo."

Crazy Mylo was actually very fond of his nickname because it kept away the vast majority of people that might come near wherever he might be located at any given moment.

The fact was actually that Mylo Phillips was not really crazy as everyone thought.

He was actually a very sane and intelligent man whose occupation was very illegal.

He grew marijuana plants for a living, deep within the many forests of Humboldt County.

He had been doing this for over thirty years, and even though a lot of people were aware of what he did, even the local law enforcement, generally, he was pretty much left alone.

He had a few friends that he would allow near him, one of them being Sleeping Beaver.

The main reason that everyone thought of Crazy Mylo to really be insane, and really crazy, was because he often would tell people that he would see the local legend… "Big Foot" very often, and was actually friends with a number of Big Foot's throughout the many forests of their beloved county.

Of course, everyone would laugh at his claims of being friends with a Big foot, but it was a good cover for Crazy Mylo to keep people away from him so he could continue doing his marijuana growing operation.

Sleeping Beaver knew where his friend Crazy Mylo was currently located, and started his hike within a few hours after waking up.

It was a very tough hike to get to the current place where Crazy Mylo made his camp and guarded his most recent marijuana grow.

He was currently watching 500 plants ranging from 2 feet too 4 and a half feet in height.

He did not ever do as other growers did and do outlandish things like set up booby traps that would harm people that came to close to the grow operation.

He did though have alarms set up to alert him when anyone came near so he could just simply hide at a pre-determined place.

If the grow happened to be found by the authorities… so be it.

He would simply start another grow, and hope that it would not be found before it was time to harvest.

In all of his years growing marijuana, only twice had any of his plants ever been found.

The reason for such good success was because of how far away and deep in the vast forests he would grow his plants.

It was generally very hard to get to one of his grow operations.

Any overhead flights by the authorities such as helicopters were pretty much unsuccessful as well in spotting his grow operations because of how he would blend in his plants in the forest.

Instead of growing the plants all together in a large patch, he would grow each plant individually near a large redwood tree.

Crazy Mylo would remember the locations of these tree's by a map that he would create while he planted the seedlings.

After each grow operation was over after harvest time, Crazy Mylo would find a new location and create a new map as he planted more new seedlings.

He would then destroy the old map of the previous grow operation, and then concentrate on the new grow.

He did not believe in chemicals, or redirecting any water from streams or rivers.

He was very meticulous with each plant.

The actual growing areas of the plants were nearly impossible to detect because the plants were not bunched together in a "patch."

Since the plants were individually located and spread out in the forest, and just enough sunlight filtering through the branches of the large trees, the actual plants were nearly impossible to be seen from above whenever the Sheriff's department did fly over's with the help of DEA in helicopters.

Whenever these "Fly overs" were being held, the agents in the operation were looking for signs of marijuana grows such as "patches," or areas where the plants were all bunched together in a group.

"Patches" were able to be detected, but even these were hard to see during the "fly overs."

Crazy Mylo would carry four "Camel" back packs full of nutrient rich water, and deliver the life giving fluid to each individual plant every other day.

It would normally take around four too six hours to do this because he would have to sometimes go back to the water source to get replenished, and then add his own special nutrients to the water.

This is why he would never have an extremely large grow operation because of how meticulous he was, and his respect for mother nature.

He thought that it was absolutely terrible to add chemicals to the ground when growing ANY plant, and redirecting water flows was simply something that he would never do.

Let the water flow as mother nature intends it to flow was his thought on that.

So now Crazy Mylo sat near a large pine tree where he had just finished his rounds of watering his plants, and was starting to drink a can of local Humboldt County beer.

It had taken him a solid five hours to water his plants today.

He had a temporary living area less than an hours walk from this location.

This particular location was a small cave on the side of a mountain, well hidden from any eyes that might be able to gaze in that direction.

It blended in well with all of the surrounding pine tree's.

This cave was one of a number of temporary living situations for Crazy Mylo.

It all depended upon where he was currently growing his latest crop of marijuana plants.

He did not believe in destroying anything from Mother nature.

He would only burn campfires from wood that he could find on the ground.

He would never reroute any water from flowing creeks or rivers.

He would certainly never ever litter anything on the ground, he would save any and all trash that he created.

Whenever he did make his way to a town to gather supplies, he would take his trash there and dispose of it.

He would recycle whatever he had saved as well while he was in town.

Usually, the only time he did really go to a town where there was a population of people, would be to deliver his crop to a buyer that was already lined up ahead of time.

Crazy Mylo definitely was not hurting for money, in fact, he was actually very well off financially.

He donated a lot of his money to wildlife and nature organizations that helped and protected plants and animals.

Some of his money was also sent to a few family members who were in need of help.

He had paid for the college education of several family members, and a few friends as well.

Even though Crazy Mylo was thought of as a crazy old coot, he was actually a very well respected person of the area in Humboldt County where he lived.

Sleeping Beaver had known Crazy Mylo almost his entire life.

He had met him as a child while he was exploring the forests with his siblings.

They had become very close friends since then, and learned a lot from each other.

Sleeping Beaver generally would keep Crazy Mylo up to date with the current events of the world, and any new things that happened in science and technology.

Crazy Mylo had taught Sleeping Beaver a lot about how to respect Mother nature.

They complimented each other perfectly.

Sleeping Beaver was not in any way involved with Crazy Mylo's marijuana grow operations.

He knew all about the grows, but never would make any negative remarks about them.

He understood how Crazy Mylo made money from the grows to help other people and Mother nature's family.

Sleeping Beaver was now in the general area of where Crazy Mylo was located.

There was a special call that Sleeping Beaver would make to let Crazy Mylo know that he was nearby.

Sleeping Beaver put one of his hands to his mouth and curved his fingers in such a way to manipulate the air flow through his hand.

He then let out a long smooth sound that had a similar sound of any number of birds.

But… there was no such bird that made this sound in nature.

This call was developed by Sleeping Beaver, and practiced with Crazy Mylo since they had become friends a long time ago.

As soon as Sleeping Beaver made this special call through the forest, Crazy Mylo had a large smile appear upon his grizzled old face.

He knew that his friend was nearby looking for him.

Crazy Mylo put his hand to his mouth and did a return call back to Sleeping Beaver.

His call was somewhat different in tone than Sleeping Beaver's, but generally the same type of sound.

They walked towards each others calls, and made more calls that were much softer as they got closer to each other.

Finally, after a few minutes of this ritual calling between the two men, they were finally face to face.

Both men smiled upon seeing each other, and then there was the usual friendly hug between them.

They started to walk through the forest at a casual pace.

They made their way towards the cave that Crazy Mylo was currently using to stay during this grow operation.

They did not talk to much as they walked.

There would be plenty of talking once they arrived at the cave.

One of the main reasons, if not the main reason that Sleeping Beaver was a trusted friend of Crazy Mylo was because he had knowledge that was shared between the two men… since they had met.

Sure the knowledge of where the marijuana grow was very important, but that secret was not as important as the one that they had shared for many years.

It was a secret that maybe no other people on the planet had.

The secret??

Bigfoot truly did exist!!

Not only did this creature exist, but these two men were actual friends of the Bigfoot population of the area, and surrounding counties as well.

They had become trusted friends of these secretive creatures long ago when they had first become friends.

It had all happened by accident… literally by an actual accident.

Crazy Mylo had only known Sleeping Beaver for a few months, and they were hiking through the forest when they heard a low piercing cry about a hundred yards away.

They cautiously traveled to the location where they though the sound was coming from, and to their shock… they came upon a scene that was the rarest of the rare to be seen by human eyes.

They stood silently looking through the bushes near a large redwood tree.

What they saw was two very large creatures attempting to move a large fallen tree that was on top of a number of boulders at the entrance to what looked like a small cave at the base of the low sloping mountain.

It appeared to be the scene of a rock slide that had been created by a large fallen redwood tree.

It looked like the large redwood tree had uprooted from the hillside up above and had rolled down the side of the mountain, bringing a number of varying sized rocks large and small along with it as it traveled down the slope.

The tree, and all the rocks had finally come to rest in front of this small cave at the base of this hillside.

It sounded as if there was someone… a smaller creature? . . . trapped inside of this small cave.

This smaller creature inside of the small cave was crying out to the two larger creatures in obvious panic and fear.

The two larger creature were moving the rocks from the front of the cave, and then trying to dislodge to large tree from it's position that held a much larger boulder in front of most of the opening to the small cave.

The two large creatures were so busy trying to help the smaller creature get out of the cave, that they did not notice, or even detect that they were being watched… silently from a distance of about forty feet away.

It was obvious to the two silent observers that these two creatures were very upset about the current situation.

These two large creatures were silently estimated by the two men to be at least eight and a half to nine feet tall easily, with no exaggeration whatsoever.

Crazy Mylo and Sleeping Beaver had stood silently for almost fifteen minutes, and then they noticed that the two large creatures appeared to be almost giving up their efforts to continue trying to release the small creature from the blocked cave.

They were simply not strong enough to dislodge the large redwood tree from it's position on top of the boulder in from of the cave.

The small creature inside of the cave went silent when the two larger creatures stopped their efforts upon the scene.

There was a detectable sadness in the air… invisible… but very obvious between the two larger creatures.

Crazy Mylo and Sleeping Beaver had the natural feeling between the both of them, to some how help these distraught creatures with their predicament.

At the same time, they also knew that these creatures could probably hurt them if they let them know that they were only a short distance away watching them.

The two men did not even dare to talk between them because of this concern for their own safety.

Yet… there was obviously a creature trapped inside of that cave, and the two large creatures outside of the cave were having a very hard time in moving the objects that blocked the caves entrance.

Mainly boulders of differing sizes, and a very large redwood tree wedging those boulders in place.

Sleeping Beaver moved a little closer to the edge of the bushes, and as he did this, a small twig on the ground cracked beneath his shoe.

Sleeping Beaver froze in his tracks, watching the creatures to see if they heard that sound that he unintentionally made.

To his utter shock, and Crazy Mylo's as well, the two large creatures has indeed heard the cracking twig!!

The two creatures immediately walked quickly over to where the two startled men stood… frozen with fear.

In almost a blink of an eye, all four… two humans… two large creatures… stood facing each other a few feet apart.

Too the surprise of both men, the two creatures did not harm them.

Instead they just stood there frozen as well… staring at Sleeping Beaver, and Crazy Mylo.

There was almost what could be construed as a look of sadness upon their faces.

Shockingly… a moment later, the two creatures turned and went back to the cave where their companion was still crying for help.

The creature that was crying inside of the cave sounded like a youngster.

Without thinking anymore about their personal safety, the two men followed behind the two creatures to the cave.

Sleeping Beaver bent down and looked closely at the debris at the entrance of the cave.

As he looked at the entrance of the cave, he could see through very small gaps of the debris, a small face that was the same as these two large creatures standing a few feet from him.

He made eye contact with this small face… the crying stopped.

Crazy Mylo was busy looking over the entire situation with these boulders, and the large redwood tree that was wedging them.

He noticed that the branches of the tree was actually what the problem was.

The tree could not be moved because the branches were preventing the tree from rolling.

Crazy Mylo pointed this out to Sleeping Beaver.

He tried to somehow show the two creatures that this was what the actual problem was.

He started to make movements with his hands in a pantomime like gesture in hopes that they would understand what he was trying to convey to them.

He grabbed at the branches.

He made a rolling motion with his hands next to the tree.

He went over to a smaller branch that he would be able to break, and snapped it away from the tree.

He grabbed another manageable branch, and did the same.

Sleeping Beaver turned away from the eyes of the smaller creature inside of the cave, and started to do the same as crazy Mylo.

After a few moments of doing this, the two larger creatures some how... maybe they understood crazy Mylo's gestures, started to break much larger branches from the tree.

It was amazing to witness how incredibly strong these creature were.

It was also incredible to see a cooperation between the two different species where civility would not be expected.

But here they were, breaking branches from a tree, side by side, with no hint or possibility of violence occurring.

All four of them worked very hard at breaking the branches from this tree for about forty five minutes before the tree was completely stripped, and now was to the point where it would be able to be rolled away from the boulders in front of the entrance to the cave, where a smaller creature awaited freedom to the outside world.

They spread out along the length of the large redwood tree and bent over to get their grips upon it's barked surface.

They could not budge the tree.

They tried very hard for several minutes, and they still could not move the tree not even a millimeter.

Crazy Mylo stood back and once again thought about the situation.

The two creatures, and Sleeping Beaver stood silently... waiting to see if he had another idea.

A smile came on his face... he did have another idea.

He walked over to one of the larger branches that had been broken away from the tree, and picked it up from the ground.

He next walked over to the spot where he had tried to roll the tree a few minutes before, and put the branch at the base of the tree to form a leverage wedge.

Instantly, Sleeping Beaver understood what Crazy Mylo was now attempting to do.

He did the same as Crazy Mylo.

He positioned himself with a large branch the same as Crazy Mylo.

Both of them tried with all of their strength to try and move the large redwood tree.

Encouragingly, the tree move a little, but not quite enough to start rolling.

Amazingly… the two large creatures acted as if they understood what the two humans were doing, and followed suit with their own much larger branches at leverage points at the base of the tree.

They used their strength, along with the two men, to finally start moving the large heavy tree.

The tree started to roll over, inch by inch away from the boulders.

They all worked together, repositioning their branches at new leverage points, after the tree would roll it's maximum distance.

After doing this for another twenty minutes, the tree was finally rolled away from the boulders enough to where it was no longer acting as a wedge.

The boulders could now be more easily moved away from the entrance to the cave.

The smaller creature inside of the cave was now making different sounds, this time it was not one that sounded like crying, but instead it now sounded a tone of excitement.

It now only took a few more minutes of moving boulders before a large enough gap was created to allow the smaller creature to exit the cave to the outside.

The two large creatures turned towards the two humans, as if to tell them to back away, as the smaller creature climbed out of the cave.

Crazy Mylo, and Sleeping Beaver backed away to a safe distance, now feeling a small amount of fear for their own safety creep back into their bodies.

They stood there silently, and watched a much smaller version of the two large creatures, exit the cave.

It looked exactly like the two large creatures, but stood half their height, and girth.

As they stood there… they were finally able to… silently… figure out the approximate height and weight of these massive creatures.

Both men secretly estimated the Bigfoot creatures to weigh around 600 to 800 lbs.

Their height looked to be an easy 8 to almost 9 feet tall.

The smaller Bigfoot was about 5 feet tall, and probably weighed around 250 lbs…. easily.

Their bone structures were very large, as compared to a man.

Their wrist bones appeared to be as large, if not larger than an average man's forearm bone.

Their heads… skulls… probably held brains within them, that were maybe a quarter size larger than an average man.

As the two men figured this out about these creatures in silence, they marveled at what they were witnessing.

They acted very similar to how a human would act when they were reunited with someone that they cared about.

Just as a human would do, they began to hug one another in obvious joy of the moment, as the smaller Bigfoot stood before them safe… finally.

None of the creatures showed any signs of caring that they were being watched by these two humans in this moment of happiness… Crazy Mylo, and Sleeping Beaver.

After about a minute or two, all eyes were upon each other once again, along with a strange silence.

Three creatures staring at two humans.

Two humans staring at three creatures.

Five beings… not knowing what to do next.

Would everyone run now in different directions?

Or… would something now happen that had never happened before?

A new friendship between a species of creatures that was more myth than proven fact, with two solitary humans who now were witnesses to the real truth.

These creatures were referred to in this area of the planet as "Bigfoots!!"

Unknowing, at this point in time, these two particular humans, would now become secret friends to these Bigfoots… forever.

The Bigfoots were very grateful for the help that the two humans had given them to save one of their youngsters.

Over time, Crazy Mylo, and Sleeping Beaver would come to know a large number of different Bigfoots… young and old, small and large.

The two men would not ever let their secret be known to anyone… ever.

The Bigfoots trusted them with their secret friendship.

So… when Crazy Mylo was telling people that he was friends with Bigfoots, he was actually telling the truth.

Because of the fact that Bigfoot was still considered a myth, and not a proven fact, Crazy Mylo was able to use that for his benefit in regards to his grow operations.

So… now the two men sat in a cave that was the current dwelling of Crazy Mylo, and started to catch-up with everyday events that had happened since they had last seen one another.

Sleeping Beaver had grown up to be a responsible man in society, and Crazy Mylo continued being… Crazy Mylo.

Crazy Mylo packed a pipe full of marijuana bud, and lit a fire upon the bowl area to cause the bud to start smoking.

He did not offer any to Sleeping Beaver because he respected his friends choice of not partaking in the drug.

They talked for several hours before making a camp fire and ate some food before going to sleep.

They decided that when they woke up in the morning, that they would go and find a few of their Bigfoot friends.

Chapter Four

S HAMIEKA FINALLY MOTIVATED HERSELF with the help of a little coffee, enough to get dressed for the day ahead of her.

Even though she would be technically on duty for the day, she decided to dress more casual, and not wear her uniform.

She was able to do this, because she was basically her own boss, with tremendous flexibility to do her job without any oversight, out in the field.

She dressed in some faded jeans, a light sweater, and covered that up with a green Carhartt's jacket.

She did wear her normal work boots though, because they were very comfortable, and she was used to wearing them out in the field.

She planned on traveling down to southern Humboldt County to hike through a forest and check out some of the wildlife, and flora.

Underneath her Jacket, she did carry a .45 caliber pistol, and a large can of Bear pepper spray.

She only had to use the pepper spray on two occasions.

One was fired at a mountain lion who decided to stalk her for awhile, and got to close to her.

The other time was a black bear that she accidentally ran into… almost literally while she was hiking.

The bear almost attacked her… more out of surprise than anything else.

So she sprayed him enough to convince him to move on.

She left her place, and got into her 4 wheel drive, government issue, green Jeep Cherokee, and drove off in a blur of speed that was illegal for normal citizens.

It took her about forty five minutes to travel to the area in Southern Humboldt County that she had chosen for the day to investigate.

She traveled along many different, old logging roads to finally get to the spot she desired, and parked her Jeep off of the road amongst the ferns and redwood tree's.

After she got out of her Jeep, she made sure that she had her cellphone, and handheld digital video recorder.

Whenever she was on official work, she always documented everything on her digital video camera.

She would later upload the video to a file on her computer and do a report on her findings. She would then send-off the report, and video to her boss who lived in one county away in Trinity County.

She casually started to walk into the forest.

Even though she was alone as she walked, she did not fear the elements, or the wildlife that surely surrounded her, hidden in the forest vegetation all around her.

Within a few minutes, she was already getting deep within this particular forest.

She had been at this location only two other times in the past, coming away with very normal… generic reports, to send to her boss.

So, she did not expect anything different this time on this assignment in the field.

Around her, there was the normal sounds of the forest… birds chirping, and a very light breeze of wind channeling it's way through the tree's, causing some of the vegetation to sway slightly.

Otherwise, there was mostly an eery silence that helped her concentrate as she walked.

As she walked, she panned her digital video camera back and forth in all directions, and made comments about various things that she was observing.

All of a sudden, she caught a glimpse of movement in the distance.

She could not tell what it was because it was too far away for exact judgment.

She changed the setting on her video camera to zoom to try and get a better look, but that still did not help clarify what she might be looking at because whatever it was, it was traveling away quickly… almost stealthily.

She quickened her pace.

She was very curious about what this thing must be.

At the same time though, she was cautious of the possibility that it could be a Bear.

Two more times in the next fifteen minutes, she was able to get a few scant seconds of video of whatever this was she was trying to track.

But… both times, she still was not able to discern exactly what this thing was.

It was certainly a living animal, most likely not human, and probably a bear as she suspected.

What was also very interesting to her was when she got to the area's where she knew this creature to be before it disappeared, she found tracks.

These tracks surely did not look like bear tracks at all.

To her amazement, the tracks had a human like appearance to them.

But… the tracks looked a lot larger than a normal human foot print.

Thought's went racing through her head that she tried to ignore.

She grew up in Humboldt County hearing all of her life about a large creature that supposedly lived in the forest's.

Everyone called this creature "Bigfoot."

She had not ever been a true believer of the existence of this mythical creature.

She had listened to many supposed eyewitness accounts about Bigfoot, but never really took the stories seriously.

Now here she stood, deep in the forest, looking at these very huge foot prints, and holding in her hands, possible video of this mythical creature… Bigfoot.

She took out her cellphone, and took a lot of pictures of these foot prints.

Shamieka also continued documenting everything with her digital video camera.

She would investigate all of this information very thoroughly before she came to her own conclusion as to what type of creature this might be.

She would also contact her boyfriend Sleeping Beaver, so she could get his opinion on all of this information she was gathering today.

She did not want to just simply turn this information in to her boss, because she feared that he might question her judgment, and start to think that she was starting to imagine things that were not real or ever proven scientifically… like the existence of Bigfoot.

She had to be very careful how she went about handling this particular case, because it could possibly impact her job, and even other jobs in the future if she was labeled a Bigfoot crackpot.

She finally gave up on trying to track this thing, and decided to head back to her Jeep, and go back home.

Once she was sitting in front of her computer, and was able to download this video, she would be able to get a better understanding what she was looking at.

Her computer had special software that was able to enhance video and increase the dot density to make the video more clear to see from a long distance.

She felt anxious to see this video as she drove her Jeep home.

What was this creature that was so good at alluding her today?

She had learned from her boyfriend Sleeping Beaver how to track things in the forest, silently, and stealthily enough, to be able to get close to many animals in the past where they did not even know she was nearby looking at them… recording them without their knowledge.

But in this particular case today, no matter how hard that she tried, this creature was able to elude her at a distance, and stay far enough away where she could not tell for sure what type of animal it was.

Hopefully her computer would be able to help her figure out what this elusive creature was, and resolve her curiosity.

She pressed down a little harder on the gas pedal of her car, and increased the speed.

She was quite anxious to get home.

Chapter Five

SLEEPING BEAVER AND CRAZY Mylo woke up from their slumber, and immediately packed up camp.

In a short while they would travel to a location where they knew they would probably be able to find one or more of their Bigfoot friends.

This place… a waterfall that cascaded down the side of a mountain, and emptying into a nearby small lake created by a beaver dam, was very special to the Bigfoots of this area.

Unknown to all humans except for Crazy Mylo, and Sleeping Beaver, this was where a centuries old secret for the Bigfoots was located.

Behind this waterfall was the entrance to a massive cave system.

This cave system is where all of the Bigfoot population of this area lived.

This cave system was also the place where the Bigfoots resided upon their demise.

If they died outside of this cave system, their body would be retrieved by other Bigfoot's, and taken to the home cave.

There had never… ever… been a case of where a Bigfoot had died, and it's remains had not been taken to this cave system.

This is why there had never… ever… been a case where a human had been able to find any evidence such as bones of a Bigfoot who had died.

The Bigfoots were actually a lot smarter than the humans would ever be able to understand.

Upon their birth, Bigfoots were taught, and reminded constantly as they grew, to be as secretive, and stealthy as possible, particularly when humans were around their area.

They understood that humans would be a dangerous race to contend with.

Their very survival as a race depended upon their being able to maintain their lifelong secrecy.

So... hence... the Bigfoot bodies always being retrieved and brought to the home cave.

The Bigfoots had, over the centuries, been spotted by a number of humans, but never for a long period of time.

Proof of their existence... luckily, was still in the category of myth with the majority of modern day humans.

But... like the Gorilla at the turn of the century, who was also in a similar situation as the Bigfoots, of whether or not they actually existed, it would only take one incidence of capture, dead or alive, to also prove that yes... indeed... these mythical creatures really do walk the same Earth as the human.

This would probably be catastrophic for the race of Gigantopithecus Apes who roamed the spot on the map called Humboldt County by the humans who decided to live in this area in centuries past.

Gigantopithecus Apes were thought by scientists of the world, to be long extinct from the planet.

There had actually been prehistoric skulls, and bones found of these supposedly extinct creatures, that were now in many museums throughout the world.

There had once been a time when these ancient creatures roamed the Earth with the humans, and were not as secretive as they now were in modern times.

These creatures had always been a somewhat gentle race as they lived among all other animals.

Their population at that time long ago, was maybe a hundred times more than it is today.

But, because of the nature of man at that time... a non feeling killer of any creature that was not of their kind... human... it was a very dangerous place for the Gigantopithecus to survive... openly.

So... as the numbers of this race of ancient apes dwindled, for survival purposes, they had to change how they lived on this planet where the human was slowly becoming the dominate race.

Because they were able to make adjustments over time in the ways that they lived day to day, they were able to survive all the way to modern times with the human race.

This race of apes were alive and well in many different areas of the planet.

The different places where they were still known as mythical creatures, they had different names given by the people that lived in those areas.

"Bigfoot."

"Sasquatch."

"Yeti."

"Abominable Snowman."

"Momo."

"Yowie."

"Meh-Teh."

"Raksha."

"Kikomba."

"The Great Bear."

"Himalayan Beast."

"Skunk Ape."

These are just a few of the names that travel the world via word of mouth by the humans.

The name of "Bigfoot" is actually a fairly new name given to this secretive creature.

It is the popular name for the creature that supposedly roams the Pacific Northwest.

Supposedly… meaning, the majority of people that hear of Bigfoot in this area of the planet, think of it as a creature that might exist, but until they see definitive actual proof, they will only think that it is possible, but not conclusive of their actual existence.

It took Sleeping Beaver, and Crazy Mylo about an hour and a half to travel to the waterfall.

The waterfall.

They sat down upon the ground underneath a majestic redwood tree and waited.

What they never did know about the waterfall was the fact that the Bigfoot's could actually see them from inside of the cave behind the flowing water, and not be seen by anyone outside.

They did this by putting both of their arms into the flowing water, and made a small window to peak through to the outside world.

There was so much water flowing over their arms while they did this, that it was virtually impossible to see them with the naked eye.

Maybe… if one were to film the waterfall with a high resolution film camera, and zoomed in, and look at each frame, millisecond by millisecond, and look at the exact spot where the Bigfoot was making his or her small window, you might be lucky to see a pair of eyes looking back at you.

Bigfoot eyes!!

So… as Crazy Mylo, and Sleeping Beaver sat at a distance, looking at the waterfall, unknown to them at that moment, they were indeed being watched by a pair of adult Bigfoot's.

One male and one Female.

They recognized their human friends, and were making sure that the rest of the area was safe to come out from behind the waterfall.

These were the only two humans on the entire planet that knew of this cave system behind the waterfall.

They spied on the two men for several minutes before coming to the conclusion that it was indeed safe to come out from behind the waterfall.

Crazy Mylo, and Sleeping Beaver had on many occasions gone through this ritual of patiently waiting at a distance for the Bigfoot's to come out and visit with them.

They did not know that they were being watched from behind the waterfall, and they could never really figure out how the Bigfoot's knew when they were there at this location, and whether or not it was safe for them to come out from behind the waterfall.

This would always remain a mystery to these two humans that were lucky to have this long term social relationship with these very private creatures.

The two Bigfoot's finally decided to make their way to the outside world from behind the waterfall, and visit with their human friends.

They both leaned up against the wall of the cave about fifteen feet from the entrance, and walked sideways to the edge of the cave entrance and the side of the flowing water of the waterfall.

One at a time, they stepped out from the side of the waterfall and onto the dry ground to the outside world.

They barely got wet from the flowing water as it fell down below to a small stream.

Crazy Mylo, and Sleeping Beaver were always amazed to witness the sight of a Bigfoot, appearing out into the open from behind this waterfall.

It was almost like watching a magician pull a rabbit out of a hat, but in this case, it was not magic, it was very much a real event.

All eyes locked onto each other… two humans… two Bigfoots.

There was always that moment of hesitation between the two species when they looked at each other.

Even though these humans were very well known by the Bigfoot's, and very trusted with the secret of their existence.

This hesitation was just a natural moment in time that would always be there… no matter how much trust was bestowed upon these humans.

Chapter Six

SHAMIEKA COULD HARDLY WAIT to get inside of her house.

She skidded her Jeep to a quick halt, and hurried into her house.

Her hands were trembling slightly, not out of fear, but from anxious excitement of what might be on the video that she carried carefully over to her computer.

She set the video camera down on the desk near her computer tower, and went to get a glass of chocolate milk.

Chocolate milk always had a way of calming her down since she was a child.

She went back to her computer, and sat down facing the computer monitor.

She turned everything on, and waited for her login to her desktop.

Shamieka reached into a drawer from her desk, and pulled out a USB cord that would transfer video from her camera to her computer monitor.

Next, she went into another drawer of the desk and retrieved a CD disc of a special software that she would use on this video to enhance the dot density of all of the video frames.

She was hoping that this enhancement would be good enough to show her some better detail of the creature that she had captured on the video from a distance.

After a few minutes of preparations with these various computer devices, she turned on the video of the video camera, and started the download.

A few minutes later, a message popped onto her screen that indicated that the download was complete, and the software was also ready to use on the video.

She sat for a moment to gather her thoughts before really getting started with this new project.

She drank a slow long sip of her chocolate milk, and closed her eyes for another few moments.

Finally, she was ready to start.

She started the video.

Because of her past experiences in shooting a number of video's in the past, there was not hardly any shakiness of the video as it started to appear on the screen.

She watched the video carefully for a few minutes, and then came to a scene that she knew was one that she would have to enhance to look at more carefully.

For a brief moment, the creature was standing at a far distance, but in open view next to a redwood tree before disappearing behind it.

It was actually a front view shot of the whole body, and face!!

Shamieka briefly gasped for some extra air into her lungs.

She freeze framed the exact area of the video that she wanted her special software to enhance.

She double clicked her mouse, and watched the software perform it's specialty.

Her eyes started to widen as the software started it's enhancement of the creature.

In a low voice she said… "Oh My God!!"

On the screen before her eyes was now a very crisp and clear still picture of the creature.

It definitely was not a Bear, or any other type of creature that she had ever seen in her entire life.

The creature was very large, standing on two legs upright.

With the exception of it's face, the entire body was covered by very dark long thick and dense hair.

She zoomed the video even more to the point of where it only looked like it was standing twenty feet away from her.

As she did this, she jumped back a little from a natural fear, even though it was only a video.

It scared her.

She drank the rest of her chocolate milk.

She now looked very carefully at the creatures face.

It looked very similar to that of a gorilla, but at the same time, different in it's own way.

It was definitely ape like… for sure.

The creature's face did not… in her opinion, show any signs of meanness.

It had an almost gentle like expression on it's face.

It looked calm, and focused.

It looked to her like the mythical creature that people in Humboldt County called… Bigfoot!!

She said this out loud to nobody in particular.

"Bigfoot!!"

"Holy crap… your Bigfoot!!"

"You really do exist!!"

Shamieka was totally stunned.

She had some very credible evidence that Bigfoot actually did exist.

This was only the first freeze frame of the video that she had enhanced with the special software!!

She had many more frames still to document!!

Shamieka spent the next several hours documenting all of the still shots on the video of the Bigfoot.

Many thoughts ran through her head about what to do with this evidence, and what the repercussions might be for her.

She could become famous in the world as the first person who actually had definitive proof that Bigfoot did indeed exist.

This was definitely not a person in a suit promoting a hoax.

It was no doubt, several good views of Bigfoot.

She thought that maybe, if she turned this evidence over to her boss, that the video would not be released to the public.

She thought that maybe she should just go public with the video, and see how things turned out afterwards.

She thought of all of the media attention that she would surely get, fame… money… a different life altogether from what it now was at this time.

Finally, after she had archived and copied, and saved all of this video, she collected her thoughts once again in a more rational manner.

Shamieka decided that she would not do anything until she was able to sit down with her boyfriend… Sleeping Beaver, and show all of this video evidence to him, and see what he had to say, and what she should possibly do.

She trusted Sleeping Beaver more than anyone in her life.

So… she picked up her cell phone, and made a call to him.

As usual, she was not able to talk to him immediately like she would have wanted too, so she left a message on his voice mail.

She did not go into any details about why it was so urgent for him to get back to her, and especially, see her in person at her place as soon as he possibly could.

She would keep all of this a complete secret until she was able to show the video to Sleeping Beaver.

She felt a tremendous amount of mental pressure to not be able to tell anyone about what she had evidence of… Bigfoot exists!!

She also started to think about how it would affect the Bigfoot, if or when she did show all of this evidence to the world of many doubters.

She felt a twinge of feeling sorry for the creature with this thought.

Would she ruin the creatures life with this exposure?

Would this evidence motivate a large amount of people to go on a massive hunt for the creature?

Maybe she would be the person who would ultimately be responsible for making this creature really become extinct, from this world of many living creatures.

That thought terrified her.

Here was a creature that had been able to stay out of the world of the humans, to a point of where it was thought of as a creature that did not actually exist… Mythical.

Now… here she was, the one person on the planet who had an opportunity to expose this creature as one of not being mythical, but of actually being very real.

A real living, breathing creature.

She really did not want any people to try to track this creature down, and capture it for their own glory, and even eventually house the creature in a zoo for people to stare at in wonder.

The more she thought about it, the more she was leaning towards keeping all of this a secret, for the sake of the continuing existence of this secretive creature who had never been proven to actually harm anyone, let alone actually existing.

But… she would for sure let Sleeping Beaver watch the video, and get his input on it.

She already thought that Sleeping Beaver would probably want her to keep all of this a secret, and let the creature continue to live in relative peace.

It was very obvious that Bigfoot did not want to become friends with the human race, because of the simple fact that it had remained so elusive for all of these many years.

At the same time… there was a very slight thought that remained within her brain… greed… that she could definitely change her life, if she did in fact expose the Bigfoot to the world.

But, this thought was very much out weighed by human compassion.

The Bigfoot creature had just as much right to live how it wanted to live as any of her fellow human beings.

She also had the thought that this Bigfoot was in all likelihood, not the only Bigfoot in Humboldt County.

It could not possibly be the one and only creature that had been sighted many times over the years by a large number of people.

Surely… there was probably a population of Bigfoots that coexisted with this Bigfoot that she had captured on video.

There were probably many adults, and young Bigfoots who lived peacefully within the vast Redwood forest.

Actually, there was probably a large population of this creature throughout the world that were known by different names that really did exist, as did this same creature caught by her video camera.

She decided to go to a liquor store and buy some hard liquor and go back to her place and get drunk.

She would wait for Sleeping Beaver to arrive, even if she had to take the next few days off.

She was basically going to keep herself private for the time being.

It was not every day when a person was able to get verifiable evidence that Bigfoot actually did indeed exist.

She needed a drink.

Chapter Seven

A S SAMUEL GOODSON WALKED across his living room of his home, he could hear the beeping from his phone recorder.

His son Augy was already in the kitchen waiting for him to get him his food for the morning.

Samuel walked over to the recorder and pressed the play button.

The red light blinked, almost urgently as the recording began.

The message was from a University professor from Washington State University.

Samuel had been having an ongoing dialog with this particular professor for almost two years.

The professor was writing a book on people who traveled the world in search of the elusive creature known by many names.

Commonly known in Humboldt County as "Bigfoot."

The professor's name was Garfield Harrison.

He wanted to have Samuel come up to meet him at the University and get together for an interview.

He also proposed a paid for, by the University, dual lecture with him about the Mythical creature… Bigfoot.

This offer intrigued Samuel.

He immediately called the professor back at his private number for discussion about these proposal's.

His immediate thought as he began contacting the professor was… his son Augy.

Normally, Augy went everywhere with him.

But, in this case, if he accepted the offer from the professor, there would be situations where it would be difficult to take care of his son while trying to do some serious business with the professor.

His mind flashed momentarily.

He thought of "Sleeping Beaver."

The phone rang three times before the professor's voice sounded on the other end.

The two men talked for a few minutes before Samuel decided that he was very interested in accepting the offer.

He told the professor that he needed to attend to his son, and that he would get back to him later on in the day to finalize when he would be able to come, and to also make arrangements for traveling up to Washington State… without his son Augy.

After feeding his son, and talking to him about his leaving for a trip to Washington State to meet someone important, and do some work, he mentioned to Augy that he was going to ask Sleeping Beaver if it would be possible for him to watch Augy.

Even though Augy was autistic, he was very able to understand what his father was telling him.

Unfortunately, he was not able to verbally relay back to his Dad that he did not really care, one way or the other.

He would rather be exploring the forest's.

So, shortly after his conversation with his son, Samuel made a call to Sleeping Beaver.

There was no answer, so he left a message on Sleeping Beaver's voice mail.

He quickly explained his situation, and asked Sleeping Beaver to please get back to him as soon as he could, one way or the other, no matter what his decision was.

There were a few other people that could be back-ups, as far as watching his son, but he hoped that Sleeping Beaver would do this for him because he would be able to take Augy out exploring the many forest's in Humboldt County.

Samuel called back Professor Harrison, and told him that he would call him with the exact time that he would be leaving Humboldt County, pending arrangements for his son Augy.

He did not hear from Sleeping Beaver that day, and decided to wait for one more day before asking someone else to watch Augy.

It was not until late in the day, just after he and Augy had dinner, that Sleeping Beaver finally did call.

Sleeping Beaver told Samuel that he would be very happy to watch little Augy while Samuel was away on his trip to Washington State.

Both men made preparations to meet the next day and have Sleeping Beaver pick up Augy.

Sleeping Beaver told Samuel that he and his girlfriend Shamieka would stop by and pick up little Augy.

Samuel immediately called Professor Harrison after hanging up the phone call with Sleeping Beaver to tell him when he was coming.

He then explained to his son again, that he would be leaving for awhile, and that Sleeping Beaver would be watching him while he was gone.

Little Augy did not show any emotion after hearing this from his Dad.

Samuel also explained to Augy that he would be staying at Sleeping Beaver's house.

Again, Augy did not seemed fazed with this information either.

Father and son, went to bed... as the stars in the night time skies twinkled like tiny diamonds.

Both were asleep within minutes.

Chapter Eight

SLEEPING BEAVER HAD JUST finished leaving the mountains where his friend Crazy Mylo remained with the Bigfoots, and his grow of Marijuana, when he noticed that he had two messages on his voice mail from his cellphone.

The first was from Samuel Goodson and the second one was from his girlfriend Shamieka.

He called Shamieka first, and asked her if she would come with him tomorrow to pick up little Augy, and she told him that she would.

She was very anxious to see him, and wanted him to come to her place for the night to show him something very important.

After he was done talking to his sweetheart, Sleeping Beaver called Samuel Goodson to tell him that he would watch little Augy for him while he was on his trip to Washington State.

After he was done with Samuel Goodson, he immediately traveled to Shamieka's place to spend the night with her.

He was always excited to see her, even if it was only a day that he had not seen her.

She was very special in his heart and soul.

She had a way of brightening up his day, no matter what his day had been like.

Sleeping Beaver was also very curious about how come Shamieka was so anxious to have him get to her place.

He wondered what she wanted to show him, that was so important.

He thought to himself that it must be something unusual.

It was dark outside by the time Sleeping Beaver arrived at Shamieka's house.

She opened the door and quickly embraced him tightly.

This surprised him a little.

She had a quizzical look upon her face that intrigued him.

What the heck was going on with his girlfriend.

He could also smell alcohol as she kissed him smooth and generously.

He could tell that she was a bit intoxicated.

He actually felt an urge to have a few drinks as well.

He knew where all of her alcohol was stored, so he went and made himself a drink… his favorite, a "Bloody Mary."

As he sat down on the couch next to Shamieka, he asked her what it was that she was so anxious to show him.

She told him a little forcefully that she wanted him to finish his drink first before she showed him what it was that she was so excited about.

This statement really made him wonder even more.

He quickly, in three gulps, downed the "Bloody Mary," and put the glass down on the table with a semi loud clink.

He smiled at her, and said… "O.K. sweetheart, I am all eyes and ears for you."

He sat there silently, waiting for a response from her.

She sat there staring at him silently for several moments as well.

Finally, she said to him… "I have some video that I shot in a forest down south that I want you to watch, and then tell me what you think that you might be looking at."

"Personally, I am shocked, but I want to hear from you what your opinion is of this video."

"I have not let any other person see this video because it is so unbelievable."

Sleeping Beaver replied back coyly… "Reaaaaalllllly?"

Shamieka playfully punched him in the shoulder.

She answered back… "This is no joke!!"

"I am dead serious, this video will make you speechless, I can guarantee you."

Shamieka walked over to her desk where her computer was located, and sat down.

She motioned Sleeping Beaver to come over and sit down beside her.

She sat in front of the computer monitor with a very serious look upon her face.

Sleeping Beaver pulled up a chair and sat down.

He thought to himself, this must be very serious, so he stopped his playful joking with her, and put on a serious expression on his face as well.

Once again, he sat silently... waiting.

Shamieka turned on her computer and waited for it to boot-up.

Within a minute, her icons on her desktop were in front of her eyes.

She went to her files section and clicked a file marked... "BF?"

Sleeping Beaver leaned forward a little and concentrated on the screen before him.

Shamieka hit play on the video, and it started to play.

The video was very high quality, and very steady.

No graininess, or shaking at all.

The video slowly panned in the direction of a figure off in the distance next to one of several redwood tree's.

Next, the video multiplied it's setting, and the image of the figure in the distance became larger on the screen, as if it were only twenty feet away.

The clarity of the video did not lose any of it's quality.

This was because of the special software that was used for this video.

The "DPI's" (Dots Per Inch) remained intact at a high resolution.

Sleeping Beaver was impressed with this feature of the video software, and told Shamieka this.

But... at the same time, silently in his head, he was starting to feel very uneasy about what was appearing on the computer screen in front of him.

Shamieka, froze the video frame on a perfect front view of the figure on the video.

She looked over at Sleeping Beaver and said... "Well?"

"What do you think?"

Sleeping Beaver did not say anything right away, because he already knew what he was looking at.

He asked his girlfriend very casually... "Is this the only shot that you have?"

She laughed at him lightly, and a bit sarcastically.

She clicked the video to play once again, and the video started to play on the screen.

They both sat there together… silently watching the video play to the very end.

Sleeping Beaver never once interrupted her to stop the video.

He was absolutely shocked at what he had just watched.

It was not a shock to see a Bigfoot on video, because secretly, he already knew all about them, he was friends with several of them.

He was shocked about the fact that the secret that he and Crazy Mylo had so carefully over the years kept from the rest of the world, was right here in full high quality video for all to see.

There was no doubt about the existence of "Bigfoot" after viewing this particular video.

The video was not altered, and was in it's original state.

All the experts in the world could view this video, and whether they were non believers or not, they would all have to definitely agree that the contents on this video, indeed proved the existence of the elusive creature known as Bigfoot.

It was not a Hollywood special effects video.

It was not a man in a high quality ape suit.

It could not be mistaken for a Bear.

No doubt about it, this video would definitely shock the world, and make believers of everyone who viewed it.

It could be compared to the time, long ago, when there was another secretive, and just as elusive creature that had been talked about for centuries, before finally being discovered, and proven without a doubt of it's existence as well.

That creature is now a common sight in almost all major zoo's around the world.

This creature is the Gorilla.

This video could now do the exact same thing in modern times as what had happened with the Gorilla over a hundred years ago.

Would Bigfoot someday become as common of a sight as the Gorilla?

In a Zoo?

Several of these thoughts raced through Sleeping Beaver's head as he sat silently next to Shamieka as the video went back to it's file on the computer desk top.

Shamieka rose from her chair and walked back over to the couch and plopped down.

She asked Sleeping Beaver to make her a drink.

Sleeping Beaver did not hesitate for a moment at this request.

He needed a few more drinks for himself as well.

After making some more drinks, Sleeping Beaver sat down next to Shamieka, and took a nice gulp from his drink.

Shamieka did the same.

She finally broke the silence between them and simply asked… "Do you think that what you just watched on that video was the legendary elusive "Bigfoot?"

Sleeping Beaver was all of a sudden boxed into an imaginary invisible corner.

He felt the same feeling as when he was a child, and his mother was putting him on a "time-out."

He felt trapped with this point blank direct question from Shamieka.

He did not answer right away.

He needed a little time to gather his thoughts, and then decide how to honestly? . . . answer Shamieka's question.

He took another large gulp of his drink.

He finally answered her question.

"Are you going to show the whole world this video?"

Shamieka did not answer his question.

She asked him to answer her question first, before she answered his question.

Sleeping Beaver, reluctantly spoke.

"Well… it sure does look like the creature that is called Bigfoot in the video."

"This video will prove to the entire world that Bigfoot does in fact exist."

"So… can you now answer my question, and then we can have a nice long discussion."

Shamieka was surprised that Sleeping Beaver answered so directly, after much hesitation.

But she was not surprised by his open honesty.

That is why she had true deep feelings for this man.

He was so completely honest.

It was really a hard thing to do in these times, to find a truly 100% honest man to be at your side.

She answered his question.

"I am also convinced that this is without any doubt whatsoever, that this in fact does prove the existence of Bigfoot."

"Technically, I am supposed to turn this video over to my boss because it was shot out in the field, and is part of my job."

"But… I have not really decided what to do with this video, because I wanted for you to view it, and hear your opinion of it's content's, and hear your personal advice on how I should proceed forward."

"There are so many different possibilities."

"Would you agree with me on that?"

Sleeping Beaver shook his head up and down silently to acknowledge that he agreed with that statement.

Shamieka continued to talk.

"I could take this video, and show the whole world, and have all of the experts look at it, and eventually make a whole lot of money from it, and be famous for being the single person who definitely showed the entire world that Bigfoot actually did in fact co-exist with us humans on this planet."

"Talk shows, lectures, a book, and of course selling the actual video to the highest bidder."

"These thoughts have crossed my mind as I sat here at home and waited for you to come here and be with me."

"At the same time, other thoughts have entered into my mind as well."

"What would be the repercussion's on the Bigfoot's?"

"Would I ruin their lives?"

"Would my selfishness and greed be the beginning of the end of their existence?"

"I would not be able to live with myself if I was to cause the extinction of a creature that has been able to live for so long amongst us."

"It would not be fair to these creatures for me to do that to them."

"They have the right to roam this planet, and live a life of freedom… as we do."

"It would also be sad to eventually watch them be tracked down and captured for zoo's like the Gorilla was a century ago."

"I am sure that there must certainly be families of these creatures, and to hear of them being hunted down, because of my actions, would be a travesty."

"So here I sit with you… torn between these thought."

"Whose world do I change, mine, or their's?"

"Or both?"

"Should I?"

"Or should I not?"

"I am leaning more towards letting these creatures live in peace."

"So… what do you think?"

Sleeping Beaver felt proud of this woman before him.

All of a sudden, he did not feel any pressure at all to answer her.

A fleeting thought crossed his mind.

Maybe he would divulge his secret about how he and Crazy Mylo have been friends with the Bigfoots for many years.

He held back on that decision for now, and decided to just talk with her about this video, and hopefully steer her in the direction that she was leaning towards.

Sleeping Beaver leaned over to her and gave her a tender kiss.

He suggested that they retire for the night, and go to bed, and that he would think about all that she had said, and what he had seen, and they could talk about it tomorrow when they woke up.

He reminded her that they needed to go and pick up little Augy Goodson the next day.

He told her that they had time to talk, but not anymore tonight.

He just wanted to cuddle up with her in the dark.

She smiled at him lightly, and grabbed his hand, and silently led him to her bedroom.

Chapter Nine

SAMUEL GOODSON HAD JUST finished packing all of Augy's clothes that he would need while Sleeping Beaver watched him.

He had already packed his own clothes for his trip to Washington State the night before while his son was asleep.

This would be the first time that he would be leaving little Augy to be watched by someone.

But... he did trust Sleeping Beaver.

He thought that his son would be alright with Sleeping Beaver because they would be doing a lot of exploring together, and little Augy really liked to explore.

He suspected that his son might experience a little anxiety when he did not come home at night, but instead spent the night wherever Sleeping Beaver decided.

He also knew that his son would be around Sleeping Beaver's girlfriend Shamieka, and he was alright with that as well.

As a matter of fact, Augy already knew Shamieka from the past few years.

As Samuel sat in his kitchen, watching his son eat breakfast, his mind started to wander, thinking about Washington State.

He was excited about this newest project.

The sun started to filter through the window of the kitchen, and the rays brightened up the room.

Augy looked up, and his father thought that it was the sunlight that just came into the kitchen, but what he did not know was that it was actually

Augy's super hearing, picking up the sound of an approaching vehicle to their home.

This vehicle was Shamieka's.

It was Shamieka, and Sleeping Beaver coming to pick up little Augy.

About twenty seconds later, Shamieka pulled up to the Goodson home and parked in the driveway.

Shamieka gave a short blast of her vehicle's horn just as she came to a complete stop.

Her and Sleeping Beaver got out of the vehicle, and walked towards the front door of the home.

Samuel Goodson opened the door before they even got to the porch, and greeted them.

There were all smiles from all three people.

Augy remained in the kitchen, meticulously devouring his breakfast.

Augy knew that there were people at the house, but he was not going to change his morning routine.

Samuel invited Shamieka and Sleeping Beaver into his home and walked towards the kitchen.

As all three adults entered the kitchen, there still was not even the smallest sign of recognition from little Augy that they were there.

His eyes did not even look up from the table.

He just continued to eat his food.

There was no shock by this from any of the three adults standing in the kitchen with Augy.

They all understood that Augy was autistic, and that he had his own daily routines that should not be interrupted.

There was actually one good thing about Shamieka being present with little Augy.

Years ago, before little Augy's mother passed away, she had been teaching her son "sign language."

Because of his speech impediment, this was going to be the way to communicate for little Augy with other's that knew how to do sign language.

But... ever since Augy's mother died, he had not done any sign language with any person since.

There were attempts by his father to continue this with his son, but Augy was not responsive, so there were no more attempts to continue the sign language.

Hopefully, there would come a time later when little Augy would be re-introduced to sign language if he felt comfortable with it.

Then it was noticed one day when Samuel had met Shamieka in Eureka by chance, and out of the blue, she showed little Augy some sign language, and to Samuel's surprise, his son started to answer her back… with the sign language!!

After he parted ways with Shamieka that day, he tried to see if Augy would respond to him if he did some sign language.

He was disappointed to see that little Augy went back to ignoring the sign language, and communicating only in his own special blabbering typing of sounds.

So… whenever Shamieka was around Augy, she would try the sign language, and his son would always respond back to her.

She sort of acted as a "go-between" for everyone, in regards to what little Augy was actually saying.

Samuel only knew a limited amount of signing, but Shamieka knew the entire special language.

Samuel and Sleeping Beaver stood there in the kitchen and watched as Augy and Shamieka communicated with each other.

She was explaining to the little boy that her and Sleeping Beaver would be watching him while his father was away on special business.

Little Augy did not seem to be irritated by this, maybe because his father had already told him about it.

Samuel never knew with his son how much was understood when he talked to him, but he had a feeling that the comprehension was pretty much completely 100%.

Samuel showed Sleeping Beaver little Augy's belonging's that they would take.

Sleeping Beaver immediately started to take these to Shamieka's vehicle to put inside.

Shamieka continued her sign language conversation with little Augy.

She could sense that Augy was actually a little excited about the prospects of a lot of outdoor exploring in the days to follow with Sleeping Beaver.

She forwarded this to Samuel, and this pleased him.

Augy finished his breakfast, and his sign language conversation with Shamieka, and walked out of the kitchen to the front room of the house.

He seemed to be anxious to leave.

This surprised his father a little.

So… Samuel went along with his son's apparent gesture, and bid everyone a farewell.

Shamieka led little Augy out of the house towards her vehicle, followed close behind by Sleeping Beaver and Samuel.

Samuel gave his son a tender hug, and watched as Sleeping Beaver and Shamieka got into the vehicle, and drove away.

It was a strange feeling for Samuel to all of a sudden to be completely alone without his son with him.

But… it was not a feeling of "freaking-out."

It was only a new feeling for him that only last for a little while.

Now he concentrated on leaving his home and traveling to Washington State.

In the meantime, Shamieka was already on the highway heading north back in the direction of her home.

She planned on spending the rest of the afternoon at home with Sleeping Beaver and Augy.

She still wanted to have a nice long talk with Sleeping Beaver about his opinion of what to do after he had seen the video of the apparent Bigfoot the night before.

As they drove on the highway, to her surprise, Sleeping Beaver actually brought up the subject of the Bigfoot video.

He started out slowly about the video.

"So… Shamieka, I have been thinking about the video of the supposed Bigfoot that I watched last night."

Shamieka instantly answered back… "Supposed!!"

Sleeping Beaver could tell by the tone of her voice that this might be a difficult conversation, but it was one that he felt comfortable having with her.

He answered back politely… "I mean, sure, it sure looked like it was what we call a Bigfoot."

"You mentioned to me all of the possibilities that were swarming in your beautiful little head."

"I am just curious as to what your final decision will be."

"Ultimately, it will be your decision, not mine."

"I can only give you my own opinion as to what I think would be the best thing for you to do."

Augy sat silently in the back seat of the vehicle, looking at all of the beautiful scenery of many types of pine tree's at 60 miles per hour.

No matter where he looked, the majority of scenery was Humboldt County's green beauty.

He was oblivious with the conversation that Shamieka and Sleeping Beaver were having in the front seat nearby.

He was in his own little world for the moment.

Sleeping Beaver continued to talk.

"Whatever decision you finally come to, I will back you up 100%, no matter if I disagree with you or not."

"I will admit to you, I do indeed believe that what you have on that video is for sure a Bigfoot."

"I have no doubt that you have captured on video, the "holy grail" of proof for all of the people in the world that doubt that Bigfoot actually does exist."

"There will certainly be major repercussions throughout the world if you decide to come forward and show everyone on the planet, this video."

"If you were to ask me what I would do if I were in your exact situation, well… that would be a bit difficult for me to answer you."

Sleeping Beaver was referring… silently, and secretly, the fact that he already knew of Bigfoot's existence.

He struggled, back and forth with a serious question to himself.

Would he, or should he tell Shamieka the truth about his years with the elusive creature… Bigfoot?

He was having a very difficult time in making a final decision.

He decided, for now, before he got too far into this current conversation in the vehicle, that he would wait and hear everything that Shamieka had to say on the subject of the Bigfoot video.

So, Sleeping Beaver backed away from the conversation, and suggested that they stop talking about it for now, and wait until they got to her place, and were more relaxed.

Maybe they could play the video again, and restart the conversation as the video played.

As far as playing the video in front of little Augy, they did not feel like he was a threat to go out and tell the whole world about Bigfoot.

How could he anyway? His language was not understood by anybody.

Shamieka agreed with Sleeping Beaver's suggestion, and stopped talking about the Bigfoot video for the time being.

She reached down and turned the radio on to a local channel, and the vehicle started to be filled with the sounds of old 80's rock music.

Everyone remained silent, listening to the music until Shamieka pulled her vehicle up to her place.

Tiny droplets of rain started to fall from the skies as they exited the vehicle.

Typical Humboldt County weather.

Not happy with the weather? . . . just wait 15 minutes.

They casually walked from the vehicle into her place.

Sleeping Beaver carried little Augy's belongings from the vehicle.

Chapter Ten

T HE TWO BIGFOOTS… A mother and her son walked stealthily through the forest towards their home.

Their home was located within a cave system hidden behind a waterfall in the mountains.

The mother's name was "Reka" and her son was called "Esher."

They were very close to each other.

Their love for each other was no different from that of humans.

Their bond was very strong indeed.

They communicated in their own language.

To a human, it would just sound like a bunch of garbled unintelligible words.

But the language spoken between the two was very much a language.

It was the ancient language of the Bigfoot creatures, and the same language of the same creatures with different names around the world.

They traveled very quickly and silently, and covered a lot of ground in a short period of time.

Reka and Esher had been out in the forest looking for food.

They had found some roots and ate generously.

They had spotted some deer, but did not feel compelled at that moment to try to capture and kill for some meat.

If they would have decided to kill the deer for some meat, they would have brought it back to their home in the cave system, and shared it with the other Bigfoot's.

They were experts at getting various types of food, whether it was plants, or animals.

Over the thousands of years, they had mastered the knowledge and techniques for acquiring both.

This was taught to all of the younger generations over time.

Esher was equivalent to the age of a ten year old human boy.

Actually, around the same maturity level as little Augy.

The ages of a Bigfoot and a human were very similar.

The Bigfoots being a little more mature at a younger age than the humans.

Esher was actually only six years in human time.

The mother, Reka, she was 18 years old in human time.

Esher liked to play.

His type of play was much different from that of a human.

He liked to show other animals that he could see them, and startle them.

This amused him.

It also was a way of training himself to be an expert of the art of "Stealth."

This was one of the most important things that any of the Bigfoots had to learn as they grew to maturity.

Failure to master the art of stealth could mean not living the peaceful life that they were used to.

It could even mean not living anymore… death.

Esher also liked to run really fast through the forest, dodging the many tree's as he ran.

Reka? She just continued to walk at her own pace as her son ran back and forth through the forest.

She had a slight smile upon her face while walking and watching her son Esher.

Yes, Bigfoots did show facial expressions on their face, almost the same as humans did.

They would frown when not happy about a situation.

They would smile when they felt happiness.

They would sneer when they felt mad.

They would gasp when surprised.

They had many other facial expressions that could be understood by other Bigfoots.

The Bigfoots were not really scared of any of the other animals of the forest.

The Bears?

They had an understanding with the Bears.

It was a very rare event, to see a Bigfoot and a Bear in mortal combat with each other.

Occasionally, a Bear might attack a smaller, younger Bigfoot, but because there was always an adult Bigfoot nearby, this would ultimately turn out to be a grave mistake for the Bear.

It turns out that the Bigfoots were so powerful, that they could kill a Bear if they fought each other.

Sure, the Bigfoot might get injured a little at first, but the Bear would be killed very quickly before it had much of a chance to do harm to the Bigfoot.

Mountain Lions?

Forget it.

They were totally afraid of the Bigfoot, even the smaller young ones.

As a matter of fact, Esher loved to try and catch the mountain Lions when he came upon them.

To him, they were like a little cat to a human.

Even a small young Bigfoot was very powerful.

A conservative estimate would be that a youngster like Esher would easily be about 4 times stronger then even the strongest human on the planet.

One could only imagine the difference in strength between an adult human and a mature full grown Bigfoot.

It was not long before Reka and Esher came to the area where the cave system was located behind the waterfall.

Both of them stopped, looked around the area for several moments, and then quickly hugged the wall of the mountain and slid behind the cascading water, and entered into a large cave.

This large cave was only the very beginning of a huge cave system that stretched for hundreds of miles in many different directions, like tentacles of an octopus.

This ancient cave system was very well hidden from the outside world where the humans roamed.

There were quite a number of exits that blended with parts of nature, such as this waterfall, and there were also many false entrances that ended abruptly once entered.

It was truly a maze on a grand scale.

If a human were to actually have the opportunity to enter this massive cave system, he or she would certainly be intimidated, and lost very quickly.

Only the Bigfoot populations throughout the planet knew where all of these caves went.

Reka and Esher were met right away by a large mature male Bigfoot.

He was one of the many leaders of this local bigfoot population.

He was also Esher's father.

His name was "Arch."

Arch gave a greeting in their language that was one of love and happiness.

He was always happy to see his mate, and son return home to the cave system from the outside world.

There was always a little bit of anxiety felt by all of the Bigfoots in the cave system whenever any of their kind exited out into the world of humans.

Arch, Reka, and their son Esher walked together at a casual pace deeper into the cave system where they were met by many other Bigfoots.

They all gave their kind happy greetings as well.

Chapter Eleven

SHAMIEKA, SLEEPING BEAVER, AND little Augy were now sitting comfortably on a couch in the living room.

Shamieka had her laptop computer set-up on a small coffee table in front of them.

Augy had a large glass with ice and soda in front of him.

Shamieka and Sleeping Beaver had glasses of Iced tea.

The computer was turned on, and even little Augy seemed interested in what would appear on the screen.

They all waited as the computer loaded up.

Shamieka went to the file marked BF, and clicked it on.

This was the Bigfoot file.

In a matter of moments, the screen started to show a video.

Even though Sleeping Beaver had already seen this video the day before, it still was a shock to him to realize that here... before his eyes, was the definitive proof for all of the world to possibly see, as he was for the second time now, real legitimate proof of the existence of a mythical creature known in this part of the world as Bigfoot.

Little Augy studied the images on the screen silently, not moving a muscle, and seemingly not even blinking.

He seemed entranced by what he was viewing.

Both adults sitting next to him noticed his total attention to the computer screen.

Sleeping Beaver made a comment... "It looks like Augy is interested in what we are watching."

Shamieka shook her head silently in affirmation to this statement from Sleeping Beaver.

All of a sudden, little Augy started to speak in his garbled, unintelligible language.

Shamieka said Augy's name aloud, and started to do some sign language.

She asked him what he had just said.

Augy looked at her for a moment before answering in sign language.

He told her that he said that he has seen these creatures before.

This shocked Shamieka to the point of utter silence.

Sleeping Beaver asked Shamieka what Augy had said.

She remained silent for almost a full thirty seconds before answering Sleeping Beaver.

"He said that he has seen these creatures before."

Sleeping Beaver answered quickly with only one word… "What!!"

Shamieka suggested that they finish watching the video before having a full conversation between the three of them.

Sleeping Beaver agreed.

The video continued to play, and all three sat and watched very carefully.

There were many times while the video played that little Augy would erupt in his special language, but not very loudly, just barely above a whisper.

Finally, the video completed it's digital course, and Shamieka turned off the computer.

Within moments, she started to engage in conversation, via sign language with Augy.

Sleeping Beaver could only sit by patiently while the two communicated in a language that he had never taken the time to learn.

Back and forth, Shamieka and Augy went in the silent language.

Many times, there were pauses to give time for each to ponder one another's questions and think of their replies.

It was interesting to watch this little boy communicate with Shamieka.

Sleeping Beaver had always thought that Augy was very limited mentally, especially in communication skills.

It now appeared to Sleeping Beaver that Augy was not as slow mentally as he had always thought.

Shamieka and Augy conversed in the silent language for almost forty five solid minutes before she finally turned to Sleeping Beaver and remarked that she was now ready to tell him what little Augy had said in sign language.

The first thing that Sleeping Beaver said to Shamieka before they started their own conversations between them was… "Do you think that you could teach me how to do sign language?"

"I would be very interested in learning, and then be able to eventually communicate with our little man here."

Shamieka promised Sleeping Beaver that she would take the time to teach him the silent language when she could find the time to do so.

This pleased Sleeping Beaver, because now that he realized that little Augy was more mentally capable then he had thought, it would be a pleasure for him to be able to communicate with the little boy.

It was already clear to Sleeping Beaver that Augy was indeed comfortable in his company.

He could see that they could possibly become friends at some point in time.

Shamieka started the conversation once again.

"Little Augy had a lot to say in regards to the Bigfoot video, and he says that he had past experiences with the creatures."

"He told me about a few occasions where he had seen a Bigfoot during his travels with his father."

"Everyone knows that Samuel is an avid Bigfoot researcher, and has traveled the world over to find definitive proof of their existence."

"It's too bad that he is not sitting here today with us and watching this video of a Bigfoot."

"I wonder how he would react?"

"I wonder if his opinion of what I should do with the video would be the same as what I think, and what you think?"

"Unfortunately, I am of the opinion that he would want to instantly tell the whole world, and share in some of the glory."

"He is a good man, but with this knowledge, I think that because of all of the years of listening to the many doubters that heckled him about his belief that Bigfoot does in fact exist . . ."

Shamieka paused for a moment before continuing.

"I think that would compel him to move forward very quickly with the proof on this video."

"It would certainly be a vindication for him, and silence all of the hecklers, and doubters."

"I myself am still not sure as to what I should do with this video."

"Technically, it is my job to just simply turn this video over to my bosses."

"But… if I do turn this video over to them, they could simply make the proof disappear, and then there would not be anymore definitive proof of this creatures existence, for who knows how long."

"Maybe that would be the best thing to do."

"If I do anything else other than turn over this video to my bosses, my career would certainly be over with."

"I am so confused Sleeping Beaver… what should I do?"

Sleeping Beaver finally made a decision, one that he thought that he would not ever make in his lifetime, a promise that would now become broken with his friend Crazy Mylo, and of course, the many Bigfoots who have trusted him with his silence of their existence for many years.

"Shamieka… I think that you should not let anyone else view this Bigfoot video."

"I have given much thought to what I have heard you talking about, and my simple conclusion is that these creatures deserve to live in peace, as they have for many thousands of years on this planet."

"Everything that you have said is very valid."

"You know the saying… "What they don't know won't hurt them?""

"In this case, I believe if the humans did in fact know, there would certainly be a great possibility of harm that might come to the Bigfoot population that survives peacefully in these mountains surrounding us."

"I say this with all my heart, and I have to now be completely honest with you."

"I will just come right out and tell you a secret that I have harbored within me for many years."

"I already know that the creatures known in these parts as Bigfoot, do in fact exist."

"The reality is that I have befriended many of these creatures over the years."

"Me and Crazy Mylo discovered these creatures years ago by accident, and we have kept a relationship with them ever since."

"I know that this sounds unbelievable, but why would I lie to you?"

"It is only because of the fact that you have captured my friends on video, that I am now forced to break a promise that I made with my friend Crazy Mylo, and the many Bigfoots that trust me."

"I also tell you this because of my deep feelings for you Shamieka."

Sleeping Beaver went on to elaborate in this conversation with his girlfriend, and tell her the complete story of how he and Crazy Mylo had come into contact with the Bigfoot's years ago.

She sat mesmerized for almost an hour, listening very intently to Sleeping Beaver's story of the many experiences with the Bigfoots.

Even little Augy seemed to be focused on what Sleeping Beaver was telling Shamieka.

In fact, after several minutes of listening to Sleeping Beaver, Augy actually started to interrupt Sleeping Beaver, and ask a question in the direction of Shamieka using sign language.

Little Augy was actually asking questions to Sleeping Beaver!!

This was a total surprise to both adults, but at the same time, a pleasure to see that the little boy was interested in interacting with them, and engage in a conversation between the three of them.

Augy had some very interesting questions for Sleeping Beaver.

The more questions that the little boy asked, the more convinced Sleeping Beaver, and Shamieka became that this boy was actually a lot more intelligent than anyone ever gave him credit for.

He asked some very intriguing questions indeed.

If his father were to hear some of these questions, he would certainly be very surprised, and also realize the real extent of the mentality that his son really possessed.

Sleeping Beaver answered all of the question that the little boy asked with much enjoyment.

As he answered these many questions to the little boy, he himself came to realize as well that he had a vast amount of personal knowledge about the Bigfoots.

It was something that he never actually realized until today.

The three of them had this special conversation for a better part of the rest of the day before Shamieka called for a time-out, and suggested that they go out for a pizza.

Sleeping Beaver and little Augy both smiled, and did not even have to answer verbally to this suggestion.

Theirs smiles were the answer.

It was a pleasurable day for the three of them.

A slow bonding was starting to happen between them.

Only as the days of the calendar disappeared into the past, would any of these three people realize how important this bond would be for them, and the many Bigfoots who lived in this area of the planet map known as Humboldt County.

They left Shamieka's place to fill their stomach's with pizza.

At the same time that the three of them were doing this, Samuel was now landing in an airport in the Seattle Washington area, anxious to start his latest project.

His mind was not even for a moment, thinking about how or what his son was doing.

He felt very comfortable about the current arrangement with his son.

Chapter Twelve

SHAMIEKA, SLEEPING BEAVER, AND little Augy returned back to Shamieka's place a few hours later, stuffed full of a pizza from a local pizza parlor.

Sleeping Beaver returned a message from a voicemail.

It was from Samuel Goodson.

Sleeping Beaver called Sameul, and had a very short conversation. Basically Samuel had a good day up in Seattle, and was getting ready for a lecture the next day at the University.

Sleeping Beaver handed the phone to Augy, and the little boy did not respond.

So Sleeping Beaver put the phone on speakerphone and told Samuel that he could now talk.

Samuel started to tell his son how much he missed him, and that everything was alright.

Samuel knew that his son could not really communicate back to him, so it was a jaded conversation to say the least.

But… at least Augy was able to hear his father's voice, even though he could not speak back in a legible language that his father could comprehend.

Augy did not seem to be affected in the very least from the voice of his father coming from the cellphone.

Sleeping Beaver spoke up in the background and told Samuel that Augy seemed to have adjusted very well with him and Shamieka.

Samuel was pleased, and comforted by this statement and finally decided it was time to end the conversation.

He told his son that he loved him and that he would talk to him again when he could… and to have fun.

Augy shrugged slightly, almost not even acknowledging his father's statement.

The phone dial tone went silent.

Shamieka made a very comfortable sleeping arrangement for Augy on the couch, and turned the television on to a cable channel showing a National Geographic special.

This seemed to get Augy's attention.

His eyes instantly focused on a gorilla on the screen.

Shamieka told Augy that she would check on him later and turn the television off for him.

Augy did not respond to her, he was focused on the gorilla.

Shamieka smiled and walked back to her bedroom where Sleeping Beaver was already comfortable on her bed.

She told Sleeping Beaver that there would not be any fun in bed tonight because Augy was here.

Sleeping Beaver understood, and just smiled.

Sleeping Beaver and Shamieka talked for a few hours before they decided to call it a night and turn out the lights.

Shamieka went to her living room to check on Augy and found him completely asleep.

She gently covered him with a blanket, and turned off the television.

The night went quickly, all three were awake around 6:00 a.m.

Shamieka started up the coffee, and Sleeping Beaver showed Augy the food cupboard.

He slowly pointed out different food items, and offered for Augy to pick something.

Augy did not pick anything, he did not even make an attempt to point anything out to Sleeping Beaver.

There was a communication problem, and Sleeping Beaver wished even more at that moment that he had the ability to do sign language like Shamieka.

He asked Shamieka to take over, and try and figure out what Augy wanted to eat for breakfast.

She started to do the silent language to Augy, and instantly Augy responded to her.

Apparently, Augy liked cereal, or English muffins with butter and grape jelly.

Unfortunately, Shamieka did not have either one of these food items in her kitchen.

Sleeping Beaver offered to go to the store to get some food items that Augy liked to eat.

Shamieka asked Augy what other types of food he liked to eat so Sleeping Beaver could buy a few days worth from the store.

Augy told Shamieka a bunch of different types of food that he liked, which turned out to be mostly junk food.

Augy at least drank some milk while Sleeping Beaver went to the store.

Augy went to the living room and sat down on the couch near the blanket and pillow that he had used for the night.

Shamieka noticed this, and walked over and folded up the blanket, and put it and the pillow away in a hall cupboard.

She then turned the television back on to a local Humboldt County morning news station to catch up on the local news.

Augy sat silently, and very politely with his hands folded on his lap.

There was not really anything very interesting on the news for the morning, so Shamieka changed the channel to a cable channel that showed animals again.

She knew that this interested Augy, and that it would keep his attention until Sleeping Beaver came back with some food.

After about forty five minutes, Sleeping Beaver was back with plenty of food for little Augy.

Augy was asked by Shamieka if he wanted to eat something in the kitchen.

Little Augy took his eyes away from the television, and went to the kitchen once again.

He sat down and ate a bowl of cereal, and two English muffins with his favorite grape jelly spread on top.

Shamieka and Sleeping Beaver ate some bacon and eggs with toast while Augy ate silently.

After everyone was finished eating, Shamieka asked Sleeping Beaver what they should do for the day.

Sleeping Beaver suggested that maybe they might go and visit his friend crazy Mylo, and do some exploring to a secret place.

This excited Shamieka, and even little Augy seemed to perk up when he realized that they might go exploring... his favorite thing to do.

So... it was unanimously agreed that this was definitely a wonderful idea for the day.

They quickly started transitioning into hike mode, and started to get dressed for exploring, and packing some food.

Shamieka was told by Sleeping Beaver that she could not bring a camera, or video recording device, and he made her promise not to use any of these functions that were available on her cell phone as well.

Shamieka promised... with no inhibitions at all with this request.

After almost an hour, they were all ready to go out for the day.

This was going to be an adventure that neither Shamieka, or little Augy would ever forget.

Only Sleeping Beaver knew this though.

He had a surprise for both of them.

This would be much better than a video.

It would be the real thing!!

He smiled a little mischievously as they departed in Shamieka's vehicle.

Sleeping Beaver also made Shamieka turn off her in vehicle GPS recorder.

She promptly did this almost immediately after Sleeping Beaver made the request.

They drove back down to the southern part of Humboldt County, and finally parked at a location off road hidden deep within a forest.

They got out and started their hike to Crazy Mylo's area of the mountain.

Once they had hiked for almost an hour and a half, Sleeping Beaver started to make his special calls that only Crazy Mylo would recognize as coming from his Native American friend.

After several minutes of making these special calls, the sound of a different called traveled through the air.

Sleeping Beaver recognized these sounds as those of Crazy Mylo.

They had found him.

Sleeping Beaver guided them in a new direction towards the calls of Crazy Mylo.

After about fifteen minutes, they came to an area of the woods that was very thick with old redwoods.

These old redwoods were very massive in size, and towered upwards to the skies above for hundreds of feet.

Crazy Mylo stood near a patch of marijuana plants that he had just finished giving some special nutrients.

He smiled when he saw Sleeping Bear, but frowned slightly when he seen Shamieka, and Little Augy.

Crazy Mylo cautiously stood where he was, and waited for Sleeping Beaver to explain why he had brought these two people with him to his secret location.

Sleeping Beaver had a broad smile upon his face.

His smile was good enough to relax Crazy Mylo a little bit.

But he still was curious as to why his friend had brought these people with him.

Sleeping Beaver spoke to his friend in a gentle tone of voice.

"Now Mylo… I know that you are confused right now, but I will explain everything for you."

"First of all, let me introduce these two people to you."

"You have known for quite some time that I have a girlfriend named Shamieka."

"Well… here she is in the flesh."

"Isn't she just beautiful?"

"Her brain is just as beautiful as her looks."

Shamieka smiled at this comment.

Crazy Mylo looked Shamieka up and down.

He silently agreed with Sleeping Beaver.

She was a very pretty female specimen.

As far as her brain… he would judge that as time went on.

He still did not comment back to Sleeping Beaver.

Sleeping Beaver motioned Shamieka to go over to Crazy Mylo.

She did this with no hesitation.

She looked directly into Crazy Mylo's eye's and as she gave him a huge Hollywood smile, she said… "Hi… I'm Shamieka, glad to meet you."

She held out her hand in a friendly gesture towards Crazy Mylo… still smiling.

Crazy Mylo took her soft hand into his and shook it gently.

He felt a slight feeling of electricity flow up his arm as he did this.

Impressive.

He quickly let go of her hand.

He answered Shamieka back in a casual voice.

"Hi… I am Mylo… people know me in these parts as Crazy Mylo."

"But my real friends just call me Mylo."

"Pleased to meet you Shamieka."

Shamieka was now staring over at the marijuana plants nearby.

Technically, as a Forest Ranger, she was supposed to report what she was now looking at to the Sheriff's Department of Humboldt County.

But… she was not on duty, and since this was Sleeping Beaver's friend, she would ignore what she was seeing.

She had done this on other occasions when she seen a number of her friends doing similar things to this.

In Humboldt County, it seemed as if everyone knew someone that grew or smoked marijuana.

It was almost a part of the local culture.

This did not mean that she never busted grow operations that she discovered in the many forest's that she traveled to.

This also did not mean that she was not a good employee of the Forestry Service either.

99.9% of what she did was by the book, but occasionally, like today, she left the realm of her official duties, and reverted back to being a normal Humboldt County resident who does not make a big deal out of marijuana… especially if it is someone she knows.

She was basically after people who came to her beloved county and tried to use it and abuse it for their own selfish and greedy needs.

She was born and raised a Humboldt County girl, and had a built in… because of the culture weaved into her as she grew up, a way of dealing with life in this special place on the world map.

If she were in the big city? . . . it would be completely alien too her and very difficult to adjust.

But for now… right now at this very moment, she stood in a beautiful area of a forested area with her boy friend Sleeping Beaver and little Augy, just enjoying life… and waiting to see what happens next.

All eyes were now focused on little Augy.

He looked down at the ground shyly.

Crazy Mylo spoke.

"So… Sleeping Beaver, who is this young boy?"

Sleeping Beaver answered back… still smiling.

"This little guy… Mylo… is my newest friend."

"His name is Augy."

"Let me explain really quickly about Augy."

"He is a special boy."

"His normal language is different from ours."

Doctors say he has an extreme form of autism.

"He communicates with a language that none of us can understand." "But Shamieka is able to communicate with him by using sign language."

"If he were to talk to you in his special language, it would sound all garbled."

"But… like I said, Shamieka is able to talk with him with the silent language."

"It turns out that Augy is actually a very bright young boy."

"The more Shamieka communicates with him, the more I realize that he is smart and special."

"I am watching him for a while for his father Samuel Goodson."

"He is in Washington State on a special assignment, and I agreed to watch Augy while he was gone."

"Augy really likes the outdoors, and especially likes hiking."

"In fact, not too long ago, I found him in a densely forested area near his home while I was out exploring."

"We need to sit down… right here on the ground, and talk seriously about something."

"There is a real reason why I brought my beautiful girlfriend, and this young boy here today to meet you."

"Not only to meet you, but to possibly do something else as well… with your blessing, my dear old friend."

"I am sure that you will be upset at first as I explain myself to you."

"All I ask for right now is for you to be patient, and hear me out all the way before flying off the handle in a rage."

"OK?"

Crazy Mylo was caught by surprise by what his friend was saying to him initially, but gathered himself, and agreed to stay silent so Sleeping Beaver could say what he felt was so important to say to him.

He only did this because of the respect and trust that he had for Sleeping Beaver.

So he nodded his head in silence, and made a hand gesture to signify to Sleeping Beaver that he could proceed with what he had to say.

"My girl friend… Shamieka, recently was on a work assignment, actually it was a normal daily work detail."

"She traveled down to the southern Humboldt County area that she had chosen to do a normal investigation in regards to her job."

"She brought her normal gear with her as she started her hiking into the deep woods."

"Part of her equipment was her video camera."

Sleeping Beaver stopped talking momentarily and glanced all around at everyone.

When his gaze came to his friend Crazy Mylo, their eyes met and transfixed upon each other for several moments.

Crazy Mylo could detect a slight uncomfortableness from the look of Sleeping Beavers eyes.

Crazy Mylo nodded his head to indicate to Sleeping Beaver that he should continue to talk.

Sleeping Beaver nodded back silently, and then continued to speak.

"Well, as I said, Shamieka had her video camera with her."

"As she hiked her way into the forested area, she noticed movement ahead of her."

"She was already videotaping at this point."

"She kept seeing this movement up ahead of her, but she could not quite figure out what type of living creature it might be, or if it was a human."

"It was just far enough away to not be identified by her eyes and stayed that way throughout the whole video."

Crazy Mylo was confused at this point, and started to really become intrigued by what Sleeping Beaver was saying.

He already had suspicions of where this story was heading to.

He did not like what he was starting to think.

But, he remained silent and let his friend continue to talk.

Sleeping Beaver continued to talk, slow and precise.

"Shamieka finally lost sight of this creature with her eyes, and decided that she was finished for the day."

"She turned-off her video camera, and left the forest."

"She did "zoom" her video a few times on the creature, and determined that it was definitely not a human."

"Shamieka was not sure what she was seeing on the video when she put the setting on "zoom.""

"She had her suspicions, but could not make herself believe that it might actually be true."

"She felt excited, and "freaked-out" at the same time."

"So all she could really do is to go home and view the video on her computer with some special software that she has, and then she would have a better chance of determining what it was that she actually had seen in the forest with her eyes, and video camera."

"She went directly home, and transferred the video to her computer."

"She then put the special software into her computer, and applied it to the video from the forest that she had just came from."

"As she started to watch this video, in much better detail, she started to really "freak-out.""

"She could not believe what her eyes were watching on the computer screen."

Sleeping Beaver once again fell into silence, and turned his head towards Crazy Mylo with a fixed stare.

Crazy Mylo figured out what his friend was about to say next.

He replied with only one word as he shook his head back and forth.

"Nooo."

Sleeping Beaver knew at that moment that Crazy Mylo had figured out what he was about to say.

Sleeping Beaver shook his head up and down, and simply replied with one word as well.

"Yes."

Shamieka asked Sleeping Beaver to continue to talk.

So Sleeping Beaver continued.

"Shamieka became 100% convinced that upon watching the entire video with the special software on her computer, that she had indeed had actual proof of the existence of what we all around these parts of the world refer to as "Bigfoot."

"Now before you say anything, let me tell you, I have also watched this video as well."

"There is no doubt in my mind that this is the real deal."

"This video shows "Bigfoot."

"Several times, and anyone who watches it would come to the same exact conclusion."

"There is no way that this video can be de-bunked as a fake, or a hoax video."

"All the experts in the world can watch this video, and they would come to the same conclusion as Shamieka and I have."

"This is the "Holy Grail" of evidence that "Bigfoot does indeed exist on our planet."

"I swear to you my friend, I am speaking the truth."

Crazy Mylo was speechless.

He really did not know what he could say at that moment.

Shamieka spoke up.

"I know that you do not know me, but Sleeping Beaver is telling the truth."

Finally, Crazy Mylo spoke.

"So if this is all true, and I guess that I have to believe it because I do trust my friend Sleeping Beaver."

"But why come to me here to tell me this?"

He was directing this question at Sleeping Beaver.

"Why bring the woman and child here to tell me all of this?"

"You could have come here alone and done the same thing."

Sleeping Beaver replied.

"This boy has also watched the video, and it appears that he has seen Bigfoot as well in the past."

"Shamieka has been able to get this information from him by the use of sign language."

"So... I thought that I would have to bring them along with me when I told you about the video that Shamieka had shot."

"I know you might be mad right now, but I felt that I had no other choice about this."

"I can only hope that you will forgive me, and understand why I am here today with Shamieka and Augy."

Crazy Mylo was not mad.

He was disappointed that the secret that he and his friend had harbored for so long was now something that was on a video tape that the whole world could watch.

He had fears that his Bigfoot friends would be harmed if the video was released to the world for viewing.

Crazy Mylo began to speak again.

"So, who else has seen this video?"

Sleeping Beaver instantly replied.

"Nobody, except me, Shamieka and little Augy have watched this video."

"In fact, nobody, except for the four of us, even know that this video even exists."

"Believe me my friend, I know what thoughts are racing through your head at this moment."

"The same thoughts also went through my brain as well after I viewed the video."

Shamieka asked a direct question that had bothered her before she even had arrived at this location where they now stood.

"Why are we here telling your friend about the video?"

"Why did we come directly here, deep into the woods at this location, to tell your friend about the video that I shot?"

"I do not understand."

Once again the two men stared at each other silently.

Shamieka continued to talk.

"You guys are holding back on something."

"Look at how suspicious you two are acting right now."

"It is obvious to me that your not telling me something."

"Can you please answer my question?"

"Why are we all here together today, and talking about the video with your friend?"

Little Augy understood what was being said by these three adults, but for obvious reasons, he remained silent.

Both men were now "on the spot" before Shamieka with these questions.

Finally, Sleeping Beaver asked Crazy Mylo a direct question.

"Shall I tell her?"

Shamieka instantly, verbally snapped, with slight irritation.

"Tell me what?"

Now all eyes were upon Crazy Mylo.

Everyone awaited for him to answer Sleeping Beavers question.

Several moments passed.

Crazy Mylo hung on stubbornly, not really wanting to answer his friends request.

But… he knew that he could not stand here all day and avoid answering Sleeping Beaver.

His shoulders slumped slightly, and he finally answered back.

"Alright, go ahead."

Crazy felt deeply disappointed at that moment.

He felt like he had just made a decision that would hurt his kind friends of the woods… the Bigfoot's.

Sleeping Beaver began to tell Shamieka the story about how he and Crazy Mylo had met the secretive creatures known as Bigfoot, and by other names around the world.

He did not leave out any details.

There were even several times when he turned to Crazy Mylo for help with their secret story.

Crazy Mylo became engaged with Sleeping Beaver in telling the story as well to Shamieka and Augy.

They talked for over an hour about when and how they met the Bigfoot's and the many other different events they experienced with the creatures leading up to the present day.

Shamieka was totally stunned by what the men were saying to her.

After the two men were finished telling their story, Shamieka wasted no time in asking a question that took both men by total surprise.

She asked if they could go to where the Bigfoot's lived and if she could meet them.

Silence became very heavy in the air after that particular question.

The two men went for a private walk to discuss how they would answer her shocking, unexpected question.

They returned about twenty five minutes later with their answer to Shamieka.

Chapter Thirteen

SLEEPING BEAVER AND CRAZY Mylo had decided, after much polite argument, that they would take Shamieka and Augy to where the Bigfoot's could be found, and meet the elusive creatures.

They both had mixed feelings about doing this, but they both had to agree that since Shamieka already now knew of the Bigfoot's existence, and the video evidence that she now had in her computer, maybe, by meeting these gentle creatures, she could be convinced that she should not ever show the video to another human being… forever.

This was the only hope that they now had to be able to protect their friends of the forested areas of Humboldt County, California.

They knew that they could not force her to not show the video to anyone else… forever, and they also knew that she had been on official duty with her job when she shot the video.

They knew that she had a professional obligation to turn the video over to her bosses in order to keep her job, or for that matter, her career.

The two men hoped that by meeting the Bigfoot's, she would be able to see for herself that they were kind gentle creatures, and should continue to be left alone to live their lives privately.

They walked back to the area where they had left Shamieka and Augy and told her the decision they had made.

They explained to her their hopes and concerns in regards to her ultimate decision as to what she would finally do with the video of the Bigfoot's.

After she listened to the two men about their decision, she shocked them once again.

She told them that she had already made a decision to never tell anyone about the video she had on her computer.

She explained how she had already done some deep

"soul searching" about what she would, could, and should do with the video.

She had similar concerns about what would happen to the population of Bigfoot's if she were to show the video to the rest of the world.

He career?

She loved her job, and yes, she was very honest, but in this particular case, it was more important to make sure the Bigfoot's were able to live in peace than any job she would ever work.

She had already made this personal decision before the men had even talked to her today.

She had a sly smile on her face as she watched how the two men's faces reacted when she quickly told them about her own decision.

Both men were speechless, and had both of their mouth's wide open in complete surprise.

Chapter Fourteen

CRAZY MYLO WAS WALKING ahead of the other three people… Sleeping Beaver, Shamieka, and little Augy.

He was leading the way to the reclusive area where the Bigfoot's could be found.

This was a waterfall that fell from the side of a secluded mountain area where the Bigfoot's cave system was hidden behind the constantly flowing water.

It took almost two hour's of nonstop hiking, up and down small hidden valley's that lay between mountains where hardly any human's may or may not have ever traveled.

The exception's being Crazy Mylo, and Sleeping Beaver.

Finally, the four people came to a peak of a small mountain that over looked a deep valley, plush with a field of various fauna, and scattered redwood tree's throughout the area, and a hardly noticeable stream of water that slowly cascaded down the side of another adjacent mountain.

Crazy Mylo stopped in his tracks.

The other three people stood silently by and watched him.

He surveyed the area slowly without the use of binoculars.

He stared mostly at an area of the mountain where the waterfall fell to create a small stream in this small hidden valley.

Sleeping Beaver was looking at an area downstream from the waterfall.

He had a fixed gaze near a thicket of redwood tree's near a bend of this stream.

Finally, Crazy Mylo silently motioned for the other's to once again follow him as he started to hike down the side of this mountain to the small valley floor towards the waterfall area.

It surprisingly took only a few minutes to make it to the valley floor, and within a few hundred feet from where the waterfall hit the ground below the mountain to start the creation of a stream.

Crazy Mylo started to talk in a low voice.

"This is the area where we will be able to see, and hopefully meet with the Bigfoot's."

"They may very well already be watching us from different area's around us as I speak to you."

"Shamieka, and Augy, I want to warn the both of you that these creatures are very large and intimidating by their normal appearances, and I am honestly not sure how they will react to seeing you two with me and Sleeping Beaver."

"I can only hope that they will be quietly cautious and civil."

"They have never shown any tendencies of violence whenever they have been around me and Sleeping Beaver."

"They are a very gentle species of animal, as much as I have ever been able to notice throughout the time period that I have been around them."

"I would say that Sleeping Beaver will say the same as I do in this regard."

Sleeping Beaver shook his head up and down in silent agreement to this statement.

Crazy Mylo asked Sleeping Beaver if he could see any signs of Bigfoot's around the area.

Sleeping Beaver answered back.

"I can see that the trail leading from the waterfall is wet from the creatures either coming or going to their cave."

"I cannot tell which direction they were traveling."

"If they did come out of their cave, they are probably hidden in different area's around us, watching us as we stand here wondering where they might be."

"I think that if I walk towards the entrance to their cave behind the waterfall, they might come out of where they might be hidden, and hopefully greet me non-violently."

"I admit, I am nervous right now."

"I have no idea of how they might react to us by having these strangers here at their private area of the world."

"But still… I will see if they might come out of hiding, if they are indeed hiding, to greet us, hopefully in a peaceful way."

Sleeping Beaver started to walk in the direction of the mountainside where the waterfall fell to the ground from up above.

When he came to within around fifty feet of where the waterfall hit the ground on the valley floor, there was a loud noise from an area where there were two huge boulders and a large amount of overgrown fern plants that almost completely hid the large stones.

Sleeping Beaver quickly glanced over to this area where he heard this sound.

The other three people did not hear this sound because it was just out of their earshot.

But they did notice how Sleeping Beaver suddenly stopped and looked over to a certain area to his right.

They all stood where they were.

Silently they stood and watched Sleeping Beaver slowly walk over to the area that he had quickly glanced at.

Sleeping Beaver walked about twenty feet, and then stopped.

He stood still and just looked straight ahead at an area that they could not see from their vantage point.

Everyone stood silently, not moving an inch… waiting to see if anything would happen.

They all stood where they were for several minutes.

It seemed as if nothing would happen.

Finally, Sleeping Beaver could see a slight movement from the area that he fixated his gaze for the past few minutes.

None of the other three people could see what Sleeping Beaver was starting to slowly see.

Behind the two huge boulder's, and thick growth of native ferns, there started to appear a large face with a thick amount of dark hair surrounding the edges of it's face.

Sleeping Beaver recognized the face to be one of a Bigfoot.

Sleeping Beaver did not make any quick movements, or hand gestures.

He just stood where he was and silently observed.

After about two minutes, in almost what seemed like a slow motion movie, a Bigfoot did walk out into the open to face Sleeping Beaver.

Crazy Mylo did not act shocked or surprised, but Shamieka started to get very fidgety and her mouth fell wide open in utter shock at what she was now seeing.

Little Augy tilted his head slightly sideways, slowly from one side to the other.

This was his was of showing silent interest and surprise at what his young eyes were now seeing.

Crazy Mylo raised his hand slowly towards Shamieka and Augy to indicate that they must remain standing where they were and not move in the direction of Sleeping Beaver.

Everyone's eyes were locked on the huge creature known in this area of the world as Bigfoot.

It turned-out that this particular Bigfoot was a female that Crazy Mylo and Sleeping Beaver knew very well.

She was one of the older Bigfoot's, sort of like a grandma type in her clan of creatures.

Crazy Mylo and Sleeping Beaver had nicknamed her "Walana."

This was a name of one of Sleeping Beaver's Great grandmother's that he remembered as a small child.

She was a gentle and kind old woman who was always telling Sleeping Beaver stories of the past about their people.

Walana had seemed very similar to his long departed Great grandmother.

Walana had always appeared to be gentle and kind whenever Sleeping Beaver or Crazy Mylo had been around her.

There was not ever any signs of violence ever detected of her from either man in all of the years that they had observed her.

So now, here she was, the apparent gentle giant, slowly walking towards Sleeping Beaver.

Walana walked to within about ten feet from Sleeping Beaver before she stopped.

She stood there, towering over him, and silently looked at Sleeping Beaver.

She had a very noticeable frown on her face.

Sleeping Beaver felt very nervous as he stood there because he had rarely ever seen a frown like this from any Bigfoot that he had been around.

Walana looked over at the other three people who remained standing where they were… transfixed.

She looked back at Sleeping Beaver, and then back at the other people… back and forth, several times, in a scary silence.

Finally, Sleeping Beaver decided to take a chance and start to slowly walk back to the other three people.

He did not feel that Walana would attack him from behind as he walked, or at least he was hoping that would be the case.

He had a slight fear within his body.

One that he had not ever felt in his entire life as he walked away from Walana with his back turned to her.

He knew that it was possible that she could attack him and snap him in half like a twig on a tree.

All he could do now as he walked toward the other three people was to hope that Walana did not do what he feared was very possible at this lonely moment in time for him.

Chapter Fifteen

CRAZY MYLO, SHAMIEKA, AND even little Augy, all had an extreme feeling of nervous fear of the unknown.

This unknown… what might happen in the next several moments as Sleeping Beaver walked towards them.

They did not see any apparent fear on Sleeping Beaver's face as he got closer to their location.

To their nervous surprise, they watched as Walana started to follow Sleeping Beaver from behind at a distance of around twenty feet.

She was now looking directly at the three of them as she walked behind Sleeping Beaver.

Little Augy started to take a few steps towards Sleeping Beaver before anyone could stop him.

Sleeping Beaver suddenly noticed what Augy did and put his hands up to make the little boy understand that he wanted him to stop.

Little Augy stopped.

Sleeping Beaver made his way to the rest of the adults and turned to face Walana.

Walana stopped about seventy five feet from the humans.

Crazy Mylo stepped forward towards Walana… cautiously taking small slow steps.

Walana's eyes widened to the point that it was obvious that she was distressed, and probably angry.

Walana opened her mouth and showed her teeth to the humans.

Her eyes stayed in the same angry position.

Walana started to make sounds from her mouth that were obviously made to call other's of her kind.

It was a slow long roar, unlike any sound in the animal kingdom.

It brought chills to all of the humans.

Within a few moments after Walana completed her roar, several Bigfoot creatures started to appear from many different directions in the small valley floor.

They all stood at a distance.

Walana made another sound that was different from her roar.

It sounded like a bunch of garbled words.

Similar to a human speaking with their mouth full of objects.

Little Augy's ears perked-up.

Nobody noticed how focused Augy was.

He did not show any fear.

He was actually acting as if there was a silent understanding being experienced by him.

He took another step towards Walana.

When he did this, Walana was startled and she started to run towards all of the humans, mainly little Augy.

Augy stood where he was as if he was totally calm for the moment.

Shamieka shrieked, Crazy Mylo bent down low to the ground, almost cowering, Sleeping Beaver was frozen like a statue in a park.

Just as Walana was about to leap on top of the little boy, Augy screamed at her in his special language that no human had ever been able to decipher.

It was always thought by everyone that his language was just a bunch of garbled, unintelligible words.

But… to the amazement of all present, humans and Bigfoot's, Walana stopped dead in her tracks, skidding on the ground for several feet, almost falling over.

She slowly bent over and looked at the little human that stood calmly in front of her, only fifteen feet away.

Walana mumbled a few short words in her language to Augy.

Right away, Little Augy spoke back to her in his special language.

Walana straightened up and stood looking at little Augy in what could be recognized as total surprise.

Walana slowly walked over to the little boy.

The rest of the human adults, and the Bigfoot's nearby, all stood motionless… watching in total shock as well.

Once Walana came to within a few feet of little Augy, she stood still and spoke again.

Once again, little Augy spoke back to her.

They were actually communicating!!

Augy's special language, unintelligible to other humans, was actually the language of the creatures known as Bigfoot in this area of the planet.

A second later, there was another shock to only the human's that were present.

Little Augy turned around and faced the three adult human's who brought him here to this secret place of the Bigfoot's, and spoke.

But this time, as he spoke, it was not the garbled language that they were used to hearing from him, and apparently the language of the Bigfoot creatures… it was something that all thought was impossible.

"Her name is Walana."

"She is very surprised that I can speak her language."

Little Augy spoke these words in perfect… English.

There was an obvious simultaneous gasp by the three humans upon hearing this from the little autistic boy.

How was Augy speaking perfect English?

Was he able to speak this all along?

Everyone was confused.

Even the Bigfoot creatures were confused by this special moment with this little human child.

Walana walked over to Crazy Mylo and stood before him.

She was no longer showing any signs of being violent.

She stood there like it was just another normal day.

She turned towards Shamieka and stared at her.

Shamieka felt immense fear throughout her entire body.

Little Augy spoke to Walana.

Walana spoke back to Augy.

Little Augy spoke to Shamieka, but not by sign language this time.

"Walana does not recognize you like she does the two men that are here."

"She is nervous about you being here."

Shamieka spoke back to Augy.

"Tell her that I will not do anything that will hurt her or the other's of her kind."

"Tell her that I will not ever tell any other human that I have ever seen her or the other's of her kind."

"Tell her that I say this with my life in her control."

"Tell her that she can take my life right now if she feels that I do not speak the truth."

"I ask for her to trust what I am saying."

Shamieka stopped talking.

Little Augy turned to Walana and spoke.

He told her what Shamieka had just said to him.

Walana stepped over to Shamieka and now stood within a foot from touching her.

She reached out and put her large hand on top of Shamieka's head.

She grabbed a whole handful of Shamiek's hair and squeezed gently, and lifted it slightly.

Shamieka almost fainted, but continued to stand still… very still.

Walana finally let go of the Shamieka's hair and took a step backwards.

She stood silently for several moments.

She stared into Shamieka's eyes.

It was as if she was looking completely through Shamieka's face, and at something else in the distance behind her head.

An obvious small smile started to spread across the face of Walana, directed 100% at Shamieka.

Walana turned her head to the rest of the humans and showed the same friendly smile.

Walana spoke once again to Augy.

Augy spoke back.

Augy spoke again to the adults… in perfect English.

"Walana wants me to call the rest of her friends and family to come over here to where we are now standing."

"She wants me to do this to show them that I can speak their language."

Sleeping Beaver finally spoke.

"Go ahead Augy, but can you answer a simple question first?"

Augy shook his head up and down to indicate that he would.

Sleeping Beaver asked his question.

"Have you been able to speak perfect English all of this time?"

"Have you just held back, and decided not to speak to anyone in English?"

"Even to your own Father?"

Little Augy spoke.

"I have never been able to speak the human language."

"Today is the first time in my life that I have spoken the human language known as English."

"I have always been able to understand the human English language, but until today, I have not ever been able to speak it."

"I do not understand why I am able to speak English right now, and also be able to communicate in the special language of these gentle creatures that everyone calls Bigfoot."

Shamieka spoke.

"I think that it is wonderful that you can speak English, and the Bigfoot language."

Sleeping Beaver nodded his head towards Augy to indicate that he could now do what Walana requested a few moments earlier.

Little Augy walked about thirty feet from the group of adult humans, and one female Bigfoot named Walana, and spoke.

Augy spoke as loud as he could for his little voice.

Me made the sounds that were the language of the Bigfoot's.

He spoke in their language for what appeared to be a small paragraph if spoken by humans.

Upon doing this, the little boy calmly turned around and walked back and stopped next to Shamieka.

Slowly, several Bigfoot creatures started to walk towards the humans, and Walana.

None of them showed any signs of anger or violence that may come from them.

They walked in almost a passive manner with their bodies slightly bent.

This was now a moment in history that might have been thought of as something that was an impossibility.

Humans and Bigfoot's actually being able to communicate between the two species.

Fortunately, this would be a part of history that would never be recorded in any books of the humans.

This day would only be a memory that would stay within the heads of the humans that were now present.

No other human would ever even know that this day had ever happened.

Chapter Sixteen

WITHIN A FEW MINUTES, all of the Bigfoot creatures were gathered around Crazy Mylo, Sleeping Beaver, Shamieka, and little Augy.

Augy was the apparent focus of attention.

He would be the one who would help in the communications between the humans and the Bigfoot's.

Walana, and now another Bigfoot who was much smaller than the rest, came over and stood directly in front of Augy.

This smaller Bigfoot appeared to be a young Bigfoot equivalent to a human child.

This young Bigfoot started to talk his language to Augy.

Augy listened, and then answered back.

Augy then spoke out loud to everyone around him, humans, and Bigfoots.

"His name is "Esher.""

Another adult Bigfoot stepped forward and stood next to Esher and started to speak to Augy.

Augy answered back.

Augy then announced to everyone that this Bigfoot was called "Reka."

He also informed everyone that Reka was Esher's mother.

Walana started to speak to Augy.

After Augy listened to her for a few minutes, He spoke to Crazy Mylo and Sleeping Beaver about what she had said to him.

"Walana wants to know why you both brought me and Shamieka here today."

"She and the others are very confused about us all being here today."

"They are also very surprised that I am able to communicate with them in their language."

"They have fears that we will let the rest of the humans of the world know about them and where they live."

"There are two males… over there… who feel like they must kill us and not let us leave today."

Augy pointed over to the two male Bigfoot's that he was speaking about.

Neither of these two male Bigfoot's showed any signs that they wanted to be violent towards the humans.

But Augy assured Crazy Mylo and Sleeping Beaver that this was indeed the case.

Crazy Mylo and Sleeping Beaver recognized one of the two male Bigfoot's.

They did not know his name, so they asked Augy to ask him what his name was.

Augy walked over to this particular male Bigfoot and stood before him calmly.

He looked up, tilting his head far back to the point of where it rested on his shoulders and asked him what his name was.

The Bigfoot creature answered a short quick word.

Augy turned towards Crazy Mylo and Sleeping Beaver and answered that this Bigfoot was called "Arch."

Crazy Mylo walked over and stood next to Augy and Arch.

Crazy Mylo asked Augy to tell Arch that he did not have to worry about any of the humans here today telling any other human about them or this place.

He asked Augy to remind Arch that he and Sleeping Beaver had known him and many others of his kind for many years, and had not ever told anyone about them.

The trust between the Bigfoot's and these humans here today could continue on into the future with no fear of any other human ever finding out about them.

Crazy Mylo asked Augy to explain to Arch about how Shamieka had accidentally discovered a Bigfoot, and had told Sleeping Beaver about the discovery.

Crazy Mylo also wanted to make sure that Augy made Arch understand that Shamieka had no intention at all to ever tell anyone of her discovery.

After saying this to Augy, Crazy Mylo stepped back a few steps and stood silently.

The little boy started to tell Arch everything that Crazy Mylo had just said to him.

Arch made a low growling type of sound as Augy spoke to him.

All of the human adults became nervous when they heard this sound from the large Bigfoot male.

Augy talked for a few minutes to Arch.

When he was finished talking to Arch, the growling stopped.

Arch made a head motion to the other Bigfoot creatures.

Upon seeing this gesture, the other Bigfoot's walked over to Arch and stood before him.

They all walked away for about twenty yards.

They were at a distance to where none of the humans could hear what they might be talking about.

They were definitely making sounds in their language with each other.

All of a sudden, in a low voice, Augy started to tell the human adults about what the Bigfoot's were talking about.

He said that he could hear them perfectly well, even from this far distance.

All of the human adults were amazed by this new development from the little boy.

At the same time, they were not really surprised, because look at what he had already done today to amaze them.

Augy started to repeat, in general, what was being said by the Bigfoot's several yards away from them.

Apparently, because of the fact that Crazy Mylo, and Sleeping Beaver had been so trustworthy for all of this time with them, they were willing to trust the two new humans… Shamieka, and Augy.

Another reason for their new trust with Augy, and Shamieka was because of the startling mysterious gift of the human child… Augy.

They were absolutely 100% amazed about the fact that this human child could understand and speak their ancient language.

The young Bigfoot, Esher, also made it clear to the Bigfoot adults that he wanted to become friends with the human child.

After Augy heard this request from afar by the young Bigfoot, he showed on his face a very rare smile.

Augy would really like for this to happen between him and the young Bigfoot known as Esher.

The human adults were pleased to hear about what the Bigfoot's were saying about them.

The nervousness that they felt for the past several minutes started to disappear.

They would be careful not to show this relief to the Bigfoot's until the adult Bigfoot's had conveyed to them, through little Augy, their decision to trust them from this day forward, as they had for all this time with Crazy Mylo, and Sleeping Beaver.

They did not want the Bigfoot's to know, for now, about little Augy's other special ability… super hearing.

What the adult humans still did not know about Augy was that he had another special ability… super eyesight as well.

Augy did not tell them about this other special ability… for the time being.

Augy himself still did not understand how he could understand the Bigfoot language, and speak it as well.

The other thing that he did not understand was how he could speak normal English to the human adults until today.

Has he been able to speak English all of this time?

He did not know this answer.

He was slightly happy about all of the new things that he could do.

He could not wait until he was able to talk to his Father… in English.

This single thought really put a genuine smile upon his little face.

The Bigfoot adults were finished talking with each other, and casually walked over to all of the humans.

Arch started to talk to Augy about their decision.

Little Augy pretended that he was garnering this information for the very first time.

In a few minutes, all of the tension was completely gone between the Bigfoot's and the humans.

Esher came over to Augy and asked him in his language if he wanted to go and play.

Augy relayed this request to Sleeping Beaver, since he was the one who was technically watching him while his Father was away.

Sleeping Beaver told little Augy to tell Esher that they could become friends, but they would have to wait for another day in the future to play with each other.

Sleeping Beaver asked Augy to also tell the adult Bigfoot's that they were going to leave to go back to their homes.

He also wanted them to know that they would come back another day, and not to worry that anything would ever be said about what had happened on this special day between them.

Augy spent a few minutes telling all of the Bigfoot's about what Sleeping Beaver wanted them to know.

Esher was a little disappointed for now, but he was also happy that someday in the near future, he and Augy would become friends, and play in the forest together.

The adult Bigfoot's agreed that it was a good idea for the humans to leave, and gave permission for them to come back and visit them in the future.

Everyone was smiling… humans, and Bigfoots, as they separated from each other in a matter of a few minutes.

Augy turned back and waved at the Bigfoot's as he walked away.

The gesture was not returned, they did not understand it's meaning.

Chapter Seventeen

ONCE SLEEPING BEAVER, CRAZY Mylo, Shamieka, and Augy were away from the area where they had just witnessed some amazing things between humans, and Bigfoot's, They stopped at a small creek to talk with little Augy.

Shamieka was the first to say something to the autistic child.

She did not bother using sign language because she assumed that Augy could now, by some miracle, speak normal English.

To her amazement, and the other's, including Augy, the words that came out of his mouth was the garbled sounds that he made before they had arrived at the Bigfoot area.

Shamieka told Augy that it was alright to talk English to her.

Augy could not do it.

He felt frustrated about this.

He was also confused as well.

He also thought that he would be able to talk English.

Finally, he started to do sign language back to Shamieka because he realized that no matter how hard he tried, he could not speak English.

Now a new mystery about Augy had come to the forefront.

How come he could communicate with the Bigfoot's in their language, which was apparently the same language that he has always spoken since he learned how to talk?

How come Augy could speak the normal human language… English… when he was in the presence of the Bigfoot creatures?

These were two very intriguing questions.

Everyone who had witnessed this phenomenon were honestly 100% baffled.

Augy was the one that was the most confused by these two questions.

Augy asked Shamieks if she could tell him the answers to these two questions.

She felt sad when she could not give him the answers to these mysterious questions.

She asked the other adults nearby if they had at least a theory that might begin to shed some light on possible answers to these questions.

Unfortunately, none of the other adults had even the slightest clue to help anyone, especially little Augy, to understand what had happened back at the Bigfoot area.

One thing that everyone did agree on though was that they had indeed witnessed something from little Augy that one might read in a book about a fictional story.

But... this was real life... right?

This is not a fictional story... right?

They were not all having a group hallucination... that is for sure something that they all knew to be a fact.

Silence fell upon the group for a few minutes as everyone gathered their thoughts.

Finally, after several minutes of silence, Crazy Mylo suggested that they start hiking once again.

They all agreed that this was a good thing to do.

So... onward everyone started, down the mountain back to where they had originally met Crazy Mylo.

Little Augy and Shamieka did not do anymore sign language between them as they hiked down the mountain.

There was relatively no talking by anyone as they progressed back to Crazy Mylo's latest area.

At the same time as they were hiking down the mountain, the Bigfoot's were also engaged in their own communications... questions about the humans that had just visited them.

Some of the Bigfoots that were finding out for the first time about what had just transpired with the humans, and especially what had happened with little Augy, were not necessarily in agreement that it was the right thing to do to let the humans leave their secluded area of the forested mountain range.

Most of the Bigfoot's, upon hearing this new development for the first time, were basically confused as to why the humans had come and gone without their knowledge.

But… Big Arch was firm about the decision to let the humans leave as the correct decision.

None of the other Bigfoot creatures would ever dare to challenge Big Arch in any decision he would make.

He was not actually the leader of the Bigfoot's.

There is no such thing as a leader in any Bigfoot community.

Big Arch just happened to be the most dominant male in this particular Bigfoot population.

Age also played a part in the respect of an individual Bigfoot such as Big Arch.

Big Arch was not actually the oldest member of this Bigfoot population in Humboldt County, California, but his age and physical dominance were enough to garner a large amount of respect.

So… if Big Arch said it was alright for the humans to leave their area with the knowledge that they now had about the Bigfoot's, there would not be any Bigfoot's to challenge his decision.

Still, even though there was not any challenge of his decision, there still remained a silent paranoia that the humans would tell the rest of the world about what they now knew about them.

But, there was one thing that the Bigfoot's knew that they were sure that the humans did not know.

This was something that would surely protect these Bigfoot's in the event that other humans were to find out about their secret area.

It was the fact that the cave system located behind the waterfall that cascaded down the side of the mountain was totally vast.

This cave system made hundreds of splits, and went on for several thousands of miles underground.

There were many dead ends as well.

If one were to enter this cave system without the knowledge of where the passages went, it would be very easy to get lost forever until death occurred.

All of the Bigfoot's since birth had learned how to safely travel these passages without getting lost.

These cave systems traveled all of the way around the world, reaching all continents.

This was the reason that there were several sightings over the centuries of different types of Bigfoots in the many areas of the planet.

Even though the names were different for the various creatures around the planet, they were actually all of the same species.

Depending on what type of environment these creatures lived, their sizes, and color of their hair varied.

So, if the humans that had left this area of the world where these particular Bigfoot creatures now lived were to tell about today's happenings to other humans, the cave system behind the waterfall would be a quick exit to safety.

It would only take a few minutes for the Bigfoots to disappear within the vast underground passages where there would not be any thought of the humans having even the slightest chance of finding them.

The humans would become lost very quickly, and maybe lost enough to where they would eventually perish.

So, as the two different species went in separate directions, many thoughts of how the future would be between them... lingered.

Chapter Eighteen

WITHIN A FEW HOURS, Sleeping Beaver, Shamieka, and little Augy had left Crazy Mylo in his area of the vast forest's of Humboldt County and had made their way back to Shamieka's place where they would stay until Augy's father returned from his trip.

He would be coming home later in the afternoon tomorrow.

Samuel Goodson was in a hotel room relaxing, and waiting for the next day to come.

He was feeling pleased with himself about what he had done on this trip.

He also missed his son Augy dearly.

The people that had asked him to make this trip were obviously quite satisfied as well.

Samuel had been very thorough when it came time for him to tell everyone about everything he knew about the elusive creatures that he has pursued for many years.

He answered everyone's questions as honestly and completely as possible.

Of course there was the usual critics in the audience that sometimes doubled as heckler's as well.

But Samuel had become very used to those people through time.

It was just part of what would be expected in the type of career he had chosen for himself.

It was always the same old conclusions by these doubters that were very repetitious.

They would always say to Samuel… where is the real proof that the Bigfoot creatures actually exist.

The only way that there would ever be 100% definitive proof of their existence would be if a body was shown to the world... dead or alive.

Anything other than that would only be considered as shaky evidence at the very most.

Sure, Samuel was secretly bothered by the fact that he could not give to these doubters some real hard evidence to really prove their actual existence.

Because of this, he had to give all appearances of a totally dedicated and honest person in search of the truth... one way or the other.

There were certainly a large number of people who definitely believed that he was not mentally stable, and in fact was a completely unbalanced crazy person who did not live in reality.

Samuel did in fact believe that these creatures do in fact exist, and he was motivated enough to prove his belief, to dedicate the rest of his life to show he was correct.

He would fantasize at times of a day in the future where he was showing the whole world real hard evidence of the existence of Bigfoot.

It was an ultimate fantasy.

Having a live Bigfoot in his possession.

Showing the whole world that they had been wrong when they had doubted him.

He wondered, if this really did happen... really happen... would it be like the old "King Kong" movies where the giant ape is on display to crowds of onlookers?

Would it be a circus like atmosphere on the border of being out of control?

Would the Government swoop in and take the Bigfoot before Samuel was able to show the world, and then leave behind their customary made-up laughable excuses that this was all a hoax or misunderstanding?

All of these thoughts swirled inside of his head when this fantasy materialized in his quiet solitary moments.

Samuel was strong minded and very "thick skinned" when it came to dealing with people that thought he was a crazy person.

He was anxious to get back to Humboldt County, California and be with his son.

Samuel reached over and picked-up his cellphone and made a call to Sleeping Beaver.

Within three rings, Sleeping Beaver answered the phone.

The two men talked for less than two minutes.

Basically all Samuel wanted to tell Sleeping Beaver was that he would for sure be home tomorrow evening.

He would stop by Shamieka's place where Augy was staying with Sleeping Beaver and pick him up as soon as he arrived back in good old friendly Humboldt County.

Samuel put the cellphone down, closed his eyes, and departed into a black abyss… the land of dreams and nightmares.

Tomorrow would be a happy day.

Chapter Nineteen

SLEEPING BEAVER PUT HIS cellphone back into his pocket after hanging up from a call by Samuel Goodson.

He quickly relayed to Shamieka and Augy that Samuel would be home tomorrow.

Augy did not show any signs of being excited by this news.

Sleeping Beaver thought that this was because of the childs autism.

Augy was in fact happy about this news, but was not able to show this feeling to the outside world.

Augy was still thinking about why he was not able to talk like the normal people around him.

He was very confused by this thought.

He wondered silently why he was able to talk their English language when he was around the Bigfoot creatures, but not able to do so when the creatures were not around him physically.

Augy pondered these questions for a few more minutes, and then pulled the blanket over his head and went quickly to sleep.

Sleeping Beaver and Shamieka went into the master bedroom and closed the door.

Once they were comfortably in the room, they both sat on the large bed and started to talk between themselves about what they had experienced, and other items of discussion.

Shamieka finally asked an intriguing question.

Should they tell Samuel that Augy was able to speak English?

Sleeping Beaver thought for a second before answering this question from Shamieka.

He spoke in a lower tone of voice because he was not sure if Augy would be able to hear them talk.

"Well… if we tell Samuel about Augy being able to speak English, we would have to tell him everything… right?"

Shamieka shook her head slightly to indicate that she agreed with this assessment.

Shamieka spoke as well in a lower tone of voice.

"I agree that we would have to tell about everything about the Bigfoots and all that we experienced out there in the woods with them."

"On the other hand, if we tell about the Bigfoots, we would be letting yet another person know about their real existence, and the possibility of losing their trust would be very probable."

"We told the Bigfoots that we would not let any other humans know about their real existence."

"But I also believe that Samuel should know that Augy is able to speak English when he is around the Bigfoots."

"As to why or how Augy is able to do this only in the presence of the Bigfoots, that is still a puzzling question that I do not have the answer too."

"I am torn between giving hope to a loving Father, and the trust of a species of animals that deserve their privacy for survival."

"It is really a tough decision for us to make Sleeping Beaver."

"I also think that Crazy Mylo needs to have a say in this decision as well."

Sleeping Beaver agreed with everything that Shamieka just said to him.

Sleeping Beaver finally, after a few moments of silence spoke again to his sweetheart.

"I think it is a wonderful thing that we have the trust of the Bigfoots, but I have to say that it would be best that we let Samuel know about everything because I truly trust Samuel."

"Samuel can be trusted."

"If we just tell him about what Augy can do when he is around the Bigfoots, he will want proof."

"I say that we show him this video as proof, for now, and after we have talked to Crazy Mylo, and the Bigfoots, maybe we can take Samuel to meet the Bigfoots."

"Samuel would be able to experience the joy of being able to finally communicate with his son in English, and also see with his own eyes that the creatures that he has spent most of his life trying to prove of their existence, actually are roaming this planet with us humans."

"Now you would probably wonder, because of the fact that Samuel has been looking for the Bigfoots for so many years, that maybe there would be the temptation of telling the world that he has been right all this time."

"Sure the temptation will for sure be there, but I think that the love for his son, and to be able to experience communicating in English with Augy would override the temptation to tell the world about the Bigfoots."

"I agree that Crazy Mylo would definitely have a say in this decision."

Shamieka slowly exhaled a large amount of air from her lungs, and rocked back and forth slowly... pondering what Sleeping Beaver had just said.

Finally she answered.

"O.K."

"Lets show Samuel the video."

"After we show him the video, we tell him everything that we know about the Bigfoots, except where they are located."

"We show him proof of their existence, tell our story, and then make sure that he clearly understands that we cannot tell where the Bigfoots are located."

"We tell him that even if Crazy Mylo agrees to an introduction to the Bigfoots, we would have to blindfold him when we take him to meet the Bigfoots."

"We tell Samuel that we would first have to go and communicate with the Bigfoots to get their permission to bring him to their location."

"We would go back with little Augy and have him communicate with them for us."

"After the Bigfoots give permission, then we would bring him to their location... blindfolded."

"We would have Augy explain to the Bigfoots that he would for the first time in his young life, be able to communicate with his father in the human language."

"Augy would explain to them that his father would not be able to tell of where they were located, even if he wanted to because he was brought to their location with his eyes covered."

Sleeping Beaver smiled, and then spoke.

"As always my dear, you are so darn smart."

"I totally agree with your plan."

"Lets see what happens."

Shamieka smiled back and reached over and turned off the lights with a little giggle.

Chapter Twenty

SAMUEL'S PLANE LANDED IN the small airport in Arcata...
Humboldt County, California early in the morning, just past 6:00 a.m.
The landing was a bit bumpy because it was a small airplane that
he was a passenger on.

He departed the airplane and called a city cab of Eureka.

He had the cab take him to a restaurant in Eureka so he could eat some
breakfast and make a phone call to Sleeping Beaver.

While he was eating breakfast, his cellphone started sounding-off in
his pocket.

He looked at the screen of the cellphone, and could see that it was
Sleeping Beaver.

Sleeping Beaver beat him to the punch on the phone call.

Samuel answered the cellphone, and started to talk to Sleeping Beaver.

He asked if Augy was awake, and Sleeping Beaver said that he was, and
he was eating breakfast with Shamieka right now.

Sleeping Beaver offered to come pickup Samuel at the restaurant.

Samuel took Sleeping Beaver up on that offer.

Twenty five minutes later, Sleeping Beaver arrived at the restaurant and
picked Samuel up.

They drove straight back to Shamieka's place.

As they arrived, Samuel could see his son Augy standing on the small
porch with Shamieka.

Augy did not show any emotion as he seen his father climb out of
Sleeping Beaver's car.

This was a normal reaction for Augy, and it did not bother Samuel at all because he was used to it.

Samuel walked over to his son and bent down and gave him a long loving hug.

He whispered into his ear that he missed him and loves him very much.

Even this did not create any type of reaction from the autistic boy.

Shamieka invited Samuel into her home.

Samuel accepted, and walked inside.

Sleeping Beaver had already told Samuel on the ride from the restaurant that he would gladly drive Samuel and Augy back to their home after he and Shamieka had a chance to show him something, and talk to him.

Samuel was intrigued by this, and kindly accepted the offer.

They all sat down, and Shamieka loaded a DVD into a DVD player and turned on the television.

She hit the pause button just before the video started to play.

She told Samuel that before she played the video, she wanted to explain to him that this was an official field operation for her job, and that what he was about to see was not edited, or faked in any way whatsoever.

This was a real actual video… 100%.

Samuel was really interested now, and anxious for Shamieka to start playing the video.

Shamieka hit the play button on the remote control, and the video started to play.

Within a few minutes of watching the video play, Samuel became stunned at what he was seeing, just as Sleeping Beaver and Shamieka had been when they first seen it themselves.

Samuel asked Shamieka several times to playback certain parts of the video, freeze the video at certain points, and zoom in on other parts as well.

Samuel was absolutely experiencing mental euphoria as he came to realize what he really looking at.

Finally, as the video ended, Samuel could not wait to ask Shamieka and Sleeping Beaver a ton of questions.

These questions were basically almost the same ones that Sleeping Beaver had asked Shamieka after watching the same video for the first time.

Samuel could hardly contain his excitement about what his eyes had just seen.

Shamieka and Sleeping Beaver answered all of Samuel's questions politely and thoroughly.

Augy just sat there on the couch quietly watching the adults.

Samuel asked if he could go to where the video footage had been filmed.

Shamieka and Sleeping Beaver had expected this question from Samuel, and so they began explaining to him what they had done with Augy and Crazy Mylo.

They told Samuel everything that had happened when they all went to visit the Bigfoot's.

They also explained to Samuel about how his son Augy could communicate with the Bigfoot's and talk perfect English when he was in their presence.

They also made a point to emphasize that they did not understand how Augy was able to do this.

They explained to Samuel that they would have to talk to Crazy Mylo, and the Bigfoot's with Augy as the interpreter, to get permission to bring Samuel to meet the Bigfoot's.

They told him that they did not want to lose the trust of the Bigfoot's, and that if Crazy Mylo agreed, and also the Bigfoots, then he would be brought to meet the Bigfoot's blind folded as a guarantee for the Bigfoot's, that no other human would know where they could be found.

All of this was almost to much information for Samuel to digest within his brain as he listened.

Secretly, he was not in agreement with the stipulations that they were putting on him so he could experience his lifetime dream to actually see a real Bigfoot in person.

He was also very skeptical of what they were telling him about his son being able to communicate with these elusive creatures.

He just could not bring himself to openly accept this as a fact.

Nevertheless, because he could not see any other way to be able to see the Bigfoot's, and also see if what they were saying about his son was true, and added to that, he could see that Shamieka and Sleeping Beaver were very firm with the stipulations, he finally agreed to what they asked of him.

So it was agreed that he would go about his normal business, and a promise of not mentioning this to anyone, as he waited to see if Crazy Mylo and the Bigfoot's would agree to their plan.

They would pickup Augy in a few days after they had a chance to speak with Crazy Mylo about the plan.

A few minutes later, Samuel and Augy were being driven home by Sleeping Beaver.

There was plenty of silence in the vehicle as they drove south down the Highway 101 to Samuel's home.

Samuel's brain was buzzing immensely in that silent car.

He was day dreaming about the possibility of finally seeing a real life Bigfoot.

He also pondered about the possibility of actually speaking to his son in English.

Was this all true?

There were so many questions jumping around in his head.

What if it was all true?

How would he react if he was actually able to see a Bigfoot in person?

What kind of conversation would he have with his son if they could converse in the English language?

Would this be the only time that he would ever be able to have these two experiences if it was all true?

At the same time, as he had his doubts about all these questions, he also realized that Shamieka and Sleeping Beaver were decent honest people that he trusted to watch his son.

They had their own legitimate reasons to give him stipulations in the event that Crazy Mylo and the Bigfoot's agreed to let this plan happen.

Would Crazy Mylo not agree to this plan made by Shamieka and Sleeping Beaver?

What would he do if Crazy Mylo squashed this plan before his little Augy even had a chance to supposedly communicate with the Bigfoot's for permission?

Were these creatures actually that intelligent?

All Samuel could do for now was to wait and see what happened in the next few days.

Chapter Twenty One

A WEEK WENT BY before Sleeping Beaver and Shamieka were able to track down Crazy Mylo.

He had relocated to a new location in a different mountain range.

He had migrated almost six miles from his previous location where they had met before.

Crazy Mylo was surprised to see the two of them so soon.

He thought that they were going to simply talk about what had happened with them when they were last together.

To his utter surprise, they came straight to the point, and explained their plan with Samuel to him, and asked for his permission to follow through with it.

They were not surprised when Crazy Mylo did not think that it would be a good idea to introduce Samuel to the Bigfoot's.

Even the idea of bringing Samuel to the Bigfoot location with a blindfold over his eyes was not good enough to convince Crazy Mylo to get his permission.

Of course, getting Crazy Mylo's permission was not something that was absolutely necessary with Sleeping Beaver and Shamieka.

The two of them just thought that out of respect, they should at the very least ask Crazy Mylo if he thought that it would be a good idea to introduce Samuel to the Bigfoot's.

Finally, they explained to Crazy Mylo that ultimately, it would be up to the Bigfoot's to actually give permission to bring Samuel to meet them at their remote location in the mountains.

Upon hearing this from Shamieka and Sleeping Beaver, Crazy Mylo finally gave in and agreed to their plan with Samuel.

He went on record still, that he did not think that it would be a good idea, and predicted that the Bigfoot's would not give permission to bring Samuel to meet them.

So it was agreed between the three of them that they would go back to Samuel tomorrow, and ask him when they could bring Augy to the Bigfoot's to help them communicate to them about their plan with Samuel.

The next day, Shamieka and Sleeping Beaver went to Samuel's home that was located on the side of a mountain at the edge of a forest, within two miles of downtown Rio Dell, in beautiful Humboldt County California.

As they pulled up to Samuel's rocky driveway, they noticed near the heavy duty built brown fence with green topper's, a familiar little boy peaking through the wooden slats that were built parallel to the ground.

He stared at them blankly, as if he had never seen them before in his life.

He made no gesture whatsoever towards them as they exited their vehicle.

But this was normal, as everyone already knew with Augy.

Samuel was silent as well, but only for a few moments before he realized who the two people were.

He walked over to one of his two gates and greeted them with a friendly smile and polite "hello."

Samuel gestured over to Augy to come over and meet his two friends.

Slowly, almost cautiously, Augy made his way over to the three adults near the side gate.

Shamieka started to do some sign language with little Augy, and finally there was a bit of recognition between the young boy and the two adults standing next to his father.

He answered back with his sign language.

Silently within his head, he was still wondering why he could not verbally talk to her as he had done when he met the large mountain creatures recently.

Samuel invited everyone into the house to get comfortable for conversation.

Once they were all comfortable in the living room, Sleeping Beaver told Samuel that they had seen Crazy Mylo the day before and had talked to him about their plan with Samuel.

Samuel understood Crazy Mylo's reluctance to follow through with the plan.

But at the same time, he felt that he was going to meet these Bigoot's one way or the other… if they in fact actually existed.

He was still slightly skeptical about whether all of what he had seen, and been told by Shamieka and Sleeping Beaver was actually in fact the truth.

Along with the skepticism that he felt, there was also an intense desire and hope that all of this about the existence of these Bigfoot's in a secret location in the mountains, was indeed a reality that he might be able to experience very soon if all went well with this plan thought up by these two friends now sitting in his living room a few feet away from him.

Augy sat still a few feet away, silently in his own little world, seemingly not caring at all about what they were discussing.

After Samuel listened to his two friends discuss their conversation with Crazy Mylo, he agreed that Augy could go with them to meet the Bigfoot's, and hopefully be able to get their permission to let him come to their location to meet them.

He agreed that being blindfolded would be the best addition to this plan that might influence the Bigfoot's to say that it would be alright to follow through and bring him to their location.

So it was agreed that in two days, Shamieka and Sleeping Beaver would come to Samuel's home and pick up Augy for a return trip to meet the Bigfoot's.

Samuel was of course excited about the possibility of having a chance to fulfill his life's dream… meeting a real live Bigfoot!!

Augy on the other hand, did not show any type of excitement at all upon getting this information from Shamieka that once again, he would be going with her and Sleeping Beaver to meet the large mountain creatures in a couple of days.

Even though Augy was not able to show any outward excitement about this return trip to meet the Bigfoot's, he was actually feeling inside of him, a slight feeling of happiness.

It was the same feeling that he would have whenever he went on one of his hikes along the edge of the forest near his home.

Sleeping Beaver and Shamieka bid farewell to Samuel and Augy, and left to go back to her place to prepare for their return trip to the mountains with

Augy to talk to the Bigfoots, and hopefully, they would get their permission to bring Samuel to meet them sometime soon.

The weather went from sunny to overcast, and then a very heavy rain in a matter of minutes, so was the natural weather of Humboldt County that all of it's residents were used to.

Augy sat at a window on the second story of his home and stared at the distant mountains where he would be traveling in a few days.

Would he be able to verbally communicate with the adults again?

This thought floated in his head like the early morning mist that came to Humboldt County every single day of the year.

Chapter Twenty Two

T WO DAYS HAD PASSED since Sleeping Beaver and Shamieka had received permission from Samuel that they would be able to bring Augy back to the mountains to meet and communicate with the Bigfoot's in hope's of getting their permission to bring Samuel to their location to meet them as well.

Samuel already had his son ready for the day.

There was just one more thing for Samuel to do with his son.

Samuel wanted to make sure that no matter what, he would be able to find out where the Bigfoot's were located.

Just in case Sleeping Beaver and Shamieka came back from the meeting with the Bigfoot's with news that the Bigfoot's did not give them permission to bring him to meet them.

In the two days that went by since last seeing Shamieka and Sleeping Beaver, Samuel had traveled up north to Eureka to a place called "CST."

This stood for... Child Safety Tracker.

This business was new to Humboldt County but not to the rest of the U.S.

What this business specialized in was selling items with GPS chips imbedded inside of the item.

This chip, once activated would be able to tracked via satellite from a laptop or desktop computer.

It also showed the entire journey of where the chip went.

This information was stored in the archives of the chip, and very easily retrievable.

Samuel decided to choose a bracelet for Augy with one of these GPS chips embedded inside.

The bracelet also had information that was readable on the front and backside.

Information such as name, address, phone number, and any medical condition.

Yes, this was a sneaky thing to do with his friends, but Samuel wanted to really make sure that he knew the entire route taken by Augy to this supposed meeting.

No matter what the outcome with the supposed meeting with the Bigfoot's, Samuel would be able to later retrack the entire route and see the Bigfoot's, if they were really there, for himself.

His friends would not even know that he did this.

So in Samuel's mind, no harm.

What they did not know, would not hurt them.

Of course, Augy did not know at all what the little bracelet was all about.

If Sleeping Beaver and Shamieka were to ask about the bracelet, he would simply tell them it was a bracelet for Augy to wear in case he became lost, and was found by someone.

The person would be able to contact Samuel and safely return his son to him.

Shamieka was finishing packing her vehicle.

Sleeping Beaver sat in Shamieka's vehicle silently waiting for her to get in and start driving.

He was slightly nervous about this day.

Thought's of how the Bigfoot's would react to their return with Augy was a reason for slight concern.

What would the Bigfoots do when they heard the request about Samuel from little Augy?

Would they react violently?

Would they agree to the plan?

Sleeping Beaver was absolutely in a state of mind numbness about how the whole day would turn out.

As a precaution, Sleeping Beaver brought his "Bear pepper spray" with him in case the meeting became uncomfortable and possible violence towards them.

He had never brought this weapon with him in the past when traveling to meet the Bigfoot's, but today, he just wanted to make sure that he, Shamieka, and especially little Augy were going to be safe at this unannounced meeting.

Deep down within his soul, Sleeping Beaver knew that the Bigfoot's were in reality a gentle race, but nevertheless, precaution would have to be taken today... just in case his inner thoughts were completely wrong.

Finally, Shamieka was done with packing her vehicle, and she got inside and off they drove... south towards Rio Dell to meet Samuel and pick up little Augy.

Within the hour they were coasting to a stop at the tip of Samuel's driveway.

They both exited the vehicle and went to the front door and rang the doorbell to announce their arrival.

Samuel answered the door with a smile and welcomed them inside his house.

Augy sat silently on the couch in the living room watching a television program about African wildlife.

Augy really enjoyed watching animal shows, even though he was not able to outwardly show his enjoyment.

Shamieka started her sign language with Augy when he looked in her direction.

She asked him if he was ready to go hiking to the mountains and see the big mountain creatures again.

Augy signed back to her that he was ready to leave to go hiking... his favorite activity.

Shamieka noticed the bracelet on Augy's wrist and asked him about it.

He signed back to her that his Father put it on his wrist this morning, and he did not know why.

Shamieka asked Samuel about the bracelet, and he calmly replied that it was simply a bracelet to help Augy get home in case he became lost and was found by someone.

He explained to her that it had all the information needed written on it to help whoever might find Augy, to contact him and help Augy get back home safely.

Shamieka read the bracelet.

The bracelet had the letters CST on the backside below all the contact information.

She did not give it a second thought as to what the CST stood for, and even if she did inquire about what it meant, Samuel would simply tell her it was the name of the company, and of course not mention that it was a GPS chip company.

CST had only been in business in Humboldt County for less than a month.

There had not been any advertisements yet to the residents of the County to explain what they were all about.

Advertisements would come in a few more weeks.

Sleeping Beaver did not think much about the bracelet either, he was more preoccupied with what he was going to do for the day, and hoped that the day would be safe for all of them.

After drinking a cup of coffee offered by Samuel, they left the house with Augy and loaded up in the vehicle.

Samuel hugged his son and bid farewell to Sleeping Beaver, and Shamieka.

The vehicle drove away, and right away, Samuel went upstair to his computer and started to track them with the GPS tracking software with the chip embedded in Augy's bracelet.

The software was working perfectly… giving chip location every seven seconds.

Samuel watched the computer screen closely as it slowly moved farther away from the Rio Dell area on the map.

He was curious if he had ever traveled to this area on the map.

It appeared that he had, so far been near the area where the chip was now located.

He watched patiently as the green dot on the screen moved.

In exactly seventeen minutes, the green dot left the highway, and started to travel into the mountains, probably along old logging roads was his best guess.

Another twenty five minutes went by as he closely watched the GPS tracker, and finally the dot stopped completely.

The green dot on the screen showed the same location for almost eight minutes.

He guessed that the vehicle must have stopped and that they were now going to proceed on foot.

His theory was reinforced shortly when he noticed that the green dot moved much slower on the screen than it did when the vehicle had been moving.

Samuel left the room for awhile to other things around the house, he would periodically check the computer throughout the day.

In the meantime, Sleeping Beaver, Shamieka, and little Augy were indeed traveling on foot to meet Crazy Mylo at his latest secret location within the mountain range.

Chapter Twenty Three

IT TOOK SHAMIEKA, SLEEPING Beaver, and Augy almost two hours to finally reach the location where Crazy Mylo was camping.

After resting for just under an hour, off they went, hardly saying a word between them as they started to walk.

Finally after hiking for about fifteen minutes in almost complete silence, Crazy Mylo started a conversation.

"You know… I am starting to have second thoughts about what we are doing today."

"We have no way of knowing how the Bigfoots are going to react after we tell them what we are requesting."

"I am sure that they will be alright with us when we first get there, but once we tell them that we are there to request that we would like to bring Samuel to their location to meet them, I really have my doubts as to how they might react."

"They very well might just decide that we have already gone way to far, and decide that the safest thing to do for themselves would be to just kill us, and that would be the end of any thoughts that they might have that they could be in danger from other humans in the future."

"Do you two actually believe that they will simply say to Augy that they do not have a problem with us bringing Samuel to meet them?"

"I think that they might already be freaked-out about how things are right now."

"They might already have decided that they made a huge mistake in letting us leave their area to go back to where all of the other humans live."

"They may very well have already decided to kill us whenever we return."

"They might not even give us a chance to even try to communicate with them."

"Honestly, I am feeling a bit freaked-out myself at the moment."

Crazy Mylo stopped talking after this last comment.

More silence followed for several long minutes before Sleeping Beaver decided to reply to his friends concerns.

"I agree with everything that you just said my friend, but I also believe that it is very possible that it might turn out to be the opposite of what you say as well."

"I had the feeling when we left them after our last contact with them that they trusted us enough to let us return in the future."

"I think that a lot of the trust has to do with the innocence that they see in Augy, and the fact that they are able to actually communicate with us through Augy."

"They can actually ask questions from us through Augy, and get answers that might quell some of the inhibitions that they have about us."

"I also realize that they might decide to just use us for the time being to communicate with us through Augy, and then, when they have satisfied all of their curiosity through questioning, they might indeed decide to kill us, and then they could feel safer about any dangers that could occur from humans in their future."

"Yes my friend, we are definitely taking a chance today."

"If you want to turn back and go back to your camp, that is your choice."

"Me? . . . I am going forward and take my chances."

"Shamieka? . . . you have been pretty quiet, what do you think?"

"Are you having second thoughts about what we are doing today?"

"Do you want to not do this and go back?"

Shamieka waited a few moments before answering.

All eyes were upon her in anticipation of what she was about to say to Sleeping Beavers question.

Even little Augy seemed to be waiting for Shamieka's answer.

"Hmm... both of you men have valid points."

"But I have to agree with Sleeping Beaver, not simply because he is my boyfriend, but because I feel that there is a genuine trust between us and the Bigfoot's."

"Sure there is a possible danger for us today, but hey, everyday there are numerous possible dangers that could harm us that we cannot predict."

"We have an opportunity to give to a Father and son something that they have never been able to experience between them."

"Real actual communication."

"We all take it for granted that we are able to easily talk with each other, but just stop for a moment and think about what Samuel and Augy have gone through mentally, in not being able to talk verbally with the English language between the two of them."

"I am willing to take the risk for the possibility that they might someday in the very near future have the chance to communicate in the English language with each other."

"Even the Bigfoot's are able to communicate with each other."

"I think that once we tell them what we are trying to do for this Father and son, they will realize that it would be a wonderful thing to see them communicate with each other."

"I honestly think that they are very intelligent creature's."

"I do not think that they are anything like the primates that we have become used to seeing in the zoo's or in the wild."

"I believe that they are more like us humans than they are with the other primates of this planet."

"I am going to continue on."

Crazy Mylo continued to walk with everyone and started to talk once again.

"I am not going to turn back my friends."

"I guess I need to be there for all of you, and take my chances."

"Hell, what else do I have planned for the day."

"If it turns out to be a bad day, then at least I will experience it with my friends."

"Does anyone have any protection in case the Bigfoot's decide to attack us?"

Sleeping Beaver showed Crazy Mylo the can of Bear pepper spray that could fire a stream of spray over twenty five feet with very good accuracy.

Crazy Mylo agreed that this might very well be a good deterrent to stop a Bigfoot just as quickly as it would with a bear.

Crazy Mylo did point out to Sleeping Beaver that the can would probably not be of much help if they were attacked by a large number of Bigfoot's at once.

Shamieka and Sleeping Beaver did agree with this assessment as well.

All that they could do for the time being is to hope that it did not even get anywhere near that point.

Hopefully, all would go well, and this meeting would turn out to be safe.

Hopefully, the Bigfoot's would agree, after communicating with the young autistic child that they would allow a meeting with Samuel to happen, so a Father and son might for the first time be able to communicate in the human English language.

Silence once again took hold of the three adults, and everyone concentrated on hiking to the Bigfoot's location.

Chapter Twenty Four

T HE YOUNG BIGFOOT… ESHER sat on a hillside overlooking the small almost hidden valley where his mother and other Bigfoot's were standing near a waterfall that cascaded from the side of the mountain. Esher heard a noise coming from the distance.

It sounded like the crackling of small dried twigs that lay on the ground.

Esher stood up on his feet and concentrated on the sounds from the direction that he had heard it coming from.

Now he heard even more of these same sounds.

He walked a few feet in that direction, and then hid behind a huge redwood tree.

He peaked around the tree ever so slightly as the sound came closer to his location.

After a few more moments, he was able to see… humans!!

He was startled for the moment before he realized that these were the same humans that he had seen recently with his parents.

He did not let the humans see him where he was hiding.

Slowly, stealthily, Esher walked sideways at an angle, and when he was away from a possible line of site for the humans, he quickly started to run down the hillside towards his mother and the other Bigfoot's that stood with her.

In large strides, Esher was able to get to his mother's location in less then thirty seconds.

He ran up to the adult Bigfoot's and quickly alerted them of the humans that he had seen approaching.

He also told them that it was the same humans that had visited them recently.

He told them that he had also noticed the human child with them as well.

Esher was excited at another chance to see these humans.

Esher's mother… Reka, quickly started to pass around the information that her son had just given to her and the other Bigfoot's.

One of the Bigfoot's that had been standing with Reka quickly ran to the cave system to alert the other Bigfoot's that dwelled within.

Just as the humans… Crazy Mylo, Sleeping Beaver, Shamieka, and little Augy reached the hillside where Esher had just been sitting, a large number of Bigfoot's had already started to gather down near a stream created from the waterfall.

Other Bigfoot's continued to come out of the cave system behind the waterfall every few seconds to also gather with the Bigfoot's near the stream.

All of the Bigfoot's stared in the direction of the hillside where the humans finally appeared, standing still looking back at the gathering.

An invisible tension floated in the air between the humans and the Bigfoot's.

The humans just stood there looking at them, not hardly moving, and certainly not attempting to communicate with them either.

The Bigfoot's acted in a similar manner, just staring at the humans, not showing any outward signs of possible aggressiveness.

Who would make the first move?

It could almost be compared to two cats circling each other, bluffing for a possible fight, but not really doing anything except staring intently at each other.

Finally, to everyone's surprise, little Augy started to run down the hillside.

The adult humans acted just as surprised as the gathering of Bigfoots near the stream.

Augy continued to run in the direction of the Bigfoot's.

He did not show any type of noticeable fear as he ran.

Moments after Augy started to run towards the Bigfoot's, yet again, another surprise all of a sudden occurred.

The young Bigfoot Esher started to run towards the hillside where Augy was coming down.

None of the Bigfoot's made an attempt to stop Esher, not even verbally.

All eyes were now concentrated on the two youngster's running towards each other. within twenty seconds, Augy and Esher met each other a few feet from the bottom of the hillside.

They stood a few feet from one another and stared at each other for a few moments.

Finally, Esher started to speak to Augy in his language.

After saying what he had to say to Augy, Augy spoke back to Esher in the Bigfoot language.

Both of the youngster's appeared to be very excited to be communicating with each other.

They were just out of earshot from the humans, but the Bigfoot's could easily hear what had been said between Augy and Esher.

Simply, the two youngster's had just greeted one another and told each other their names.

They continued to talk for a few more minutes before Esher invited Augy to come back with him to where the other Bigfoot's were gathered.

Crazy Mylo, Shamieka, and Sleeping Beaver continued to stand silently on top of the hillside where Esher had been sitting before he heard them approaching.

Moments later, Augy and Esher stood before a very large group of Bigfoot's.

Augy still did not show any type of fear in anyway.

He looked as if he was totally comfortable standing alongside this large group of Bigfoot's.

The fact was that Augy was indeed feeling very comfortable with himself as he stood with Esher and the other Bigfoot's.

The other fact was that the three adult humans on top of the hillside were feeling very nervous.

They had a feeling of helplessness for the moment as they watched Augy down with the crowd of Bigfoot's.

They waited for some type of sign from the Bigfoot's that it would be alright for them to come down to where they were all gathered.

They stood there on top of the hillside for several minutes, patiently, and nervously waiting.

They watched little Augy talking with the Bigfoot's, obviously in their language.

Crazy Mylo whispered to his friends… "I told you both this was a mistake."

"The Bigfoot's don't look like they are going to be friendlier with us this time."

"Look at how many are down there with Augy, and look at the waterfall area, they are still coming out."

"Maybe they have decided to kill us after all, just like I said."

"Maybe they all want to be witness to our death's for reassurance that they will be safe in the future from humans."

Shamieka spoke in a slightly higher whisper in response to what Crazy Mylo was saying.

"Stop sniveling."

"I think that you are going to be wrong in your theory of them wanting to kill us."

"I think that because not all of them had a chance the last time we were here to see us, maybe this time they decided that all the Bigfoot's could have a chance to see the humans that know where they live."

"I am also sure that there are many Bigfoot's that feel like we should not be here in the first place."

"Yes… I am nervous, but confident that because Augy is here to communicate with them, that we will be safe at this meeting."

Sleeping Beaver stayed silent as his two friends whispered with each other.

He was carefully watching everything down below, waiting for some kind of sign or signal from the Bigfoot's.

A few more minutes went by, and then Augy turned around to face the three adults on the hillside.

He did not make any type of hand gesture.

After a few moments, Augy, and then Esher, started to walk in the direction of the hillside.

They slowly made their way up to the top of the hillside.

Within two long minutes, Augy and Esher were standing in front of the three nervous adults.

As before on their last visit, Augy started to talk to them in the English language.

His tone of voice seemed to be happy.

Maybe he was a bit happy as he realized that he was talking in English to them.

Augy spoke almost casually to them.

"This is my new friend "Esher," and he came up here with me to let you all know that we all have permission to come down from here to meet with them."

Slight smiles appeared on all three adults.

They were certainly still nervous though.

So the three adults, along with Augy and Esher, started to walk down the hillside towards the now very crowded area with what looked like over fifty Bigfoot's.

As they came close to the crowd of Bigfoot's, one of the Bigfoot's stepped out of the crowd to meet them.

They recognized him from their last meeting.

It was "Arch."

Their was no handshakes like the normal human tradition, just a simple head nod seemed to be the greeting from Arch.

Arch started to talk to Augy in the Bigfoot language.

Augy answered back to Arch.

Then Augy turned to Sleeping Beaver and said… "Arch wants to know why we are here today."

Sleeping Beaver answered back slowly to Augy.

"Tell Arch that we have come here today as friends with a request."

Augy told Arch what Sleeping Beaver said.

Arch said something to Augy, and then appeared to be waiting for an answer.

Augy spoke once again.

"Arch is surprised to see us here today, he invited most of the other Bigfoot's out here to be able to see the humans that know where they live."

"Arch said that there are many of his kind that want to hurt the humans."

"They are scared that more humans will come to this place and hurt them and there young."

"Arch has told them not to do anything to the humans."

"He says that you all can feel safe today."

"He wants to know what the request is."

Shamieka spoke this time.

"Tell Arch that we appreciate him making sure we are safe today, and that we understand the concerns of the others around him that do not feel safe with us here and their not trusting us is a normal feeling that we understand them to have."

"Tell Arch that we have a request concerning your Father."

Augy looked at Shamieka momentarily after she said this.

He turned back to Arch and relayed all of what Shamieka said back to him.

Arch spoke to Augy again, and then waited again for an answer.

Augy spoke again to his human adult friends.

"Arch is confused when you mention my Father."

"Arch wants us to walk over to another spot and sit down to continue talking."

Shamieka nodded her head towards Arch as she told Augy that they were ready to go sit down and talk some more.

Arch nodded back to Shamieka as Augy told him his friends were ready to go sit down to talk some more.

Arch made no motion with his hands, he just simply turned around and started to walk away.

As he walked, the crowd of Bigfoot's parted to make a clear path for everyone to follow Arch.

There was what appeared to be mumbling throughout the crowd of Bigfoot's as the humans walked by them behind Arch.

Crazy Mylo felt very petrified as he walked through the crowd of Bigfoot's.

Arch led them to an area near the waterfall and abruptly sat down on the ground near a redwood tree.

The three human adults quickly sat down near Arch, forming a small circle.

All of the Bigfoot's that had been gathered in a crowd were now forming a large circle around the entire area.

It seemed to be an invisible perimeter or sorts.

It seemed as if they were guarding the entire area to make sure that the humans did not leave this area.

Crazy Mylo whispered to Sleeping Beaver.

"Look at what they are doing."

Sleeping Beaver heard his friend whisper, and answered back in a normal tone of voice.

"It looks like they are taking a normal precaution to make sure they are safe."

"I do not feel paranoid."

"Lets see how this all turns out my friend, try to relax."

Arch looked over at Crazy Mylo quizically.

Crazy Mylo bowed his head to not look at Arch's eyes.

Augy remained standing with Esher at his side near Arch.

Once they were all sitting for about a minute, Arch spoke to Augy once again.

Augy once again started to speak back to his friends.

"Arch wants to know why we mention my Father today."

Sleeping Beaver was the person who spoke this time.

"Tell Arch that we want to be able to have you… Augy… for the first time in your life, talk with your Father in the human language that we call English."

"Tell Arch how normal it must be for him and his kind to be able to talk to their young."

"Tell Arch that you and your Father have never been able to talk to each other in the human language we call English."

"Tell Arch that we have discovered, and we do not know why, or how, but we discovered the last time that we were here, and he can also see today, that you are able to speak the human English language when you are around his kind who we as humans call Bigfoot's."

"We would like to get permission from the Bigfoot's to bring your Father who is named Samuel, to this place so that you will be able, for the first time, talk to your Father in the human English language as you are doing here today."

"We would make sure that your Father would not actually know where this place is located because we will put a cover over his eyes so he cannot see where he is going."

"We will hold his hand while his eyes are covered, and guide him to this place."

"Tell Arch that if the Bigfoot's decided that they do not want to give permission to bring your Father here so that you will be able to talk to him in our language, we would honor their decision, and we promise to not bring your Father here… ever… if that is what the Bigfoot's decision turns out to be."

Sleeping Beaver stopped talking to Augy, and went silent.

Augy spent the next several minutes explaining to Arch what Sleeping Beaver had said to Augy.

Many times during the conversation between Augy and Arch, Arch made slight grunts that did not appear to have a nice feeling.

These grunts once again put the three adult humans in a nervous mode.

Back and forth the conversation went between Augy and Arch.

Finally, after several nerve racking minutes, Augy once again turned to his human friends.

Augy spoke.

"Arch understands how important it would be for me and my Father to be able to talk with each other in the English language."

"He understands this because he knows how bad he would feel if he was not able to speak with his kind, old or young."

"Arch wants us to wait here while he goes to talk with the rest of the Bigfoot's about our request about my Father."

"He says that he would give permission to have my Father come here, but he wants to hear from the other Bigfoot's to know what they want."

"He say's that he alone, cannot make this decision for all of his kind."

Sleeping Beaver nodded in Arch's direction.

Arch nodded back as he rose from the ground and walked away to the other Bigfoot's.

Augy and Esher walked alongside Arch talking energetically with each other.

Esher actually had what appeared to be a smile upon his face as he talked to Augy in the Bigfoot language.

Augy did not actually smile, but the tone of his voice indicated that he was in what could be determined as a happy mood as well.

Arch was gone for what seemed like over an hour, talking with the other Bigfoot's.

The reality was that he had only been talking to the other Bigfoot's for only slightly over fifteen minutes.

One of the things that Sleeping Beaver did while Arch was busy talking to the other Bigfoots was to collect some hair samples that he had noticed in many of the areas on the ground where they were now sitting.

Without anyone noticing, he collected two large handfuls of this hair and casually put the hair into his pants pockets.

If this turned out to be the hair from the Bigfoot's, which he was sure that it was, then later, he would try an experiment with the hair based on a theory of his that he had not mentioned to anyone so far.

For now, it was more important to concentrate on the moment, and later he could try out his experiment with the hair.

Augy and Esher were running around with each other gleefully and obviously enjoying each other's company.

They looked like they were now truly friends.

Young human… young Bigfoot… friends.

As Arch made his way back to the three adult humans, Augy and Esher came back with him, once again at his side.

Arch sat down where he sat before.

Augy once again remained standing.

Arch spoke to Augy for about a minute before going silent to wait for Augy to translate what he had said back to the three adult humans.

Augy spoke.

"Arch spoke to the other Bigfoot's about our request, and they have decided that they do not want any other humans to know about this location where they feel safe from humans."

"Arch also says that we will be allowed to come back here in the future to visit."

"Arch, and the other Bigfoot's have noticed that me and Esher like each other as new friends."

"The Bigfoot's think it would be a good idea to have me and Esher continue to be friends in the future."

"They have also said that if we break our promise and bring another human here ever again, besides who is here today, that they will have to kill all of us."

"They understand how good it would be if me and my Father could have a chance to talk with each other in our human language, but they do not trust what could happen in the future if another human knew where they are located."

"That is their decision today."

After hearing this from Arch and the other Bigfoot's, Sleeping Beaver told Augy to tell Arch that they would honor the Bigfoot's decision that they made today, and that they will not bring your Father, or any other human to this place... ever... in the future.

He also asked Augy to tell Arch that he and the humans who are here today are glad to hear that they have been given permission to return for future visits.

"We have also noticed that you and Esher like each other as new friends."

Augy relayed this message back to Arch.

Arch nodded his head that seemed to affirm his understanding what was said by the humans.

After another half of an hour sitting on the ground, still surrounded by many Bigfoot's, Crazy Mylo suggested that maybe they should leave and hike back to their homes and leave the Bigfoot's in peace.

The other adults agreed with this and had Augy tell Arch of their intentions.

Arch agreed with them and walked them out of the area towards the hillside.

Most of the other Bigfoots started to walk back into the cave system behind the waterfall. Within minutes, only a few Bigfoots remained in the area as the humans started to climb the hillside and disappeared over the ridgeline into the forest.

Meanwhile, several miles away near Rio Dell, Samuel sat at his computer and noticed that the GPS tracker had stopped at one location for quite awhile, and now the green dot was backtracking in the direction it had already went.

This indicated to Samuel that they were on their way back home.

It also indicated to him that the spot on the screen where the green dot had stopped had to be the spot where they had met with the Bigfoot's.

It was the farthest spot away on the screen that they had traveled.

Samuel was excited.

Was this truly the actual spot where he was going to travel with his friends to meet with the Bigfoot's?

Samuel did not know that the Bigfoot's had decided that he would not be allowed to travel to their location.

But... Samuel had prepared for this possibility just in case.

He had the GPS tracker identifying the location.

If need be, he would go to that location himself and see the Bigfoot's anyway, regardless of the Bigfoot's decision.

This was his lifelong dream, and nothing was going to stop him for this opportunity.

He was not thinking about a chance to speak English with his son, because he had doubted that this part of their story to be true.

He thought that this was impossible, and had to be an exaggeration by his friends.

He turned the computer off, and went downstairs to wait for his friends, and son to return.

Samuel had a smile on his face.

Chapter Twenty Five

I T WAS ALMOST THREE and a half hours before the vehicle drove-up to Samuel's house containing Sleeping Beaver, Shamieka, and his son Augy.

Crazy Mylo had been left at his usual place in the mountains.

Samuel greeted everyone with an extra amount of exuberance.

Of course, Augy did not show any outward sign of joy or any other emotion to his Father.

They all went into the house.

Secretly, Samuel was hoping to hear from his friends the best possible news.

Hopefully they would tell him that the Bigfoot's had given permission for him to hike to their location to meet them.

The adults sat down in the living room.

Augy wandered off to another part of the house, not at all interested in what the adults would talk about.

Fact of the matter was that Augy was still thinking about the Bigfoot's, and especially his new friend Esher.

Augy had not said even a single word, or made a sound with his special language near the adults since the very moment that they had left the area where the Bigfoot's were located.

He had not even made an attempt to communicate with Shamieka with the silent sign language on the trip back either.

Back in the living room, the three adults started to talk... casually at first about the day.

Finally, Samuel wanted to "Cut to the chase" . . . and asked point blank what the decision had been with the Bigfoot's.

Sleeping Beaver and Shamieka looked at each other momentarily. Shamieka nodded at Sleeping Beaver to indicate that he would be the one to give the news to Samuel about what decision the Bigfoot's had made.

Sleeping Beaver sighed slightly, and then spoke.

"Samuel, your son Augy did very well today."

"He was able to communicate with the Bigfoot's in the same way that he had done before in our last visit."

"He was also able to speak in the English language when he was around the Bigfoot's."

"He even made a friend today with a young Bigfoot named Esher."

"Augy and Esher obviously enjoyed each others company."

"Now... as to what decision was made by the Bigfoot's, unfortunately the news for you is not good."

"The Bigfoot's did not give permission for you to visit, even if it was blindfolded."

"They already feel uncomfortable about how many humans already know where they are located."

"There was a short period of time where we felt that we might be in danger."

"But that feeling was put to rest after they talked to Augy."

"On the other hand, they did give us permission to return in the future with Augy so they can continue talking with us, and they think that it is a good idea for Augy and Esher to be friends."

"Maybe, over time with other visits, maybe Samuel, they might change their minds."

"But for now, that is their decision, and we have to honor it."

"I know how important this is for you Samuel, and I know that you are very disappointed, but it is what it is."

"I am so sorry my friend."

Shamieka repeated how sorry she felt for Samuel about the decision that the Bigfoot's had made.

She reached across the small coffee table to comfort Samuel as she spoke.

She grasped his hands gently, and smiled her million dollar smile to him.

Surprisingly, to their amazement, Samuel did not react towards this news as they thought he would.

He just simply shrugged his shoulders and spoke in a normal tone of voice and answered with a nonchalant reply.

"Of course, you are correct when you say that I am disappointed with this news, but hey… what can I do?"

"I can only hope that they might change their minds, and give me permission in the future after they have been around both you and my son Augy."

"Yes, I do give permission for Augy to return for future visits."

"Now, if that is all there is to say about this subject, I would like to spend some time with Augy and relax for the rest of the day."

"I'll walk you two out to your vehicle."

Samuel rose to his feet and motioned them towards the door.

Within minutes, they were gone.

Samuel sat again in his house after they left… smiling.

Chapter Twenty Six

I N THE NEXT FEW months as time passed ever so slowly in the well isolated coastal region of Humboldt County, Samuel allowed his son Augy to travel with Shamieka and Sleeping Beaver to visit the Bigfoots.

Mainly the young Bigfoot named Esher who had become Augy's friend on previous visits.

During this time, Samuel was busy plotting a plan that he thought would make him rich and famous throughout the world.

Also during this time, as little Augy spent more time around Esher and the other Bigfoots, he began to understand more and more how they lived their every day lives in the vast mountains.

Augy actually felt more comfortable being around the Bigfoots than he did around humans.

During the times that Augy spent playing in the mountains with Esher, Esher taught him things about nature that he never knew.

At the same time that Esher was showing Augy new things about nature, Augy started to teach Esher the human silent language that he practiced with Shamieka.

Sign language.

Esher realized quickly that this was a good way to communicate in silence from distances that were far apart.

The two youngsters would practice sign language with each other as they sat far apart from each other up to a hundred feet away.

They had fun with this game.

After Augy would leave and go back to his home in the human world, Esher began teaching all of the other Bigfoot's how to do the human sign language.

The other Bigfoot's liked this new way of communicating because they also realized, as had Esher, that they could talk with each other silently without having to vocalize loudly with their voices.

They themselves started to practice the silent language with each other more and more as time went on.

They also realized that their stealthiness improved when utilizing the silent language.

If they were in a situation where humans might be near them, they could, instead of howling, they could just sign each other.

They also realized that this was only good to use in the daylight because the hand signals had to be deciphered with their eyes.

Nevertheless, it became a new useful part of their everyday lives during the daylight hours.

At night time, they would resort back to their normal way of communicating with each other by use of loud vocalizations such as howling.

Months went by and all seemed to be peaceful and normal in the world of the Bigfoot's.

Little did they know, in the near future, their world would experience some traumatic events that would turn the peaceful times into a time of stress and extreme negative feelings towards the human race.

Less than a few hours away from their peaceful location, the Father of the human child... Augy... who visited them regularly to play with Esher, was plotting a very devious plan.

Samuel was very close to finishing his plans about the Bigfoots... very close indeed.

On most of Augy's recent visits, Shamieka would be the only other human at their location.

The Bigfoot's had also become comfortable with this adult human female.

Because the Bigfoot's were becoming fairly good at the use of sign language, they enjoyed communicating with Shamieka because she was very good at the silent form of talking.

While Augy and Esher would be playing in the nearby mountains, Shamieka would spend her time talking silently with the Bigfoot's.

As Augy had with Esher, Shamieka was also learning new things about the Bigfoot's that she could not even ever imagined on her own.

The Bigfoot's taught her much more about nature that she simply did not even ever think about as someone whose job was working within the many forest's of Humboldt County.

So the Bigfoot's began to trust Shamieka to the point that they felt confident they she would not ever in her life ever betray them.

Unfortunately, the plan that was almost at it's completion by Samuel would impact this trust in the future.

This trust, once Samuel's plan went into effect, and if successful, would certainly be tested.

Samuel knew exactly where the Bigfoot's were located because of the GPS bracelet worn on Augy's wrist.

The location was validated many times during these month's when Augy visited the Bigfoot's.

Samuel could easily see that the green dot on the computer screen always ended up at the same exact location by use of the GPS software.

Samuel's plan was well thought out.

He wanted to make sure that the chances for success were very good.

Simply... he wanted to capture the young Bigfoot named Esher.

Samuel wanted to bring Esher back to the human world.

He wanted to show all of the people that ever doubted the existence of a species of primates nicknamed "Bigfoot" in the Humboldt County area, that they did indeed live privately in the many surrounding mountain forest's.

He would be vindicated throughout the world of people who had basically laughed at him for his belief of the existence of this secretive animal.

Surely, Samuel was being selfish with this plan.

He did not stop to think of the ramifications that would become a reality if the world did finally find out that Bigfoot's actually did exist.

He did not think how this would affect the Bigfoot's themselves.

He was basically only thinking about himself.

Samuel also thought of how famous he would become.

The thought of how he would more than likely become very rich crossed the pathways in his brain as well.

He also did not think how this would affect his son Augy.

He did not realize how much Augy enjoyed being friends with Esher.

He loved his son dearly, but this selfishness blinded his Fatherly love for his special son.

Samuel felt very strongly that there was not anything in the world that was going to stop him from carrying out his plan to capture Esher,

It was now only a few days away from the day that Samuel would start to carry out his plan.

Chapter Twenty Seven

T HE DAY WAS GETTING close to when Samuel was going to start carrying out his secret plan.

Samuel had modified a small house that was in his backyard into an area that he would be able to keep Esher in captivity once captured.

It was sound proof.

It had walls reinforced by quarter inch iron sheets.

The floors were repoured with a strong industrial cement.

The inside door was custom made from iron, and had bars that were over an inch in diameter.

It had the look of an old wild west jailhouse cell.

This door was backed up by another reinforced steel door to open to the outside.

The locking system of this iron door was coded from a key pad on the outside wall of the small building.

Of course, only Samuel would ever know the codes to open the lock of both door's.

The first code would open both door's, and then if you wanted to just open the outer door and not the inside iron bar door, you would press an additional code after the first code.

There was also a special slot to insert food into the room.

This slot was similar to the old style of post office mail boxes that citizens used to drop off their mail.

There was also a sliding latch lock attached to this food slot.

This was installed on the food slot to prevent Esher from making sounds that could be heard from the outside if the slot was in the open position.

Samuel knew that Esher, because he was a Bigfoot, would be very strong physically.

So he made sure that everything was very heavy duty and reinforced to withstand Esher's natural strength.

There were three slots also built into the floor area to capture all of Esher's urine and feces.

Through these slots was a drain that carried the bodily discharges to the main sewage system of the main house where Samuel and Augy resided.

Samuel had been very meticulous in converting this little house into a place where he could keep Esher until the time came where he could introduce the young Bigfoot to the entire human world.

In a few hours, Samuel would begin his plan.

First of all, he would travel on the highway to where it would be the closest distance to the area of where the Bigfoot's supposedly lived.

At this point in time, Samuel 100% believed that this area did in fact exist.

He would not have gone through all of this trouble if he did not think this was true.

He would be towing a horse trailer behind his truck.

Inside of this trailer would be a very powerful All Terrain Vehicle (ATV) "Quad" commonly used by many ranchers and hunters of this massive beautiful county.

Behind this Quad was also attached an open flatbed trailer.

At the head of this flatbed trailer was mounted a small electric winch.

If needed, this winch would be able to help put Esher onto the flatbed trailer.

On the bed of this trailer laid a "body board".

It was the same used by paramedics or firefighters to transfer bodies.

If all went right, if Samuel was successful in capturing the young Bigfoot, he would have him laying down on this body board securely strapped to the flatbed trailer.

He would then drive the Quad into the horse trailer and secure the back door.

Samuel had also modified the horse trailer so there was not any way for anyone to see inside of the trailer once the door was shut.

A totally enclosed horse trailer with no open slots where normally people would be able to see part of a horses body when it was being transported.

Samuel had a large can of powerful "Bear spray."

This was in case he had problems with any adult Bigfoot's that might interfere with his plan.

As a back-up to the Bear spray he also had a .357 magnum pistol to only be used if his life was 100% in danger.

He honestly did not want to ever kill any Bigfoot, but he would if his life was threatened.

Lastly, Samuel had his main item for this plan.

He had a high powered "air gun" rifle that would be used to silently shoot a tranquilizer dart into the body of Esher.

He estimated that Esher would weigh a few hundred pounds at the very least.

Hopefully his calculations would be correct in how much of the chemical should be used to quickly make Easher unconscious.

He had talked to a few of his rancher friends who would sometimes use this chemical on various animals, on how much they used per pound.

He reinforced their knowledge passed on to him by also researching the internet with the same inquiries about the chemical.

He did not want to use to much of this chemical to knock-out Esher.

It would be horrible if he used to much of the chemical, and accidentally killed the young Bigfoot.

So… now Samuel was confident that he had the chemical measured at a safe amount to do the job without fear of accidental overdose to Esher.

Esher… Esher… soon to be the most famous animal in the world.

Samuel also felt confident that his plan would be carried out without anything going wrong.

He had a feeling of immense confidence that he would soon have Esher stored away in the little house in his backyard.

It would be a way of getting close enough to Esher and bait him into an area close enough for him to successfully use the air gun.

Samuel would have to first bring the Quad to the location where he would want to load up Esher on the trailer's body board on the flatbed.

He spent the next seven hours doing this.

He drove to the closest area of the mountains near where he wanted to go and parked.

He then drove the Quad to the desired location that he had chosen on the map, and then parked the Quad and trailer.

He hid them by laying a light green blanket over them under some redwood tree's.

Samuel then hiked back to his truck and drove home.

Little did Samuel realize was that when he was parking the Quad at his hidden location, there were several eyes upon him.

Mainly the eyes of some Bigfoot's.

The Bigfoot's did not get very alarmed when they observed what Samuel had done because they had seen in the past this being done by the human hunters.

The human hunters would store a vehicle the same as Samuel had done, and then they would kill some deer and put them on a trailer that was towed by a vehicle the same as Samuel's.

The Bigfoot's over the years had observed many hunters using this technique to transport the killed deer from the mountains back to where the humans lived.

So when Samuel left the Quad behind at his chosen location, the Bigfoot's did not feel threatened.

They just thought that Samuel was probably another hunter that would soon return and kill a deer, and transport the deer away from the mountains as other hunters had done in the past.

The Bigfoot's went about their day after Samuel left, like any other normal day.

Chapter Twenty Eight

T HE DAY HAD FINALLY arrived for Samuel to start carrying out his plan to capture Esher.

Samuel would use his son Augy to lure the young Bigfoot within range.

His quad was already stored at his chosen location as well, so he would be able to quickly load an unconscious Esher onto the trailer that was attached to the rear of the quad.

He realized that his son Augy would probably become distressed by what his father had just done with his Bigfoot friend, but Samuel was now beyond caring about the feelings of his son.

Samuel's selfish feelings had officially taken over his brain that controlled his body.

He was now ready to get started with this plan.

Everything was loaded up to go, with the exception of the Quad that was already in place, and now all he had to do was go and get his son who was at this moment, sitting in the backyard watching the many birds that liked to land in the nearby trees.

Samuel walked to the backyard and leaned out the door and called to his son.

"Augy" . . . let's go hiking.

Augy slowly got to his feet and walked towards his father, not knowing what the day had in store for him.

He did not have the slightest clue as to what traumatic event he would become witness too on this day.

Within a few minutes, Father and son were on their way down the highway towing a horse trailer behind their truck.

Meanwhile, miles away, Esher played on a hillside with another young Bigfoot.

They were totally unaware of the fact that danger was approaching them and getting closer to their location as every minute disappeared into measured time.

They were playing by practicing the silent sign language that was quickly spreading throughout the Bigfoot population.

The other young Bigfoot was named Cin Cin.

She was a year older than Esher, but not much bigger in size.

This was because the male Bigfoot's were larger in body size than the females.

So it was common to see a younger male Bigfoot that might be the same size as an older female Bigfoot, or even a little larger.

They ran with each other, enjoying the freedom of their existence in these beautiful forest's that blanketed the many mountains of this special place on the globe.

They made happy vocal sounds towards each other, very similar to those that a human child might also make.

Their world was generally a very happy world.

They were slowly being taught by the older adult Bigfoot's about the many dangers that exist beyond their happy world of the mountain forest's.

Because the only humans they had ever met were the ones that visited their area, these young Bigfoot's did not yet have the realization that there were many humans beyond the forest's that could be dangerous to them.

Unlike the adult Bigfoot's who had grown to understand the dangers that the humans could bring towards their kind, these two young Bigfoot's... Esher and Cin Cin were very ignorant simply because they were still very young and had not yet lived long enough to learn, and observe the humans as they traversed through the forests and mountains.

What a lot of people did not actually realize, because of the rarity of the event, it was quite common for young Bigfoot's to climb upwards into the many types of tree's within the forest's.

They were able to do this as youngsters because their body weight was still light enough as compared to the much heavier adult's.

They did not swing in the tree's as other primates common did, they would simply climb as high as they wanted up into the tree, and then sit on a thick branch that could sustain their weight safely, and observe.

It was common for a young Bigfoot to spend hours sitting up on a branch, high off the ground… just observing their surroundings in the distance.

Cin Cin, especially liked to climb up a tree and observe her surroundings.

Esher was more of a roamer, occasionally he would climb a tree, but he enjoyed roaming much more.

So after playing with each other for awhile, Cin Cin decided that she wanted to climb a nearby redwood tree and do some observing.

Esher told her that he would be in the area walking around, and when she was finished observing in the tree, she could come find him, and then they could go back home to where the other Bigfoot's were.

Up the tree went Cin Cin, climbing with surprising agility.

Esher slowly walked away, disappearing in the forest in a matter of moments.

Esher started to think of his other friend.

His human friend Augy.

He wondered when he would see him again.

Esher never knew when Augy would show-up… he would just show up randomly.

Esher was always very happy when Augy showed up in the mountains for a visit.

Many of the times when Augy would show up, Augy would try to spy upon Esher without Esher even knowing he was being watched by his human friend.

Once Esher would realize that "Augy" was peaking at him from a distance, Esher would try to find Augy as quickly as he could.

Augy would peak at him, and then run to another spot to peak at Esher again.

It was a form of the human game of "hide and seek."

This would go on for several minutes until Esher was able to finally catch up to Augy, and then they would have fun hanging out together doing various things, mainly talking.

Esher found a spot at the bottom of a small mountain ridgeline, and sat down to rest for awhile.

As he sat there resting, Samuel and Augy were quickly approaching the same mountain range from the human road they called a highway.

Samuel and Augy would be at the area where they would be parking their truck in less than an hour.

Chapter Twenty Nine

SAMUEL SLOWED HIS TRUCK down, and pulled off to the side of the road and coasted to a stop near a shaded area of large redwood tree's. This is where he had parked when he had brought the Quad up to the mountains to stash away until today.

Once they stopped, he motioned his son Augy to get out of the truck and to grab his bottled water.

Augy did this, and then waited nearby as his Father unloaded other items from their truck.

In a few minutes, they left the truck behind, and started to hike into the forest of this mountain.

Augy recognized this forest area from the many times that he had already visited recently to see his Bigfoot friends, mainly Esher.

Augy wondered why this time, his Father hiked with him in this forest instead of the other adults like Shamieka or Sleeping Beaver.

Augy did not understand what his Father was going to attempt to do with his friend Esher.

In fact, Augy did not really understand that it was not alright for his Father to be traveling in this area towards the area where the Bigfoot's lived.

Augy did not understand that the Bigfoot's had already said to Shamieka and Sleeping Beaver that his Father could not come to the area where they could be found.

For Augy, today was just another day of hiking in the forest's, and mountains.

It was just another day to Augy, the only difference being that he was hiking this area with his Father instead of the other adults who normally would be with him.

Augy was starting to feel slightly excited, even though he did not show any outward signs to his Father.

He thought that it would be nice for his Father to meet his friend Esher.

Inside of his head he had the thought that he might finally have the chance to speak to his Father today in the English language the same way he was able to do when other adults were with him at the Bigfoot location.

He thought that Esher would like his Father.

If Augy only understood what his Father actually had planned for Esher, he would surely not feel this way at this moment.

So onward they hiked, almost the same exact way that Augy was used to hiking with the other adults.

Augy did not understand that his Father knew where he was hiking because of the GPS bracelet that had been around his wrist.

The GPS bracelet was no longer on Augy's wrist.

Samuel had decided that the bracelet was no longer needed, and also did not want Shamieka, or Sleeping Beaver to figure out what the bracelet actually did in fact do, so he detached the bracelet from his sons wrist a few weeks prior to today.

The bracelet GPS had already reassured Samuel that the location on his computer screen was in fact the location where the Bigfoot's would be found.

It took a little longer to hike to the area where Samuel had stashed the ATV Quad vehicle and the flatbed trailer that was attached to it's rear because Augy always walked a little slower when he was hiking.

The reason was because he was constantly observing things around him.

Finally Samuel and Augy arrived at the location where the Quad was parked with it's flatbed trailer.

Samuel immediately uncovered the vehicle and folded the blanket up and stored it on the flatbed trailer.

Next, Samuel made sure that the air rifle was loaded with the chemical that would knockout Esher very quickly, within a few seconds after the dart penetrated the young Bigfoot's skin.

He made sure to top off the gas tank as well.

While his Father was doing these things, Augy wandered slightly away from the area, but still within sight of his Father.

His Father glanced up and noticed this and in a low voice called his son to come back near him.

Less than two hundred yards away, Cin Cin sat on a large branch, high in a redwood tree.

Another fifty yards closer was Esher, calmly sitting under another large redwood giant.

Each of the two young Bigfoot's were totally unaware that there were humans so close to their locations.

It did help Samuel, as far as being out of sight, that he had a mountain ridgeline between him and the young Bigfoot's.

Samuel also did not realize how close he actually was to being able to see a Bigfoot for the first time, after so many years of trying.

Samuel sat down on the flatbed trailer, and motioned Augy to come sit next to him.

Even though Samuel had always been unable to communicate with his son via the English language, he was in fact always able to at least talk to his son and Augy would be able to understand what his Father was saying.

If Samuel said to his son that he could go outside and play, Augy would understand that, and go outside and play.

If Samuel said any number of things to Augy, his son understood what was being said, and reacted appropriately..

So… as Augy sat down next to his Father on the Flatbed trailer, Samuel started to explain to his son that he wanted him to do something for him.

Augy sat silently next to his Father and listened.

"Augy, I know you understand what I am saying to you."

"I would like for you to go and find your friend Esher, and bring him here to meet me."

"I will wait here for you."

"Do you understand what I am saying to you Augy?"

Augy tilted his head sideways and made a mumbling sound to his Father.

This was how Samuel knew that his son was basically saying yes to him.

If it was a no, Augy would have turned his back on his Father and made a different mumbling sound.

So Samuel continued to talk to Augy.

"Augy, I know that you are able to communicate with Esher, in Esher's language."

"Sleeping Beaver and Shamieka have told me this."

"So, I am asking you to bring Esher here to meet me, but I do not want you to tell Esher that he is going to meet me."

"I want it to be a surprise for Esher."

"Do you think that would be fun?"

"Fun to surprise your friend Esher?"

Augy, once again tilted his head and made the same gesture, indicating a yes to his Father.

This pleased Samuel.

"Alright son, go ahead and find your friend Esher and bring him here to meet me."

"It will be such a fun surprise."

Augy started to walk away.

Samuel called his son back to him and gave him a hug.

Samuel also handed Augy his bottled water to take with him.

Augy walked away from his Father, starting upwards instead of down as Samuel had thought his son would go.

Augy disappeared very quickly in the shadows of the many large redwood trees.

To Samuel's surprise, a few minutes later, Augy returned from the direction from where he had walked when he left his Father.

What Samuel did not realize was that his son had found a high point of the mountain ridgeline, and had scouted the area at a long distance.

Samuel thought his son was returning to him, so he spoke to his son as he approached.

"Son, are you going to find Esher?"

As Augy passed near where his Father sat, he kept going without acknowledging his Father's question.

Now he started to travel parallel to the mountain ridgeline, and once again disappeared in the vast forest of redwoods.

Samuel did not attempt to stop his son, he knew that Augy understood what he had asked of him, and was just basically going about his own way in his own little world.

Samuel walked to a very large redwood tree about fifty feet from the Quad, and positioned himself slightly behind it, barely in view.

He had the air rifle in his arms, ready to shoot a dart at Esher as soon as he was within his sight.

All he could do now was wait for his son to do as he had asked.

Samuel had an excited feeling swelling within his body, an anxiousness unlike he had ever felt in his entire life.

He has a smile on his face as he waited.

Chapter Thirty

AUGY WALKED A ZIG zag pattern through the many redwood tree's that surrounded him.

His friend Esher had taught him this technique.

Within ten minutes of traveling the mountain ridgeline doing this technique, and stopping here and there, Augy noticed something near another tree near the ground.

He recognized his friend Esher sitting on the ground by that tree.

Esher did not see Augy.

Augy realized this, and quickly slid behind a tree.

He peaked around the corner of the tree at his Bigfoot friend.

Esher continued to sit calmly, not showing any indication that he knew that his human friend was nearby watching him.

Augy darted to another tree, and peaked again towards his friend Esher.

This time, when Augy peaked to see Esher, Esher was not there.

The game was on.

This was the hide and seek game that they liked to play with each other whenever they first came together.

Augy did not move.

He was now using his super hearing to help him locate Esher.

Moments later, he heard a soft shuffling sound over to his left about eighty feet from where he now stood.

Augy slowly circled around the tree, and then darted forward to another hiding area, this time behind some wild black berry bushes that filled in a depression in the ground between two tree's.

Augy stopped once again to listen.

A moment later, once again he heard some more soft shuffling.

This time, the sound came directly behind Augy from where he had just been hidden.

Augy now knew that Esher was close by, hidden behind the tree where he had just been.

Augy did not move a muscle, he just waited.

He knew that in a few moments, Esher would show himself to Augy.

Augy was correct.

Only a few seconds passed before he could see Esher peaking from behind the tree, and giving Augy some silent sign language.

The sign language was just a basic greeting to Augy.

They made eye contact with each other, and Augy gave a sign language greeting back to Esher.

They both walked out from their hiding spots and walked towards each other.

They walked to within a few feet of each other and stopped.

Esher started to talk in his normal verbal Bigfoot language.

He asked Augy why he was alone.

He asked Augy where a human adult was.

Augy answered Esher back that he was not alone, and that there was a human adult with him. Esher looked around.

He did not see another human.

He was confused.

Esher asked where the adult human was.

Augy told him that the human adult was his Father, and that he was just over the mountain ridge, just out of sight.

Augy asked Esher to come follow him to where his Father was waiting for him to come back.

Augy told Esher that his Father was a nice human, and that he would like for Esher to meet him.

Because Esher totally trusted Augy, he quickly agreed to follow Augy to where his Father was on the other side of the mountain.

If Augy would have known what his Father had planned for Esher, he certainly would not have invited his friend Esher to follow him to where his Father waited.

They walked together a few feet apart, but side by side.

Esher stopped at the top of the mountain ridge.

He looked around down the slope.

He did not see any signs of where Augy's Father was.

He asked Augy where his Father was.

Augy looked down the slope as well, and did not see his Father where he should have been waiting.

Augy shrugged his shoulders.

He told Esher that his Father was down in a particular area, and pointed in that direction.

Even though Augy could still not see his Father, he assured Esher that his Father was somewhere down in that area.

So they continued their walk together, not knowing what horrific event was about to unfold at the hands of Augy's Father ...Samuel.

Even though Augy and Esher could not see Samuel, Samuel was having a fit of extreme excitement that he had never in his life experienced.

He could hardly contain himself when he actually, for the first time, seen a real live Bigfoot!!

He was at the same time, in a sort of physical shock, slightly paralyzed.

His brain and body were temporarily not in sync with each other.

He could not hardly believe what his eyes were projecting to his brain... a Bigfoot!!

A Bigfoot!!

A Bigfoot!!

WOW!!

Samuel tried as best as he could to calm down enough to continue with his plan.

He would have plenty of time to analyze this Bigfoot once he was captured.

He steadied his air rifle as he watched his son walk with what was obviously a young Bigfoot.

They came closer and closer to where he was.

They obviously did not know that he was behind a tree... waiting for the opportune moment to shoot a dart with a chemical that would quickly make Augy's friend fall asleep.

Samuel now had his scope of his rifle aimed directly at the young Bigfoot.

He waited for the young Bigfoot to get well within range.

Augy and Esher walked casually together all the way to the area where Augy had last seen his Father.

They stopped together.

They both looked around.

They did not see Samuel nearby with a rifle pointed at Esher.

Esher started to do the silent sign language with Augy.

Samuel watched this in amazement… still aiming his air rifle, on the verge of pulling the trigger.

He aimed at Esher's lower backside.

Esher asked Augy where his Father was.

He also asked Augy what the object was a few feet away.

It was the ATV Quad and trailer.

Augy told Esher that it was his Father's vehicle to travel instead of walking.

Esher was slightly confused, and was still to young to even begin to comprehend what this vehicle was all about.

Just as he was about to take a step towards the Quad to take a better look at it, Samuel pulled the trigger.

The dart traveled silently through the air and embedded itself into the skin in the lower back area of Esher.

Esher felt the sting of the dart and jumped forward a bit, almost falling down to the ground.

Augy noticed his friend making this sudden movement, and stood where he was, surprised and confused at the same time.

Esher looked back at Augy.

He had a look of fear and shock.

He tried to take a step back towards Augy.

He felt very dizzy.

His eyes lost focus on everything around him.

Esher fell to the ground with a hard thud.

Augy ran over to his friend and bent down and looked at him.

Augy was to confused to do anything for Esher.

Moments later, Samuel came running out from behind the tree where he was hiding.

He ran over to Augy and lifted his son up to a standing position.

He told Augy to stand nearby while he helped his Bigfoot friend.

Without Augy seeing what he was doing with a quick slight of hand, Samuel pulled the air dart out of Esher's backside, and put the dart into his pocket.

Next, Samuel walked over to the Quad and put the hoist into the neutral position and started to unwind the cable towards Esher where he laid upon the ground as if he was sleeping.

Samuel wrapped the cable around Esher's chest just under the armpit area's.

He connected the cable hook back onto itself.

Samuel next went to the Quad and retrieved the body board from the trailer bed.

He took the body board over to where Esher still laid and put the board next to the young Bigfoot.

Samuel then rolled Esher over on his side and slid the body board in place.

Samual then rolled Esher back onto the body board.

Samuel secured the four straps on the body board across and back tightly to hold Esher in place.

Once Esher was secured tightly to the body board, Samuel walked back over to the Quad and put the hoist into the drive mode.

He pulled the control handle.

Slowly the body board started to slide on the ground towards the trailer behind the Quad.

Augy stood by watching.

He did not show even the slightest emotion as he watched his Father do this to his friend Esher.

His only thought was that his Father must be helping his friend because he had fallen down.

He did not realize that this was all a planned event by his Father Samuel.

As the body board came to the lip of the backside of the trailer, Samuel had to lift it up a little so that it would not get caught up and stop moving.

Just this moment of lifting on the body board by Samuel showed him that this young Bigfoot was very heavy.

He estimated a few hundred pounds at the very least.

The board slid into place on the bed of the trailer.

Samuel then quickly secured the board to the trailer bed so it would not fall off when he started to drive the Quad.

Samuel ran back to the tree where he had taken the shot at Esher with the air rifle.

He picked up the air rifle that he had dropped on the ground in his excitement of seeing the chemical dart knock-out Esher.

He came back to the Quad and put the air rifle on the back of the Quad.

Augy noticed the air rifle, but still did not understand what had just happened with the fire arm.

Samuel motioned for his son to climb onto the back of the Quad.

Samuel started the Quad up and put his son in front of him between his legs.

Samuel revved the throttle a few times.

The sound that the gas throttle made was very loud.

Moments later, Samuel started to drive the Quad back in the direction from where he and his son had hiked earlier.

Samuel felt extremely excited.

The excitement could be compared to that of a person doing something dangerous and illegal, like robbing a bank.

He traveled at a medium speed down the mountain, being careful not to go so fast where the trailer might trip over sideways.

Augy was now very confused, he thought that his Father would be taking Esher back to the other Bigfoot's.

Onward they traveled, slowly but surely in the direction of where the humans lived.

Poor Esher was sound asleep, oblivious to what was now happening to him.

Chapter Thirty One

CIN CIN HAD WATCHED Esher walk back away where she sat in a tree, towards the mountain ridge.

She also noticed that the young human named Augy was walking with Esher.

She was curious, so she climbed down from out of the tree and started in their direction.

She did not try to hurry because she thought that it would be fun to sneak up on them and surprise them.

She followed them at a distance just enough to still be able to see them, and also far enough for them not to detect her as she walked stealthily through and around the many surrounding redwood giants.

She watched Esher and Augy stop on top of the ridgeline.

She stopped as well, just secretly watching them.

Once they resumed walking, they disappeared over the mountain ridgeline.

Cin Cin hurried up her walking pace to try and get to the top of the mountain ridgeline so she would not lose sight of them.

She finally made it to the top of the mountain ridgeline and stopped to look over the surrounding area below.

Moments later she was able to once again find the young Bigfoot, and young human with her eyes.

She cautiously followed them at a safe distance, still well out of sight if they happened to look back in her direction.

Cin Cin noticed them stopping at a particular area.

There seemed to be some type of object that she did not recognize near where Esher was standing.

This was the ATV Quad.

Cin Cin crept closer, tree by tree, very quickly.

She found a spot and stopped, just to watch and see what Esher and Augy would do next.

Cin Cin did not see Samuel behind a tree nearby with the air rifle.

Within a few seconds, to her total surprise, and horror, she saw Esher fall to the ground.

She was about to run towards Esher and Augy to see why Esher had fallen, and to try and help her fellow Bigfoot, when all of a sudden, an adult human that she did not recognize, came running out from behind a tree and was upon Esher in moments.

She stopped herself out of fear of this unknown adult human.

She secretly watched in horror as Samuel put Esher onto the strange unknown object.

She was helpless for the moment.

She continued to watch.

After a few minutes of watching Samuel put Esher on the flatbed of the trailer she became even more frightened when Samuel started the Quad's engine.

When he cranked the throttle a few times, this noise startled her very badly.

She now watched as the Quad started to drive away from her direction towards where the humans lived.

Cin Cin did not attempt to follow, instead she started to run back towards where her kind lived.

She needed to tell the adult Bigfoot's what she had just witnessed.

She needed to save Esher!!

Chapter Thirty Two

C IN CIN RAN AS fast as she possibly could.

Compared to the speed of a human, this was very fast.

A normal Bigfoot would be able to easily leave even an Olympic track runner well behind if they were to ever have a race with each other.

Onward Cin Cin ran towards her home.

She was making distressful sounds as she ran.

She accidentally ran directly into a tree and fell down hard to the ground.

As she got back to her feet she felt a sharp pain in her upper thigh of her right leg.

She tried to run again but now found out that her thigh was going to slow her down.

Instead of running at a full pace, she was now relegated to a half jog because of the pain in her thigh.

Nevertheless, she continued onward as fast as she could with this aggravating pain shooting through her leg on every stride.

She was so very worried about her friend Esher.

The unknown of what might happen to Esher made her experience a negative stress that she had never felt in her entire young life.

As Cin Cin made her way toward the Bigfoot area, Samuel was getting closer to the highway in the other direction.

It took Cin Cin a little over an hour to make it to the top of the mountain ridge that overlooked the small valley where the rest of the Bigfoot's could be found.

If there were no Bigfoot's within eyesight, then she would proceed to the cave system where She would for sure find other Bigfoot's.

She stopped for a moment and looked around at the small valley in the distance.

She could see two adult male Bigfoot's standing near the stream that cascaded off of the mountain wall and at the same time hid the entrance to the cave system.

Cin Cin made a very loud howl towards the two male Bigfoot's in the distance.

Immediately, both of these two male Bigfoot's turned their heads towards Cin Cin.

They both recognized that this particular howl from this young Bigfoot was one of extreme stress.

Cin Cin started down the mountainside towards them, not really going to fast now because she was exhausted, and her leg was hurting her in the worst way possible.

The two male Bigfoot's, at the same time as Cin Cin started down the mountainside quickly started to run towards her.

Within a minute, they were all together.

One of the male Bigfoot's noticed how Cin Cin was laboring with her walk, and so he picked her up from the ground and cradled her in his arms.

He started back to the cave system along with the other male Bigfoot.

Cin Cin started to tell the two adult Bigfoot's what she had seen happen to her friend Esher.

Both of these adult Bigfoot's started to make sounds that could easily be deciphered as sounds of extreme anger.

Cin Cin made sounds of fright and sadness.

They walked parallel to the side of the mountain stream and followed it to the wall of the mountain.

They quickly followed the wall to a section of the waterfall and stepped down a few feet and then turned sideways and slithered between the falling water on a small ledge for another few feet.

They barely got any water on their fur as they turned torward an opening in the rock wall hidden behind the waterfall.

This was the entrance to the massive cave system that was well hidden from the outside world.

The male Bigfoot who was carrying Cin Cin now put her gently down on the ground inside of the cave.

The other Bigfoot quickly ran off down the tunnel howling what amounted to an alarm.

Very quickly, several Bigfoot's started to appear throughout the cave system.

Now the cave system started to get filled with a large amount of noises from the many Bigfoot's.

The one Bigfoot had started to tell the other Bigfoot's what he had heard from Cin Cin.

Within a few minutes, a mob was created… a Bigfoot mob.

They all congregated near the frightened and hurting Cin Cin.

From the crowd of many Bigfoot's that now numbered well over fifty, Big Arch stepped forward with his mate Reka.

Reka was making sounds of terrible spine chilling stress as she stood next to Big Arch.

Big Arch asked Cin Cin to repeat back to him what she had told the two male Bigfoot's who had brought her inside of the cave.

Cin Cin told Big Arch what she had observed.

She cried as she relayed to Big Arch how his son was taken away by an adult human.

She also told Big Arch how she had seen the young human Augy with this adult human.

This confused Big Arch, but at the same time he thought that Augy was probably just as surprised as his son Esher had been when he was taken.

Cin Cin said that she did not recognize the male adult human.

Lastly, Big Arch asked Cin Cin in what direction the adult human was taking Esher.

She told Big Arch that the adult human was traveling towards the human road that she was not allowed to go near.

Immediately upon hearing this last bit of information from Cin Cin, Big Arch departed the cave system.

A large amount of other adult male Bigfoot's also exited the cave system behind Big Arch.

They numbered about twenty.

They spread out from each other, but all of them traveled in the same direction that Cin Cin had told Big Arch that the male adult human was going with Esher.

As these Bigfoot's started to quickly traverse the many mountains and valleys that led towards the human road… the highway, Samuel was getting ever so close to his truck and horse trailer.

The Bigfoot's made-up ground very quickly between them and Samuel.

Samuel was still driving the Quad at a semi slow pace.

Samuel was now only within about ten minutes from his truck.

The Bigfoot's that chased him were still about twenty minutes from Samuel even though they were making up a whole lot of the distance between them, it did not look like they would make it in time to rescue Esher.

Time ticked off of the clock ever so slowly for both the Bigfoot's and Samuel.

Both parties wanted so badly to get to where they wanted to be.

Big Arch wanted to get to his son Esher.

Samuel wanted to get to his truck and load Esher inside of the horse trailer.

Finally, as Samuel came around a bend of a wild blackberry patch, he could see his truck and horse trailer in the distance.

Samuel now stopped the Quad.

He reached down and got the blanket that had covered the Quad while it was stored in the mountains, and covered Esher completely.

Samuel next got a couple of stretchable rubber cords and secured the blanket.

The shape of Esher's body now looked more like a human underneath the blanket than that of a young Bigfoot.

Even this would look suspicious to anyone who might look at this before Samuel had a chance to load the Quad into the horse trailer.

Samuel slowly drove the Quad to within thirty yards of the horse trailer and stopped once again.

He motioned his son Augy to follow him as he went over to the parked truck.

He opened the door to the truck and again motioned his son this time get inside the cab of the truck and buckle-up.

Samuel closed the door to the truck and left his son without saying anything to him.

Samuel was now to excited at this moment.

He was also very nervous because there was always a chance that someone could come upon him and notice the suspicious trailer behind the Quad that was being loaded into the horse trailer.

If by chance anyone was able to see Esher wrapped-up on the bed of the Quad trailer, they would certainly inquire as to what it was, and at the same time as they asked the question, they would suspect that what they were looking at was a human body under the wrapped blanket.

They would also, for sure, certainly call a law enforcement agency very quickly.

Samuel had no choice at this point.

For a few minutes, he would have to take the chance of being discovered.

To minimize the amount of time it would take to load the Quad into the horse trailer, Samuel opened up the back doors of the horse trailer.

He next put a pair of motorcycle ramps between the horse trailer and the ground.

As he was doing this, Big Arch was making very good progress towards Samuel.

Big Arch was a few minutes ahead of the rest of the other Bigfoot's because of the adrenaline that pumped through his massive veins in his massive body.

He was very angry and stressed at the same time.

The love for his son made him travel at a speed that he never in his life had ever experienced.

Maybe there was a chance that he would be able to arrive at the location where Samuel was, before he disappeared with his precious son Esher.

Anything smaller than a tree, Big Arch did not bother to go around, he just plowed through them as if they were not even there in his path.

The only objects that he dodged were the large redwood tree's that now surrounded him in the thousands.

Chapter Thirty Three

SAMUEL WAS NOW READY to load the Quad and trailer that it pulled with Esher on it's bed, into the horse trailer.

Samuel sat on the Quad that was now running on idle.

Big Arch was quickly approaching the area where Samuel now sat on the Quad.

Augy watched his Father from the side rearview mirror as he sat quietly in the truck.

He watched as his Father looked around for a minute, and then started to drive the Quad towards the back of the horse trailer.

Samuel got to the back of the horse trailer and lined up the wheels of the Quad to the two motorcycle ramps.

Big Arch came closer to where Samuel's truck was still parked.

Samuel looked around in both directions of the highway.

A vehicle was approaching in the distance about a quarter of a mile away.

Samuel turned the throttle on the Quad and started to drive-up the ramps.

Closer the vehicle in the distance came.

Closer Big Arch came.

Just as the Quad made it inside of the horse trailer, the approaching vehicle passed without even slowing down at all.

Samuel breathed a sigh of relief.

Samuel did not realize that he was still not yet safely finished with his secretive task with Esher.

He did not realize that he had a very angry male Bigfoot… Big Arch, on the verge of appearing before him to try and rescue his young son Esher.

Even without this knowledge, Samuel still did not slow down.

Samuel quickly secured the Quad and it's trailer that still held a sleeping Esher to the inside of the horse trailer with wheel chalks and chain gripes.

He wanted to make especially sure that the young Bigfoot did not become injured during the trip back to his house.

Samuel exited the horse trailer and grabbed the two motorcycle ramps.

He put them inside of the horse trailer and secured them so they did not slide around.

Closer Big Arch came to where Samuel now stood, outside of the back of the horse trailer near it's two swinging door's.

Samuel reached out to the two door's and shut them.

He locked the door's with a tempered steel circular lock that was nearly impossible to cut with bolt cutter's.

Samuel walked over to the driver's side of his truck and opened the door to the cab where Augy sat silently looking straight ahead through the front windshield.

Samuel climbed inside of the cab next to Augy and secured his seatbelt.

He next put his key into the ignition and just as he started the truck's engine, Big Arch reached the outer edges of the nearby forest.

He was not able to see Samuel had loaded Esher into the back of the horse trailer.

But he was at just the right angle to be able to see the young human Augy sitting inside of the human vehicle.

Big Arch now knew that his son was there.

Esher was probably inside of that other object… the horse trailer… that was connected to the human vehicle… the truck.

Augy turned his head sideway, sensing something, and immediately seen Big Arch in the distance.

Augy made a sound of surprise like trying to take a small breath of air… a gasp.

Samuel noticed this from his son.

He looked over in the same direction that Augy was looking.

Samuel did not gasp, he mumbled a number of derogatory words in connecting sequence.

At the same time, Samuel instinctively realized why Big Arch was now approaching his truck very quickly from the distant redwood forest.

Samuel punched the gas pedal on the floorboard of his truck.

His truck jolted forward with the horse trailer banging into the tow-ball on the rear bumper of the truck.

Samuel slowly started to drive his truck away as Big Arch narrowed the gap between them.

Esher still laid in the back of the horse trailer, silently sleeping, and oblivious as to what was happening outside of his confines.

Samuel's truck made it to the tarred pavement just as Big Arch made it to where the truck had been parked. Big Arch did not care at this point whether any other humans were to see him.

He ran towards Samuel's truck.

Augy watched silently from the rearview mirror.

Samuel floored the gas pedal, and his truck started to gain immense speed.

No vehicles were present from either direction of the highway.

Big Arch's strides were now almost equivalent to short leaps as he tried with all his physical strength and agility to catch the human vehicle.

Unfortunately for Big Arch, the speed of Samuel's truck was now just to fast to catch.

Big Arch still tried to catch the truck, but now every stride was a waste of time.

Big Arch finally realized that his efforts had fallen just short to rescue his son Esher.

He veered back over into the direction of the forest and sat down on the ground just within the treeline.

Big Arch, for the first time since he was a young Bigfoot, cried.

Real tears.

The tears cascaded down his face.

His emotions at the moment were uncontrolled.

His anger was unmeasurable.

He sat there on the ground grieving loudly for several minutes.

After a few minutes had passed, some of the other male Bigfoot's started to show-up.

Instantly they were able to find the grieving Bigfoot Father by his stressed vocalizations.

Big Arch did not have to tell them vocally that he had failed to rescue Esher.

They knew, just by how Big Arch was acting at this very sad moment.

It would not be until a while later when they, along with Big Arch, were traveling back to the Bigfoot area, when he was able to tell them what he had seen, and what he had tried to do with obviously no success.

An anger towards the human race was now officially multiplying as Every second clicked on a time piece.

A few hours later, this group of angry Bigfoot's finally made it back to the cave system.

Big Arch immediately found his stressed mate Reka.

He explained to her about how he had failed to rescue their son Esher.

The other male Bigfoot's that had went with Big Arch quickly passed the word around to the other Bigfoot's about what had happened.

Anger swelled within the cave system towards the humans.

This was the first time that anything like this had ever happened with any Bigfoot's… anywhere… anytime… ever!!

There was a realization with the Bigfoot's that the humans would now know that they did indeed exist.

They knew that the humans had seen them many times over the years, but now the humans would truly know that the Bigfoot's lived in the vast forests around them.

Also, there was a fear for Esher.

What would the humans do to the young Bigfoot?

Where did this unknown male adult human take Esher?

Why was Augy with this adult human who had taken Esher?

These unanswered questions lingered, and fueled the fire of anger amongst the many Bigfoot's who lived within the cave system.

What would the Bigfoot's do now?

If they knew where Esher was located, should they try to rescue him?

What would they now do if they ever seen any humans within the forest's.

At the moment, their anger pointed towards violence if there was any encounter with a human.

As this anger multiplied with the Bigfoot's, Samuel was now just arriving at his home on the outskirts of Rio Dell.

He backed his truck up the driveway and positioned the horse trailer to one of his two garages.

He lined-up with the garage that had a direct pathway to the small house that was in the backyard… waiting for Esher.

Augy got out of the truck and stood nearby watching his Father.

Samuel was extremely excited.

He opened the garage door, walked inside to the back of the room, and opened another door to the backyard.

He next went to the two doors on the backside of the horse trailer and unlocked the security lock.

He opened the doors and noticed that Esher still laid relatively motionless.

He could see a slight movement of Esher's chest as he breathed underneath the wrapped blanket.

Samuel retrieved the ramps and lined them up to the Quad wheels and the ground in front of the garage.

Samuel started the Quad's engine, and put the gears in neutral.

He next took the wheel chalks away from the Quad tires.

He then released the chain gripes from the Quad tires as well.

Slowly Samuel backed the Quad and it's trailer down the ramps, putting on the brakes every few seconds, being overly cautious.

Finally the Quad was on the ground with it's trailer… safely, no harm to Esher.

Samuel then backed the Quad and trailer all the way to the back door of the garage.

He parked the Quad for the time being, and went back outside and put the ramps away, and closed the horse trailer's back door's.

Samuel motioned over to Augy to come inside of the garage with him.

Samuel turned on the over head light's in the garage and then shut the large front garage door.

Samuel, Augy, and Esher, were now officially safe and hidden from the rest of the world.

Samuel sat down for a few minutes, thinking of what to do next with Esher.

The small house in the backyard was already ready to house Esher in complete silence from the outside world.

So far Samuel's plan had worked perfectly.

He felt very satisfied with himself.

Augy did not show the satisfaction that his Father was exuding on his face.

The young boy just stood there looking at the blanket where his friend Esher laid sleeping from a chemical that had been shot into his body by his Father.

Finally, Samuel started the task of transferring Esher into the small house in the backyard.

It took much effort, and almost an hour and a half of huffing and puffing with a few breaks along the way, but finally, Samuel was able to secure Esher within the confines of the small house.

He locked up the small house, and went inside of his much larger house with his son.

He would come back and check on the young Bigfoot in a few hours.

It would be probably a few more hours before Esher woke up from his chemically induced slumber.

Poor Esher, how would he react when he awoke?

Samuel was anxious to find out the answer to this question, but for now, he needed to eat and make plans for what he would do next with Esher.

Samuel could not erase the smile from his face, he was so happy.

Chapter Thirty Four

THE TELEVISION BLARED IN the background as Shamieka and Sleeping Beaver sat on a nearby couch.

They had just finished a nice big breakfast.

A commercial came on the television set.

It was a commercial that had recently in the past few days started to run.

This was just another repeat for maybe the hundredth time since it's inception on air.

The commercial was about a new business that was pushing their GPS product's.

Their most popular product being the children's GPS bracelet.

Sleeping Beaver and Shamieka watched this commercial, and a few moments after the bracelet was showed on the screen with an enlarged close-up view, they both looked at each other in astonishment.

Both of them thinking of the same question within their brain cavities.

This bracelet looked very similar to the one that they had noticed Augy wearing recently as they made their many trips to visit the Bigfoot's.

Was this the same bracelet.

They also realized the last time that they visited the Bigfoot's that Augy was not wearing his bracelet anymore.

They did not think anything of it.

But if it was in fact a GPS bracelet that could be monitored on a computer, did this mean that Samuel had been monitoring their travels to the Bigfoot area?

Sleeping Beaver spoke first to Shamieka, almost taking the same words out of her own mouth as well.

"Was that the same bracelet that Augy was wearing when we visited the Bigfoot's?

Shamieka answered almost instantly.

"I am 100% sure that the bracet we saw on Augy's wrist was the same as this one on the commercial."

"I am sure, because I remember that logo of the company that sells the bracelet was next to Augy's name on it's front side."

"I am positive."

Sleeping Beaver made a facial expression that Shamieka at once recognized.

He was getting mad.

Sleeping Beaver very rarely got mad about anything.

So Shamieka knew that he was getting in a mood that would linger throughout the day.

Shamieka did not get mad right away.

She was more levelheaded for the moment.

They both talked about the possibility of Samuel tracking their travels to the area where the Bigfoot's could be found.

They also remembered how Samuel was so nonchalant about the Bigfoot's decision not to let him come to meet them.

Maybe he was nonchalant because he already knew where to find the Bigfoot's, by secretly tracking their travels to the Bigfoot's area, by using the suspected GPS bracelet that Augy wore on his wrist.

If this turned out to be true, then Shamieka would really become very upset at Samuel for his deception.

They also remembered that Augy had not been wearing that bracelet recently.

Maybe Samuel had no use for it anymore.

Was Samuel going to go on his own to the Bigfoot area?

This possibility worried both of them.

Shamieka suggested that they go for a visit to see Samuel and Augy.

Sleeping Beaver disagreed with his girlfriend.

He thought that maybe it would be better if they visited Crazy Mylo first and tell him about their suspicions about Samuel using the GPS bracelet to find out where the Bigfoot's area was located.

Sleeping Beaver then thought that it would be a good idea for Crazy Mylo to go and visit the Bigfoot's and warn them about what they suspected, and while Crazy Mylo did that, they would go back and meet with Samuel and Augy.

Shamieka pondered this suggestion quietly for a few minutes, and then agreed that what Sleeping Beaver had just suggested was a good idea.

They quickly packed provisions for the day, and left within the hour to go and find Crazy Mylo.

Chapter Thirty Five

SLEEPING BEAVER AND SHAMIEKA drove as fast as they were legally able to do in her vehicle without being pulled over by a Highway Patrol and given a citation for speeding above the speed limit.

They parked her vehicle in the normal area where they usually did when they were going to visit Crazy Mylo or go to the Bigfoot area deep in the vast mountain range.

Depending on the time of year, Crazy Mylo could be found in various locations.

He rotated to different area's.

Sleeping Beaver knew these area's, and knew Crazy Mylo's special calendar cycle.

The particular area where Crazy Mylo was now located was actually the farthest away from the Bigfoot area if compared on a map with his other locations.

This location was where he would have his largest grow operation.

So it took over an hour and a half longer to find Crazy Mylo then it normally would if he was at one of the other secret locations.

When Sleeping Beaver got within range of where Crazy Mylo should be, he hollered out his special call to find his friend.

Within a minute, through the air traveled a return call that Sleeping Beaver recognized as that made by Crazy Mylo.

The two men, along with Shamieka, found each other within a few minutes after the special calls were made.

Crazy Mylo asked both of his friends to follow him to where he had his camp set-up.

Once they got to his camp, Crazy Mylo asked them why they came to visit him today.

Both Sleeping Beaver and Shamieka started to talk at the same time, and then they both went silent, giving each other the chance to speak first.

Sleeping Beaver sighed.

"I will tell him."

"You know Samuel, Augy's Father."

"We think that he did something very bad, very sneaky, without us knowing."

Crazy Mylo had an instant frown on his face upon hearing this initial statement from Sleeping Beaver.

He remained silent.

Sleeping Beaver continued on with what he needed to say.

"Me and Shamieka had noticed a bracelet that Augy had been wearing on his wrist a while back when we made several hikes to visit the Bigfoot's."

"We asked Samuel about the bracelet, and he did not tell us the truth about what it really was."

"We believed him, and did not think to much about it until this morning after breakfast."

"We watched a commercial on the television set that caught our attention."

"Normally we do not care about the commercials on the television, but this particular commercial caught our eye's and ear's."

"Shamieka recognized the logo of the company that was selling their product's on the commercial."

"She is 100% positive that the logo on the commercial is the same as the logo that she looked at on Augy's bracelet."

Crazy Mylo now had a frown, and a quizzical look upon his face as he continued to listen to his friend talk.

"It turns out that this company on the commercial was selling various GPS tracking devices."

"One of these devices was the bracelet that Augy wore on his wrist when we visited the Bigfoot's."

"The bracelet could be tracked on a computer screen."

"We suspect that Samuel had Augy wear this bracelet so that he could track on the computer, where we went when we visited the Bigfoot's."

"We think that Samuel has the knowledge of where to find the Bigfoot's."

"We have not confronted him about our suspicions yet, but we plan to do that today after we leave this location."

"We think that the Bigfoot's definitely need to know what we just told you."

"They need to be warned that if this is true, then they need to decide what they want to do."

"While we go back to talk to Samuel, we were hoping that you would go and warn the Bigfoot's."

Crazy Mylo instantly agreed that he would do this.

He was so upset about this new information that he wanted to do it as soon as possible.

So they agreed to meet back at this camp the next day and talk about what had transpired on their visit's.

Sleeping Beaver and Shamieka left Crazy Mylo's camp after resting for a few more minutes while Crazy Mylo gathered up some gear.

Crazy Mylo started his hike to the Bigfoot's a few minutes after his friends left his camp to go and visit Samuel.

Chapter Thirty Six

WITHIN A FEW HOUR'S, Crazy Mylo was getting close to where the Bigfoot's were located.

He was totally unaware of what Samuel had done with Esher.

He was also unaware that the Bigfoot population in this area were very upset at humans right now.

There was a noise in the distance that caught his attention.

It sounded like wood branches cracking from several directions.

He stopped to listen more carefully.

Moments later, from five different directions to his present spot where he stood, came five large male Bigfoot's.

Crazy Mylo recognized one of the male Bigfoot's as Big Arch.

Crazy Mylo became very startled because of how they approached him.

All five Bigfoot's stopped almost at the same time, surrounding Crazy Mylo to where he would not be able to go in any direction if he wanted to do so.

Luckily, Crazy Mylo had been learning how to communicate via sign language, from Shamieka, when it became known that the Bigfoot's were also learning how to do this silent language from Augy and then Esher.

Crazy Mylo felt scared at this moment.

The Bigfoot's had never shown any type of aggression to him or anyone else in all of his times in their presence.

Crazy Mylo was mystified by how they were now acting.

Crazy Mylo started to do some sign language to the Bigfoot's.

As he started to do this, one of the Bigfoot's raised his large arms in a manner that suggested that he was going to attack Crazy Mylo.

Big Arch reached over with one of his massive arms, and stopped this Bigfoot from attacking Crazy Mylo.

The Bigfoot put down his arms... for the moment.

Big Arch made a hand sign to Crazy Mylo.

He told Crazy Mylo that he could talk to him by using the silent language.

Crazy Mylo trembled as he started to use the sign language to Big Arch.

He was able to tell Big Arch about what was suspected of Samuel by Sleeping Beaver and Shamieka.

He tried his best to assure Big Arch that he did not know about any of this until today.

He said the same thing about Sleeping Beaver and Shamieka as well.

Crazy Mylo asked Big Arch why it appeared that he and these other male Bigfoot's were angry.

Big Arch flinched slightly when asked this question.

Moments later, Big Arch told Crazy Mylo what had happened to Esher.

Crazy Mylo was stunned.

His body was frozen in the spot where he stood.

He could see the hurt and anger in Big Arch's face.

Again, Crazy Mylo tried to reassure Big Arch that he and his friends who had told him about their suspicions about Samuel, did not know anything until today.

Big Arch signed one more thing to Crazy Mylo.

He told Crazy Mylo that he did not trust him any longer and that he needed to leave the area and not come back because he might get hurt if he did.

Before Big Arch could stop him, one of the male Bigfoot's grabbed Crazy Mylo and threw him violently at a nearby redwood tree.

Crazy Mylo flew threw the air like small sack of potatoes.

He bounced off of the tree very hard, and then fell to the ground in a heap of flesh.

Pain shot through Crazy Mylo's body as he lay on the ground.

He thought that he now only had a few more moments of life to live.

He cowered, waiting for the end to come.

Fortunately for Crazy Mylo, Big Arch was able to stop the male Bigfoot from doing anything further to Crazy Mylo.

Big Arch made some loud sounds to this male Bigfoot, and in return the male Bigfoot made what sounded like a small submissive reply.

Big Arch looked at Crazy Mylo.

Crazy Mylo stared back at Big Arch.

Big Arch waved his arm towards the direction where Crazy Mylo had come.

This was his warning to Crazy Mylo that he wanted him to leave the area.

Crazy Mylo forced his body to get up from the ground.

Luckily, there did not appear to be any broken bones.

He would be able to walk back to his camp.

Each step would bring much pain throughout his body.

He turned his back on the five male Bigfoot's and started to leave the area as Big Arch wanted him to do.

He did not look back.

The only thing he could think of at the moment was that he was glad to be alive.

His next thought would certainly be that he needed to tell his friends what had happened to Esher.

He also needed to warn them that the Bigfoot's were angry, and that it was not safe to go anywhere near the Bigfoot's area.

Chapter Thirty Seven

A S CRAZY MYLO MADE his way back to his camp to wait for his friends to return the next day, Sleeping Beaver and Shamieka were close to arriving at Samuel's house.

They turned off the exit of the freeway, made a right turn at the stop sign, and traveled almost a mile down a road that was parallel to the highway.

They then turned left up a small hill and turned onto a road that ran parallel to a nearby forest.

They could now see Samuel's house a few hundred feet from a beautiful redwood forest.

Samuel's vehicle was parked in a gravel driveway leading to the house.

As they came closer, they were able to see Samuel in his fenced front yard.

Augy was nowhere in sight.

Augy had just quietly snuck through the two garages, spending a few minutes in the second garage that led to the backyard and little house where Esher was being held.

While Augy was inside of the second garage, he noticed with his great eyesight, small bunches of curly dark hair on the floor.

This was the spot that was the staging area that Samuel had used as he transferred Esher into the little house in the backyard.

Augy bent down and picked up several samples of this hair.

He looked all around, and found more samples of this hair.

He was able to gather enough of this hair to make up a considerable amount in his hand.

Augy rolled all of this hair into a large ball in his hand, and put it inside of his pants pocket.

Augy put his hand that just held this hair to his nose to smell.

He was surprised to realize that the smell of this hair had the same scent as that of his friend Esher and the other Bigfoot's that he had been around in the past few months.

Augy then quietly entered the backyard.

Samuel was not aware that his son Augy was in the backyard next to the little house where Esher was located.

Esher had awoke out of his chemically induced sleep a few hours ago.

He had woken to an unfamiliar world.

As he had looked around the room upon waking, Esher felt confused, and also started to feel frightened.

He had no idea where he was, or how he got here.

He screamed out in his language, hoping that he would hear another Bigfoot answer his cry.

He got to his feet and walked around the room.

He made several other cries as he walked around the room.

To his dismay, there were not any return calls from another Bigfoot.

Minutes before Esher had woken-up, Augy had went into the backyard to the outside of the small house in the backyard.

Augy stood there looking at the outside wall of the little house.

He stood near a small opening that had a handle in it's hole.

Augy walked over and pulled the handle.

It was a flap that rotated as the handle was pulled in a circular direction.

Augy could hear Esher walking around and making distressful sounds in the Bigfoot language.

Augy bent down towards the open flap and put his mouth a few inches away from the opening.

Augy made a sound in the Bigfoot language that Esher would be able to hear, and understand right away.

Esher heard this sound and stopped walking.

Esher answered back.

Augy answered in return.

Esher recognized his human friend and ran over to the hole in the wall.

Esher bent down to the ground and started to talk to Augy, asking the young boy many quick questions.

Augy answered back to Esher as much as he knew.

The two youngster's communicated for several minutes, each eager to see each other.

This was not possible at this moment.

Augy heard a sound in front of the house that he recognized as being a vehicle driving up the gravel driveway.

The sound of the gravel crunching under the vehicles tires was very distinct.

Augy told Esher that he would return to talk to him when he could.

He told Esher that he hoped that he would be alright, and remain safe until he returned.

Esher told Augy that he was scared, but did not see any danger in the room.

He would wait until Augy returned.

Augy let go of the handle, and the circular flap closed, silencing the outside world to where Esher remained… sitting scared and lonely.

Esher for the first time noticed a long rectangular pan mounted to the wall near the door.

He went over and looked at this strange thing.

It turned out to be a water trough for Esher to drink water.

It had an automatic feed that replenished the water as it was being drank from the trough.

Esher dipped his hand into the trough and wet his fingers with the water.

He put his wet fingers to his lips.

He realized that he was indeed very thirsty, and at once, bent over and put his face just at the top of the surface of the water and started to lap the clear fluid into his mouth.

After doing this until his thirst was quenched, Esher now realized that he was hungry as well.

He looked around the room, but did not notice any food that he could eat.

What Esher did not realize yet was that Samuel would be feeding Esher through another slot at the top of the door.

Samuel had already taken the time to make up what he thought would be food that Esher would eat.

Esher sat down once again… waiting.

Augy had stood next to the small house for several minutes while Esher was inside drinking the water from the trough.

Finally, Augy walked over to a side fence and climbed onto a cross beam that connected the post's in the ground.

He peered over the fence slightly, not showing himself.

He watched a vehicle that he recognized come to a complete stop in the gravel driveway.

It was Shamieka and Sleeping Beaver.

He watched his two friends get out of the vehicle.

He heard them greet his Father.

He next heard his Father greet them back.

His Father did not invite them inside of the house.

Augy stood there on the fence, listening.

Chapter Thirty Eight

BOTH SHAMIEKA AND SLEEPING Beaver approached the fence where Samuel stood inside the yard waiting.

They did not go to one of the two gates unless invited.

Samuel did not invite them into the yard as he normally did.

They both thought this was odd, but it matched how they thought he would act if he was in fact guilty of what they suspected him of doing.

Samuel walked over to the fence and spoke first.

"So… what brings you out this way… unannounced?"

"Usually, one of you will call first before coming here."

"Neither of you look very happy."

"Is there something wrong?"

Sleeping Beaver answered this question.

"Well Samuel, me and Shamieka were watching the television this morning and noticed a new commercial that is starting to play."

"The commercial is about a new company in the area that sells GPS products."

"One of the GPS products that it is selling is a GPS bracelet."

"Of course, all of these GPS products, including this bracelet, can be tracked online with a computer."

Samuel answered swiftly, and short.

"Is that so."

Sleeping Beaver, trying his best to contain the anger that simmered within him, answered back just as fast.

"Yeah… that's a fact."

Sleeping Beaver started to talk again, but was now interrupted by Shamieka.

Shamieka spoke with her voiced raised slightly because she was just as upset as Sleeping Beaver.

"Me and Sleeping Beaver asked you about a bracelet that we seen Augy wearing recently before we started to take the trips to visit the Bigfoot's."

"You told us it was basically an informational bracelet for people to notify you in case Augy got lost."

"You did not mention that the bracelet was also a GPS device."

Samuel stood silently and did not answer right away.

Sleeping Beaver now spoke.

"Samuel… was that bracelet one of those GPS products that we seen on the commercial this morning?"

Again Shamieka jumped in verbally, this time directing herself towards Sleeping Beaver.

"You know it was the GPS device."

"I saw the logo on Augy's bracelet that matched the company on the commercial that we watched this morning."

"That bracelet was a GPS device."

Now Shamieka directed herself towards Samuel.

"Samuel… you acted so nonchalant when me and Sleeping Beaver told you that the Bigfoot's did not give you permission to have us take you to their location to meet them."

"Now I know why."

"It was because you had Augy secretly wearing the bracelet without us knowing, and you tracked our entire hikes to and from the Bigfoot location on your computer."

"You already knew where the Bigfoot's were located when we told you that the Bigfoot's did not give permission for you to visit them."

"I cannot believe that you did this to us."

"We trusted you Samuel."

"We did not think at all that you would ever stoop to doing such a sneaky thing behind our backs."

"You also used you son Augy without his knowledge as well."

"If Augy knew what you were doing, I am sure that he would not have cooperated with your sneaky plan."

Samuel took on the same expression as his son Augy normally did as Shamieka spoke... blank, and non-emotional.

"How could you do this Samuel?"

"Are you going to talk?"

Samuel shook his head, and answered her back.

"Shamieka, Sleeping Beaver, you are both totally wrong about what you are accusing me of."

"Yeah, I bought a bracelet from that company, but I only used the bracelet for the information that was printed on it's surface."

"I had the option of activating the GPS if I wanted to do so, but I chose not to activate the GPS for now."

"Maybe sometime in the future, I may actually activate the GPS."

"To activate the GPS, there is another separate charge, and I do not have that within my budget at this time to do that."

"I am very disappointed that you both would think that I actually would do something like that to both of you and my son Augy."

"I am so disappointed in fact at this accusation, that I am not sure that I will give you permission to take Augy to where these Bigfoot's... are supposedly located."

"You are both suggesting that I know where the Bigfoot's are, and that either I am going to go to their location, or that I have already been there and seen a real live Bigfoot."

"Believe me... I have still to this day, have not ever seen a Bigfoot in person."

"I still long for the day for that to happen."

"Remember, I told you that you could continue to bring my son to that location in the hopes that maybe eventually a trust could be grown to the point that the Bigfoot's would change their minds and finally allow me to come and visit them."

"That was my hope, and I have been very patient with both of you."

"Maybe this thing that you are telling me today is just a ploy to make me not want to ever get the chance to ever see a Bigfoot in person."

"My lifelong dream."

"Maybe your doing this on purpose to make me mad so you can cover up a lie."

"Maybe all of this talk about the Bigfoot's has actually been a lie, and you are both trying to weasel out of the whole thing."

"Basically covering your tracks on a big fat lie."

"If indeed you are both lying about the Bigfoot's, it makes me wonder what in the heck you both have been doing to my son when he was supposedly being watched by you."

"I guess I did not know you two as well as I thought I did."

"To think, I actually trusted both of you to watch my child."

Augy still stood on the fence crossbeam on the side yard at the backside of the house out of eyesight of the adults in the front yard.

He listened carefully to the adults talking.

His great hearing easily picked up on every word spoken.

Augy realized as he heard his Father talking, that his Father was not talking honestly with his friends.

His Father always told him to tell the truth… no matter what.

He was confused as to why his Father was lying.

Finally, after listening to his Father lying to his friends for a few more moments, something inside of the little autistic child exploded.

Augy screamed out in anger as loud as his small voice could.

The sounds that came from his mouth were not the usual garbled sounds that only the Bigfoot's could understand.

The sounds were in human English!!

As Augy screamed out in English, all three adults heads turned in the direction where the sound came from… the back yard side fence.

All mouth's of the three adults were wide open in surprised silence.

What Augy hollered was… "My Father is lying to you."

Samuel was momentarily shocked to hear his son speak the English language for the first time.

He quickly caught himself.

He hollered very loudly at his son, realizing that he was near the little house in the back yard.

He also did not want his son to say anything more, like letting Sleeping Beaver and Shamieka know that Esher was in the little house in the back yard.

Samuel hollered almost violently towards his son.

"Get back inside of the house Augy!!"

"Do not say another word until I get inside of the house with you!!"

Augy became frightened by the tone of his Father's voice, and stopped talking."

Augy immediately did as his Father ordered him to do, and jumped off of the fence and went directly into the house.

He disappeared from the line of sight of the three adults in an instant.

It was so quick, that neither Sleeping Beaver or Shamieka had a chance to try and talk to the little boy.

Immediately upon Augy's disappearance from the back yard, Samuel turned to Sleeping Beaver and Shamieka and asked them to leave his property.

He turned around right away and walked back to the front door of his house.

He turned around before going back inside and spoke once more.

"Get out of here!!"

Shocked… Sleeping Beaver and Shamieka did not attempt to even try to speak with Samuel any longer.

They now knew that Samuel was lying to them, and what they suspected was in fact true.

Samuel knew where the Bigfoot's were located.

If they only knew the rest of what was true about Samuel.

The truth was less than a hundred and fifty feet away in the little house in the back yard.

They both walked back to their vehicle and climbed inside.

Both… without the knowledge that Samuel had kidnapped Esher, and now had him as a captive in the little house in his back yard.

They drove away upset, and not knowing the whole truth, it was obvious to them that little Augy knew the truth, but was not given the chance to tell them.

Sleeping Beaver and Shamieka now concentrated their efforts on getting back to their friend Crazy Mylo and tell him that their suspicions had apparently been valid.

They hoped that Crazy Mylo was able to warn the Bigfoot's about the possibility of Samuel making an appearance at their location.

Shamieka backed out of Samuel's driveway, throwing gravel in all directions as she punched the gas pedal down to the floor board.

The thought as to how little Augy was able to speak in the English language here, as he had in the mountains did not occur in their brains yet.

They were too upset at the moment to think 100% rationally.

Samuel stood inside of the house, peaking from the side of a curtain, watching them drive away.

Augy sat on his bed upstairs, waiting for his Father to come and talk to him.

He would now have a conversation in English with his Father for the first time in his life.

He felt scared and mad at the same time.

Chapter Thirty Nine

SAMUEL WALKED AWAY FROM the window after Sleeping Beaver and Shamieka disappeared from view.

His thought now was of his son Augy.

Augy had spoken the English language outside only a few minutes ago.

It was the first time ever, since Augy was born, that he had ever heard his son speak anything other than a garbled sound from his mouth, let alone the English language.

Samuel now started to think about what Sleeping Beaver and Shamieka had been telling him about the unexplainable abilities of Augy when he was around the Bigfoot's.

Supposedly, his son was able to speak the English language when he was in the proximity of a Bigfoot creature.

It must all be true.

His son had only been a few yards from a Bigfoot, even though there was a wooden wall for separating the two of them.

So, maybe because this young Bigfoot, who was in close proximity to Augy… somehow… it was true that his son had the ability to speak… English.

What bothered Samuel at the moment, along with this surprise of his son's apparent ability to speak English when near this young Bigfoot, was that Augy had basically "snitched his own Father off to Sleeping Beaver and Shamieka.

Samuel called up to his son from downstairs.

"Augy… come down here right now, we need to talk."

Augy heard this request from his Father, and did not verbally answer as he knew that he could.

Augy reached into his pants pocket and retrieved the ball of hair that he had found in the garage where Esher had been.

He knew that this hair was his friend Esher's, and wanted to keep it in a safe place.

Augy quickly walked over to his dresser and opened the botton drawer.

He reached down and lifted all of the folded clothes in the drawer and placed the ball of hair in the backside of this drawer.

He gently placed the folded clothes back on top of the ball of hair.

Augy shut the drawer quickly and stood back up.

Augy walked out of his bedroom and went downstairs to where his Father stood silently near the couch.

He walked over to Samuel silently, slightly nervous.

Samuel reached out to his son.

Augy did not go into his Father's arms as was usual.

Samuel detected that his son was a little scared of the moment, and so he just pointed to the couch.

Augy went over to the couch and sat down quietly, and lowered his head.

Samuel pulled an ottoman nearby over in front of the area where Augy sat.

Samuel sat down gently on the ottoman.

Samuel spoke very softly to his son.

"Augy… you spoke real words outside."

"Son… you are able to talk to me."

"That is wonderful, we can now talk to each other."

Augy did not answer his Father.

Samuel continued to speak.

"Augy… Augy… talk to me like you did outside."

Augy remained silent.

Samuel became irritated by this silence.

"Augy, I want you to talk to me now!!"

Augy raised his head and looked at his Father.

Augy spoke as his Father requested, but instead of the English language, it was the same garbled sounds that he had always made.

Samuel hollered at his son.

"Don't play games with me Augy, I know that you can speak the English language, I heard you talk English only a few minutes ago from the backyard where your friend is in the little house!!"

Augy was just as confused as his Father was, as to why he was not able to speak English as he had a few minutes earlier in the backyard.

After saying this to his son, Samuel realized why his son could not speak English.

Augy was not near a Bigfoot.

Samuel stood-up and motioned Augy to do the same.

Samuel had a hunch, and now he was going to do an experiment... a safe experiment to see if his hunch was correct.

Samuel started to walk to the backside of the house, and he motioned Augy to follow him.

He spoke to his son.

"Do you want to see your Bigfoot friend in the little house in the backyard?"

Augy did not say anything, he just followed his Father towards the door that opened to the backyard.

They both stepped out into the backyard and proceeded around to the other side where the little house was located.

Samuel walked up to the little house and stopped near the door.

Inside, Esher could hear some movement from outside.

Augy stood next to his Father near the door.

Samuel reached up and grabbed a sliding metal panel that was at the top of the door.

He slid the panel open.

From inside, Esher heard a sound near the door.

Esher seen an opening appear at the top of the door.

It was the panel that Samuel had just slid open.

Esher rose to his feet slow, and cautiously, and walked over to the door.

Esher stood a foot from the door and looked up at the opening... the panel.

Samuel reached down and picked up Augy into his arms.

He lifted Augy up the height of the open panel at the top of the door.

He spoke to his son.

"Augy… look inside, can you see your friend?"

"What is his name again, I forgot."

Augy leaned forward from his Father's arm's and peered inside of the open slot.

He instantly seen Esher.

At the same time, Esher seen Augy.

Augy spurted out… in English… "Esher!!"

But after saying this in English, Augy realized that Esher only understood the Bigfoot language, or the silent sign language.

Augy started to speak in the Bigfoot language… the garbled sound that Samuel was used to hearing.

But Augy had just spoken English!!

Samuel's experiment was successful.

He quickly put Augy down to the ground next to him.

He did not want his son to speak any further to this young Bigfoot.

He now knew that this young Bigfoot was indeed the one that Sleeping Beaver and Shamieka had spoken of as Augy's young Bigfoot friend… Esher.

Samuel told Augy to go back inside the house and not to come back outside in the backyard unless given permission.

He said this to Augy in a raised tone of voice.

Augy lowere his head once again, and did as his father asked.

He went back into the house.

Once Augy got into the house though, he quickly ran upstairs to a closet at the top of the stairs.

There was a window on a side wall of the closet that had once been a bathroom.

Through this window, if one were to look through it, the little house could be seen.

Not just the little house and a good part of the backyard, but specifically, there was a clear view of the door of this little house.

Augy looked out of this window down at his Father who still stood by the door.

He watched his Father look into the open slot, and then closed the panel door.

He next watched his Father reach down and open another thing.

It was a small box that covered a key pad inside.

It had ten numbered buttons on the pad... 1,2,3,4,5,6,7,8,9, and lastly 0.

There was one other button... oblong shaped, that spelled out the word UNLOCK.

Samuel looked as if he was going to use this pad, and then decided otherwise and shut the box up over the keypad as it was moments before.

Augy somehow realized that this had to be used to be able to open the door where Esher was inside.

He watched his Father leave the area of the little house and walk back in the direction of the back door.

Augy heard the back door open and then close.

He knew that his Father was back inside of the house.

Augy left the closet and walked back to his bedroom.

He wanted to see his friend Esher.

He decided that he would watch his Father from the closet window, and try to get the code of numbers that would open up the door to the little house.

His Father did not know that he had what amounted to almost "Super" Hearing and eyesight.

Augy would use these super qualities to his advantage, in the hopes of getting a chance to be able to see Esher as soon as possible.

He knew that his young Bigfoot friend was scared.

Augy was scared as well.

Augy went over to his bed and laid down upon it, wondering why he could only speak the human language when he was near Esher, or any other Bigfoot.

He laid there... wondering.

Downstairs, Samuel was in the kitchen area getting out from a cupboard an airtight sealed container.

He had made-up weeks before, his own recipe of what he thought would be a food that the Bigfoot would eat.

It was a mixture of crushed pine nuts, egg yolks, flour, and other ingredients.

He rolled it up between both of his hands.

It had the texture of clay.

Next Samuel went to the other room and retrieved a small quantity of the chemical that he had used to make Esher go to sleep.

He put this chemical into the doughy food in his hands and worked it in very thoroughly.

The Bigfoot had to eat and drink water.

Samuel hoped that the Bigfoot had figured out how to drink the water that was inside of the little house.

Samuel emptied this special food into a plastic baggy and walked back outside to the backyard.

Augy heard the door open and shut again to the backyard.

He quickly got up from the bed and went back to the small windowed closet.

He looked down through the window, and watched his Father once again without him knowing, walk back over to the door of the little house.

He watched his Father open up the sliding panel at the top of the door.

Samuel looked through the opening of the panel.

Esher stood there a few feet away, looking at him.

Samuel reached up with the baggy and tore it open, and dropped the contents through the panel opening.

The doughy food dropped down to the floor in front of Esher.

It was obvious to Esher that this human was giving him some food to eat.

Normally Esher would not ever eat a strange food that he was not used to eating, but he was extremely hungry at this moment.

He reached down and picked up the food that Samuel had just dropped onto the floor.

Esher held the odd food in his hands for a few moments… looking at it curiously.

He put it to his nose and smelled it.

There were some familiar smells that he recognized.

Moments later, Esher started to eat the strange food given to him by this adult human.

This pleased Samuel.

He thought that it would be a lot more difficult to get this Bigfoot to eat, but to his surprise, the young Bigfoot was eating a food that he had made up himself without the real knowledge of what these primates actually ate.

Augy watched his Father very intently through the small closet window.

Augy watched his Father stand there near the door looking through the panel opening for several minutes.

Inside, Esher ate the food that Samuel had given to him very quickly.

He was surprised that this food's taste was acceptable.

Esher did not know that the food that he just ate was drugged with the sleeping chemical.

He felt dizzy and tired.

Esher laid down on the floor.

Samuel also watched Esher lay down on the floor.

After a few minutes, Samuel was convinced that Esher was really asleep.

He did not know that his son was watching from above.

Augy watched closely as his Father reached down once again and opened the box that covered the keypad.

His Father reached down with one of his fingers and pressed the following buttons.

8235929772761.

Samuel had wanted to make sure to do a long code instead of the usual short code, so it would be nearly impossible for anyone to randomly crack the code and be able to open this door.

Augy memorized this code easily.

Repeating it back to himself several times silently.

Augy now had the information to be able to open the door to the little house and see his friend Esher.

He watched his Father open the door and disappear inside where Esher laid on the floor asleep.

Augy left the closet and went back to his room, and once again laid down on his bed.

He wondered what his Father was doing with his friend Esher.

He wondered why his friend Esher had not ran out of the room when his Father opened the door.

Augy was obviously unaware that Esher had been drugged once again by his father.

Even though Augy was autistic, he had the ability to think like anyone else.

It's just that other's around him were not able to understand the world that he had to live in.

It was a totally separate world from the normal world where the majority of humans lived and died.

Augy was able to understand what he heard from people around him, but was not able until recently, to be able to communicate back to these people.

What was normal to Augy, was unfortunately construed to be a handicap by the people that did not understand his world.

Augy had recently, after meeting the Bigfoot's, become more comfortable with them than the humans that surrounded him most of the time, including now… his Father.

There was an anger swelling up within the autistic boy that was directed at his Father because of what he was doing to his friend Esher.

Augy closed his eyes and went into a deep slumber.

Chapter Forty

S AMUEL WALKED OVER TO Esher and bent down and touched his neck area.

He wondered if he could check the neck area for a pulse like a human.

He felt through the thick fur and indeed detected a heartbeat throbbing inside of the young Bigfoot.

The heartbeat was not racing… it beat slow and steady.

This pleased Samuel.

He would spend the next twenty minutes examining Esher very closely.

After doing this, Samuel left the room, and locked it securely.

The code was reset, and he went back into the house.

The rest of the day was uneventful for everyone, Samuel, Augy, and Esher.

The night skies turned dark, and turned back into light for the next morning in what seemed like a blink of an eye for Sleeping Beaver. Shamieka had the same feeling as well as she rose from the bed and went directly to the bathroom.

Sleeping Beaver went to the kitchen to start the coffee.

They had already packed the night before what they would need for today when they went to see Crazy Mylo.

Shamieka decided to make a small quick breakfast for her and Sleeping Beaver.

She was anxious to get on the road with Sleeping Beaver and get to where their friend Crazy Mylo was waiting for them.

They were both finished and out the door within an hour after waking up.

There was a rare wreck on the highway that slowed them down in their efforts to get to Crazy Mylo's location.

The wreck was a logging truck that had jack knifed and dumped it's load of logs.

Upon doing so, a chain reaction occurred involving three more vehicles.

There were no fatalities, but one individual had to be taken to the nearest hospital.

Sleeping Beaver and Shamieka were finally able to get around the wreck after almost an hour of stop and go with flag people directing the way.

They continued on their journey to the remote mountain area where they would find their friend.

They finally made it to the area where they normally parked for this hike, and unloaded their gear quickly.

They did not bother to rest, they immediately took off towards the forest, and up into the mountains.

There was an urgency to the pace that they hiked.

It was almost as if they were competing for a gold medal in the Olympics.

They did not know that Crazy Mylo awoke this morning very stiff, and in much pain from the ordeal yesterday with the male Bigfoot's.

Their only thought was the information that they were sure was correct, could be passed on to Crazy Mylo, and get his opinion about it all.

They also hoped that Crazy Mylo had been successful in finding the Bigfoot's and warning them about the possibility of an appearance by Samuel to their area.

If they had only known what Crazy Mylo knows right now.

They would have acted different when they were back at Samuel's house.

Halfway during their hike to Crazy Mylo's location, Sleeping Beaver stopped in his tracks.

Shamieka almost ran into him, he stopped so abruptly.

Shamieka asked Sleeping Beaver what was wrong.

Sleeping Beaver spoke.

"It just dawned on me."

"When we were back at Samuel's house, Augy spoke to us in English!!"

Almost immediately, Shamieka figured out what Sleeping Beaver was now saying to her.

She spoke to him with her eyes closed.

"Augy spoke to us in English."

"Augy only speaks in English, only if he is near a Bigfoot."

Sleeping Beaver interrupted her for a second.

"I have this theory that I was going to figure out with an experiment and see if it was correct."

"I think that Augy only has to be near some hair of the Bigfoot's for him to be able to talk English."

Shamieka asked how he was going to do an experiment.

Sleeping Beaver told Shamieka that he had gathered some Bigfoot hair secretly, and was going to put it near Augy's face to see if his theory was correct.

He had left the hair sample back at his place, and was waiting for the perfect time to try the experiment.

So Sleeping Beaver added that if the hair experiment proved his theory to be correct, then maybe Samuel had been able to gather some Bigfoot hair if he had already gone to the Bigfoot location.

Shamieka agreed that maybe this was something that was also possible.

Neither one of the two could even imagine that it was not just the Bigfoot hair that Samuel might be in possession of, but in reality an actual Bigfoot!!

This thought did not even come close to entering their minds to ponder.

They both agreed that Samuel more than likely had hiked to the Bigfoot area by use of the GPS information from Augy's bracelet, and retrieved some Bigfoot hair samples, and had then probably experimented with Augy and the hair sample to see if his son would indeed speak English to him.

These thoughts spurned Sleeping Beaver and Shamieka to actually pick up their pace to get to Crazy Mylo's location even quicker.

After hiking at a considerable pace in almost complete silence for almost two hours, they came near the area where they should be able to find Crazy Mylo.

Sleeping Beaver made his normal call to his friend, and was quickly answered.

As they came up to the area where Crazy Mylo was, they noticed their friend lying on the ground on his back.

He had his head propped up on a folded sleeping bag.

Shamieka ran over to Crazy Mylo and bent down over him.

She spoke frantically.

"What is the matter with you?"

Sleeping Beaver went down to one knee next to his friend, and waited for an answer to Shamieka's question.

Crazy Mylo spoke in a tone of voice that was considerably lower than normal.

"I was able to come into contact with some Bigfoot's."

"But before I was able to tell them about Samuel, they became angry at me, and a male Bigfoot threw me like nothing against a tree."

"I asked them by using the sign language that Shamieka taught me, why they were so upset."

"I did not even have to tell them about Samuel."

Crazy Mylo made a face of pain to his friends before trying to talk again.

"I have some very bad news."

There was a pause of several seconds.

Silence owned the air at the moment.

Sleeping Beaver bent down to his friend and gently asked him to continue.

"The Bigfoot's, one of them was Esher's Father Big Arch, they told me that a male human, and I already knew it had to be Samuel, this male human captured Esher… kidnapped him from these mountains."

"Samuel took Esher from these mountains to who knows where!!"

"Those Bigfoot's are very mad, and I am lucky that they let me leave alive."

"Can you believe that?"

Shamieka bent down and placed her hands gently on Crazy Mylo's ribcage area.

She pressed down a little and felt at the same time.

Crazy Mylo squirmed with pain. Shamieka could easily feel several broken ribs on both sides of his ribcage.

She told both men what she felt, and they all immediately agreed that it was more important to get Crazy Mylo to a hospital before anything else.

They could always figure out what to do next in relations to the Bigfoot's after Crazy Mylo was taken care of.

They quickly made a temporary stretcher for Crazy Mylo, and started their hike out of the mountains to get to a hospital.

They would deal with Samuel as soon as they could, but for now, their friend was more important on the priority list.

It was very hard to carry Crazy Mylo back out of the mountains, but they were able to get back to the vehicle just before it became dark.

They took him to a hospital in a town called Fortuna… known as "The friendly city."

Chapter Forty One

SAMUEL DECIDED THAT HE needed to speed-up his plan about Esher because he was now sure that Sleeping Beaver and Shamieka would figure out what he had done.

He based this reasoning on how they had acted the day before.

He also knew that they would eventually find out when they had contact with the Bigfoot's again.

Of course, he could deny everything, and simply not let them on his property.

What could they do?

Go to a law enforcement agency and tell them that he had kidnapped a Bigfoot?

Law enforcement could not even get a legal warrant to search his property based on what would appear to be crazy allegations.

Their accusations would still not be taken seriously, even though they were both very well known and respected members of the Humboldt County area.

He could simply deny everything that they said, and refuse to let anyone on his property.

That was his legal right as an American citizen.

Nevertheless, Samuel still decided to make his plan happen faster then he had originally wanted.

Samuel wanted to be able to announce to the whole world that he had indeed finally attained indisputable proof that the Bigfoot creatures did in fact exist.

He wanted to make arrangements with the very large media outlets around the world, and set a date and time to where he would unveil his proof... Esher.

First of all he got on the computer and contacted an old friend of his that was in the newspaper business.

Within an hour, his friend contacted him back.

He wanted to break the news to his longtime friend first because he trusted him.

He trusted that his friend would not leak out to the world media the information that he was going to tell him.

At the same time, his friend had many contacts in the massive media world, newspaper, and television, and could be used to make all of the important contacts for him a lot quicker then he could do himself.

He arranged a meeting in person with his friend for late that afternoon.

His friend would meet him at a small restaurant in Rio Dell.

He would tell his friend that he had indeed captured a young Bigfoot, but he would lie to him and tell him that he was at a secret location nowhere near his home.

This was just in case he was wrong about his friends integrity.

If he knew that Esher was actually at his home in his backyard, he might be tempted to see for himself if there was any truth to what Samuel was telling him.

His friend might use the excuse that he had to see Esher with his own eyes before he went out on a limb for Samuel with this unbelievable breaking story.

He could either have the story of this new young century, or be the most laughed at person and ultimate fool of the decade.

But Samuel planned to tell his friend that if he would just believe him, he would be given the first exclusive right to see Esher before anyone else on the same day of the first showing of Esher to the world media... and ultimately to the whole world.

He could go down in media history as the man who was the first to see a real Bigfoot and pass it on to the rest of the media outlets throughout the globe.

Samuel would also reassure his friend that if it turned out to be a hoax, he himself... Samuel Goodson would take all of the criticism.

He would take all of the blame, and assure everyone that he had hoaxed his unsuspecting friend with an unbelievable lie.

So what would his friend have to lose with this offer from him?

He felt confident that his friend would agree to the terms, and go along with his plan.

While Samuel was busy making his plans with his friend about Esher, his son Augy was also making his own plans as well regarding his young Bigfoot friend who was locked up in his backyard.

A few hours passed, and Samuel left his house for the meeting with his friend.

He brought Augy along with him.

Chapter Forty Two

SAMUEL ARRIVED WITH AUGY at the small restaurant a few minutes before his friend arrived.

The name of his friend was Harley Beau Rhodes.

Everyone called him "HB."

HB walked over to Samuel's table and put out his hand for a customary handshake.

Samuel stood up and returned the handshake with HB.

Next, HB looked over towards Augy and offered the same gesture.

Augy ignored the gesture.

HB was already aware of how Augy was, and simply shrugged his shoulders and sat down across from Samuel.

They had a table in the very back of the small restaurant.

There were no other patrons at the time in the restaurant.

There was light music playing in the restaurant from the area of the cook and dishwasher.

It was just enough to be able to drown out any conversation that Samuel and HB would have.

After the two men ordered a Mexican meal, they waited for the waiter to disappear before starting their conversation.

HB started the conversation.

"So Samuel, it sounds like you have one heck of a story to tell me."

"I have been thinking about what you might be getting ready to tell me since our conversation yesterday."

"Since I know your background fairly well, I have come to the conclusion that it must be something about what you have been doing all of these years."

"Is it related to Bigfoot's?"

Samuel was not surprised that HB was already so close to the answer because of his background in the media.

Samuel smiled back at HB silently.

HB smiled back, but only quiet for a moment before continuing to talk to Samuel.

"I knew it!!"

"So let me try to guess more of the story."

"So maybe you found some hair, and had it tested scientifically."

"The results came back as primate?"

"Or let me rephrase that, the hair came back as an unidentifiable primate?"

"A primate whose DNA is not on record in the science community?"

Samuel continued to smile back at HB.

HB tilted his head sideways, still smiling.

"You know Samuel, even if what I have just pondered is true, that does not necessarily prove that you have undisputable evidence of the existence of a Bigfoot here in Humboldt County California."

Samuel still held his silence with a smile.

He wanted HB to exhaust all of his guessing before dropping the real actual truth about Esher.

HB continued to talk.

"Your still not saying anything Samuel, but your smiling."

"I must be somewhat close to the truth, or you would not be smiling like you are."

"But maybe I am not quite correct, and that is why you are still silent, but smiling."

"If it's not the hair… then maybe you have video evidence."

"Now that would be a bombshell if the proper video forensic people could analyze the video and come to the conclusion that the video is valid, and not edited in any way whatsoever."

"If you have video evidence that is proven to be valid, and a sample of hair that has been DNA tested to prove it is an unidentified primate, then I would say that you are very close to proving the existence of a Bigfoot."

"But you know how it is Samuel… people will still say that the evidence, even this type of terrific evidence, would still not be enough to convince the world of the existence of a Bigfoot, or a primate known around the world by other names."

"They would say that anything less than a body or bones would not be enough."

"You want me to be able to notify the rest of the world, with an exclusive, that your evidence is like the holy grail in the world of truth in regards of the Bigfoot."

Samuel still smiled without a word yet.

HB frowned a little now, not really knowing what to say next.

Finally he said one more thing before putting the onus on Samuel to tell him the truth.

"Is this about a Bigfoot Samuel?"

Samuel stopped smiling and spoke.

"Yes… it is definitely about Bigfoot."

Now HB sat silently, waiting for Samuel to tell him everything.

"Now HB you would not do anything like record what we are saying would you?"

HB answered back quickly that he definitely was not recording their conversation.

Samuel continued his conversation.

"Everything that you just surmised about the Bigfoot was partially true, but not quite correct."

"What I have is what everyone would want to see that would 100% prove the existence of the primate that we here in Humboldt County California refer to as Bigfoot."

"I have captured a Bigfoot."

HB gasped and became light headed upon hearing this from Samuel.

"I have in my possession, a young male Bigfoot who is very much alive and well at a secret location miles away from where I live."

"I know that you are at this moment probably very shocked and skeptical."

"I would expect that to be the normal reaction after hearing this."

"It would be almost as shocking to say that Jesus is sitting over at another table in this restaurant."

"HB… I know that you will probably want to see with your own eyes, this young Bigfoot that I have captured and stored away before you would really believe me, but let me assure you, I am very much telling the truth."

"I am prepared to offer to you the exclusive story about this young Bigfoot, and how I was able to capture him, if you will just trust me, and make preparations to the vast media's of the world for a date and location to show the world that I am indeed telling the absolute truth, and that I am not crazy."

"If it did somehow turnout that I am lying to you, and this is a stupid hoax, I would step forward and admit that I hoaxed you, and that you are a completely innocent victim."

"I assure you HB, on my dead wife's grave and my son Augy that I am telling you the absolute 100% truth."

Samuel stopped talking, waiting for a reply from HB.

HB let this information sink into his brain for a few minutes as Samuel patiently waited for a reply.

Finally, HB gave a reply to Samuel.

"Alright Samuel, only because we are close friends, and I am very sure that you would not ever do anything stupid like lying about something of this magnitude, and risk our longtime friendship, I will go out on a major limb and basically risk my career, and believe what you have just told me."

"Exclusive rights to the whole story?"

Samuel shook his head to indicate a yes to HB.

HB started to talk again.

"Wow Samuel, this is incredible."

"This is going to make you the most famous person in the world for awhile."

"You will definitely get your 15 minutes of fame whether you are telling the truth or not."

"But of course, I do believe you, so your instant fame will come as being the person who has finally proven to everyone on our planet who has ever questioned whether the Bigfoot exist's as a fact that the creature does in fact share this planet with us humans."

"What date have you set to announce to the world about your captured young Bigfoot?"

Samuel answered almost immediately.

"I want as much media as possible for the announcement that I have in fact a live Bigfoot in my possession."

"You go and contact all of the media outlets that you have been chosen as the person to contact the media outlets of the world to announce, that you know the person who has in his possession, a living breathing, healthy young male Bigfoot at an undisclosed location."

"Tell them that this person will remain anonymous until the date of the showing to the world this young male Bigfoot."

"Tell them that a date will be set by this anonymous person to show the young male Bigfoot to the world for the first time."

"So HB… I suggest that you get right on it today if possible."

The waiter came with the food, but Samuel asked him to bag it up and that they had changed their minds about dining, and would instead take the food home to eat."

Samuel gave the waiter a generous tip.

HB and Samuel rose from the table after the waiter returned with their food all bagged up as requested.

They left the small restaurant and went separate directions to their vehicles and left… both men smiling.

Samuel and Augy drove home.

HB drove straight to where he worked at a local newspaper in Eureka less then forty five minutes away from Rio Dell.

He could hardly drive in a normal legal manner because he was so excited about what he was going to be doing for Samuel.

If one were to follow behind him on the freeway, it would be thought that he was driving under the influence.

Luckily for HB, there was no Highway patrol in sight.

He got to his destination feeling like he was floating on air, or like he had just hit the California Lottery.

Chapter Forty Three

SHAMIEKA AND SLEEPING BEAVER picked up Crazy Mylo from the hospital in Fortuna.

They brought him to Sleeping Beaver's place where he would recuperate until he was healed.

They would not let him go back to the mountains until they knew for sure that his body would be able to handle it.

He was already complaining that his current grows would suffer without his attention.

He tried his best to convince his friends that he was well enough to go back to his grow locations deep in the mountains.

Both of his two friends were firm with him, and did not relent to his complaining.

Sleeping Beaver assured Crazy Mylo that the worst that could happen is that the plants would only grow larger, or maybe someone could find the grows and steal them.

He convinced Crazy Mylo that his health was more important than his grows in the mountains.

Crazy Mylo would just have to trust that his plants would still be there when he went back in better health.

Crazy Mylo finally stopped complaining, and settled down at Sleeping Beaver's place to recuperate his injured body.

Shamieka wanted to go and visit Samuel with Sleeping Beaver as soon as possible.

She was furious about what she now knew about Esher.

She could hardly contain her anger.

Her anger was very obvious on her face.

Sleeping Beaver was just as upset, but did not openly show the same anger as his girlfriend.

After they were both sure that Crazy Mylo was totally comfortable at Sleeping Beaver's place, they made plans to go back to confront Samuel about what they now knew.

They left Sleeping Beaver's place within the hour.

This time, they would try harder than they had before to get Samuel to talk to them.

They would not beat around the bush, they would come right out and tell them what they now knew.

Their drive back down south to Samuel's was as quiet as outer space.

They also both realized that it would be stupid to contact the authorities about what they knew.

For one, they did not know where Samuel had Esher located.

Two, they knew that the law enforcement authorities would be very doubtful of their allegations towards Samuel.

Three, and finally, they did not want any harm to come to Esher.

Silent anger filled the air in the vehicle as they came closer to Samuel's place.

Chapter Forty Four

SAMUEL WAS UPSTAIRS AND seen the vehicle containing Sleeping Beaver and Shamieka arrive.

He knew that they would return.

He also knew that they probably now knew the whole truth about Esher, except for the fact that he had the young Bigfoot hidden away in a small dwelling in his backyard.

The vehicle pulled up to the same place as it had when they were last here.

Both Sleeping Beaver and Shamieka got out almost immediately from the vehicle and started to walk towards one of the front yard gates.

Samuel was not alarmed or in a rush to go and meet them.

He already had a few different plans on how to deal with these two obviously mad people.

One of the plans would surely work, he was very sure of himself.

Samuel watched the two people who might not be his friends anymore, go through one of his front yard gates and walk straight to his front door of his home.

Moments later, his doorbell rang it's sound throughout the house.

It was a doorbell chime that his wife had picked out many years ago when they first moved in the house.

Augy heard the chime of the doorbell as well.

Augy rose from his bed and walked over to his bedroom window and looked outside.

He could see his adult friends standing on the porch.

Augy casually walked out of his bedroom and went straight downstairs towards the front door.

He saw his Father approaching the door just as he got down to the bottom of the stairs to the front room.

Samuel turned around and seen his son across the room.

He motioned his son to come over to him.

Augy went over to his Father and stood next to him.

Samuel opened the door to the front porch.

A security screen separated him from Sleeping Beaver and Shamieka.

Samuel greeted the two people through the security door.

"I knew that you two would be back, even though I did not invite you both to come out here today."

"I am not going to be rude to you both and make you stay on my front porch, so if we can all be civil I will let you in."

"I know that you are both angry, and I expected that, but we can talk about everything in a civil matter... right?"

"Otherwise I will simply shut this door and ask you to leave my property again, and ignore you in the future."

Sleeping Beaver answered for himself and Shamieka.

"Alright, we can talk civilly."

"You are right, we are mad, but we'll talk as calm as we can."

"We do not want to upset Augy."

Upon hearing this from Sleeping Beaver, Samuel opened the security screen door and let the two people into his home.

They walked over to the front room and took their seats around the room.

There was a large sectional couch that took up over half of the front room, and a recliner chair.

Samuel sat in the recliner, and the other's, including his son, sat on the sectional couch across from him.

Samuel started to talk before the other's had a chance to start speaking.

"So... what do you both know?"

"Or should I ask, what do you suspect?"

Samuel sat silently, waiting for an answer from one of the two people.

Sleeping Beaver started to talk.

"Samuel... me and Shamieka went back into the mountains and found Crazy Mylo."

"He was injured."

"The Bigfoot's hurt him."

"We brought him to the hospital and now he is recuperating at my home."

Samuel answered back that he was sorry to hear that about Crazy Mylo. Sleeping Beaver continued to talk.

"Crazy Mylo told us something that definitely has us upset."

"The reason the Bigfoot's hurt him, and he is lucky that they did not hurt him even more than they did, they hurt him because one of their young had been taken by an adult human."

"It was the same young Bigfoot that had become friends with your son Augy."

"We now know for sure that you did lie to us about using the GPS bracelet to track us when we hiked into the mountains to visit the Bigfoot's."

"When Augy hollered from the backyard that you were lying to us... in English, we did not at that time figure out everything as we have right now."

"We were so upset when we left that we did not realize that there must be a Bigfoot close by Augy in order for him to speak English."

"So... after hearing what Crazy Mylo told us about what the Bigfoot's had told him, we knew that the adult human male that had taken the young Bigfoot, and by the was his name is Esher, we figured out that the human that the Bigfoot's were referring too was in fact... you."

"We thought about how Augy had spoke English to us when we were last here, and we have concluded that you have Esher somewhere around here as a captive."

"Of course, we realize that it would be stupid to go to the authorities about what our suspicions are about what you have done."

"They would laugh at us and think that we must be high on something, or need to take our medication."

"So we are here today to flat out confront you about what we think is true, and ask you to tell us the complete truth."

Shamieka looked over at little Augy and started to do a sign language to him.

Samuel spotted this and immediately asked her to refrain from doing the signing to his son, otherwise he would have Augy leave the room.

Shamieka stopped the signing to Augy.

Augy started to sign back to Shamieka, and Samuel stopped him as well.

Samuel started to talk after Sleeping Beaver had said his initial statement.

"Sleeping Beaver… Shamieka… we do not need to be angry about all of this."

"Just let me come right out and say it."

"Yes, I did capture the young male Bigfoot in the mountains."

"Yes, I did deceive both of you by using the GPS bracelet to track your movement."

"I feel bad that Crazy Mylo was injured by the Bigfoots, but you know what, I almost got hurt as well."

"Once I had who you call Esher, the Bigfoot's somehow figured out that I had him, and they chased me all the way to my vehicle."

"They came very close to catching me, and they were surely angry enough to do great bodily injury to me if they would have caught up to me."

"Luckily, I made it away just in the nick of time."

"So I do know that the Bigfoot's are for sure very angry about the current situation about Esher."

"I would warn the both of you not to travel up into the mountains anymore, for your own safety."

Shamieka's mouth dropped completely open upon hearing what Samuel had just said.

She was utterly speechless for the moment.

Samuel continued to talk.

"I want to tell you right now, I did have Esher here at my place when you were here and Augy spoke to you in English, but after you both left, I moved him to another location."

"I was sure that you would figure out that he was here, so I had no choice but to move him to another secure place for the time being."

"I want to offer both of you a chance to be a part of history."

"Since the both of you were a part of the story in finding the Bigfoot's, I feel it is only right to at least offer both of you a chance to experience the fame that will come when the world finds out that the Bigfoot primates do in fact exist on this planet."

"If you both turn down this offer, well… I guess that is your choices."

"I can't force you both to agree to have a chance to be famous."

"But let me tell you both something… I intend to become famous as the person who showed the entire world that their doubts, all of this time, that the Bigfoot's did not exist, were wrong."

"I have spent many years to have this opportunity."

"When my wife was here with me, she spent a lot of her time in the same venture."

"Fame will also bring me enough money to be able to give Augy a much better life than he has now."

"Don't get me wrong, life for me and Augy are great here in Humboldt County, but there are many more things that could make our lives much better that are not here in this wonderful place."

"I have thought that Humboldt County was the best kept secret in California."

"If all of the rest of the Californian's knew how wonderful this place was, I am sure that there would be a mass migration to come here."

"I love the seclusion and the privacy to be able to live in such a beautiful place, but Humboldt County does not offer many things that could be found elsewhere."

"I want Augy to have a chance to experience those other things that he cannot get here."

"I have already put the ball in motion to announce to the world that I have captured a living, breathing, healthy young male Bigfoot primate."

"I intend to show the world Esher very soon."

Sleeping Beaver and Shamieka were absolutely shocked at what their ears had just heard.

Samuel stopped talking momentarily to offer the two shocked people a drink or something to eat.

Both people shook their heads to indicate that they would decline the offer.

Samuel shrugged his shoulders and asked them if they had anything to say.

This time, Shamieka spoke.

"Samuel… I am shocked!!"

"You have taken from the Bigfoot's one of their youngster's!!"

"How would you feel if Augy all of a sudden was not here, and you did not know where he was?"

"I can answer that for you."

"I am sure that you would be just as upset as the bigfoot's are about Esher."

"You do not have the right to kidnap somebody's child."

Samuel interrupted Shamieka for a second and spoke.

"Esher is not a human child, he is basically a large ape... not human."

"So I did not kidnap a child."

"What I did is not even illegal."

"Unless you know of a law that I do not know that say's that it is against the law to capture an unknown primate in the forests of these vast mountains."

"So go ahead and continue to speak, I just wanted to correct you in your statement."

Shamieka escalated to another level of anger upon hearing this from Samuel.

She could not contain herself.

She stood up and lunged towards Samuel.

Sleeping Beaver immediately grabbed her to try and settle her down.

As he grabbed her, her momentum made both of them fall down on the carpeted floor.

Samuel hollered at Augy to leave the room.

Samuel got up from his recliner and then hollered at Shamieka and Sleeping Beaver to leave his house immediately.

Samuel ran over to his front door and opened it and the security screen door as well.

He hollered at the two angry people as they got to their feet.

"Get out of here, and do not ever come back here!!"

Samuel moved over behind a dining room set, and motioned them towards the opening to the outside.

Sleeping Beaver had Shamieka in a strong enough hold to be able to control her and guide her out the door to the front yard.

As they went through the door opening, Shamieka screamed at Samuel.

"I swear to God Samuel, you will not get away from this, and you will for sure regret doing what you have done... I promise you that!!"

Sleeping Beaver did not say a word as he guided Shamieka outside.

But he did give Samuel a look on his face that he felt the same as what Shamieka had just screamed at Samuel.

Augy did not leave the room entirely, he watched from a distance, not really showing any emotion externally, but he did feel sad inside for his adult friends.

Samuel slammed the door, and walked over to a curtain of one of his front windows.

He watched from the side of the curtain as Sleeping Beaver and Shamieka left his property.

He hoped that this would be the last time that he would see them, but he knew otherwise.

Hopefully, it would be long enough for him to have a chance to follow through with his plan about Esher with the help of his friend HB.

Samuel looked over at Augy and asked him if he was hungry.

Augy silently walked towards the kitchen.

It was back to the same routine for Father and son, as was the usual case between parents and their autistic children.

Just another day for Augy.

Chapter Forty Five

HB SAT AT HIS desk in front of his desk top computer.

He had just finished e-mailing several people in the media world that he knew personally, and many more that he did not know at all.

The initial e-mails did not go into detail as to what Samuel had told him, but HB did go out on a major limb and promise all of these people that he e-mailed that he had the story of this young century so far.

He told these people that he would give them more details if and when they contacted him back.

Basically, HB was going to tell these people as they got back to him, that he was hired by someone to announce to the world by as much media as possible, that a young male Bigfoot had been captured, and that there would be a date and time set to show the people of the world this young male Bigfoot.

Of course, HB would not disclose who had hired him.

No matter how hard HB was pressed, he would not give up Samuel's name or whereabouts.

Within an hour of making his last e-mail, he started to get people who were curious, and were already getting back to him.

So, the first person who inquired was a reporter from the Associated Press.

He wanted some more information from HB.

HB e-mailed this person back and gave him his personal cellphone number.

Minutes later, this Associated Press reporter phoned HB.

As HB was getting ready to answer this phone call, he noticed that there was now a growing number of contacts who were returning his e-mails.

He answered the phone.

"Hello, this is Harley Beau, everyone calls me HB."

The AP reporter said his name in return, and right away started to pump HB for information.

HB started out slowly with this reporter, trying to lay the groundwork as he would with all the others who were now waiting to talk to him.

He told this reporter that the information that he would relay to him would sound very unbelievable.

He explained that he had not independently verified the information as 100% fact given to him by the person who hired him, but at the very least it would be a story that many people would be interested in whether it turned out to be true or not.

The AP reporter already started to sound skeptical and went into a cautionary mode.

HB expected this from him as he would with all of the others that he would soon be having almost the identical conversation.

The AP reporter got very blunt with HB, almost rude.

He asked HB to just come right out, and get to the point of this supposedly unbelievable story.

So HB started to tell this reporter what Samuel had told him about Esher.

He did not divulge Samuel's name or whereabouts as promised to Samuel.

After a few minutes, HB was finished telling this reporter the possible bombshell story.

The AP reporter, as expected was now in 100% skeptical mode with HB.

But HB did remind him as he already had told him, that even if this story turns out to be false, and a complete hoax, could the reporter afford to ignore this story?

What if the story turned out to be real?

This reporter had to agree with HB on this point.

So... the AP reporter asked to be on the list of people to be contacted when a date and time was announced so that he could make arrangements to have a camera crew at the appointed location when supposedly, this young male Bigfoot would be shown to the world for the first time.

The AP reporter's final comment to HB was that he did not believe the story, and predicted that it would turn out to be a hoax, or very weak evidence that still would not prove the existence of Bigfoot's.

HB understood his opinion, and answered back that he would not believe this story as well, until he seen this young Bigfoot with his own eyes.

He was only trying to have this story come to a conclusion as soon as possible, whether it turned out to be true or not.

HB spent the next several hours talking to a large number of media people, basically getting the same opinions, and same results of request's to be contacted for the same reasons as the AP reporter had given.

A predictable thing also started to happen with HB.

The people that he had talked too, started to tell other's in the media world, and those people, who HB had not even reached out to, started to contact HB as well.

HB felt so important at this moment as he held the same conversation's with those people too, and made the same arrangement's as he did with all the other's that were now on a growing list.

HB thought to himself, what if it turned out that this story was true?

HB was promised by Samuel the first exclusive on this story.

If it turned out that this story about Esher was in fact true, HB would become famous as the reporter who reported to the world that Bigfoot's really did walk this Earth with the human race.

HB daydreamed for several minutes before getting refocused with his brain.

The e-mail's just kept coming onto his e-mail account.

It reminded him of a large amount of spam mail invading his computer that he would normally spend a few minutes deleting whenever he logged onto his e-mail account.

In this case though, he was not deleting these e-mail's, he was answering every single one.

After spending several hour's of tireless talking with interested and curious people, HB got a knock on his office door.

He did not think anything of it at first, and hollered across the room that he was busy, and that he would come out in awhile.

The knocking persisted.

HB thought that this was very unusual… and borderline rude, so he got up from his desk and went and answered the door to his office.

He opened the door abruptly.

His eyes widened slightly when he seen who was standing there a few feet away in front of him.

It was his boss, and two men dressed in very nice black suits.

Both men instantly pulled out identification badges to show that they were agents for the FBI.

HB was not scared, but this did surprise him, and made him slightly nervous.

HB knew that he had not broken any federal laws, so why were these two FBI agents now walking into his office at his job site?

HB walked over and sat down at his desk.

He motioned the two FBI agents over in the direction of two plush chairs that he kept on the far side of the room.

His boss walked over and stood beside HB.

This actually made HB more nervous than the FBI agents did.

His boss looked nervous, confused, and a hint of being upset.

All of this could be read on his facial expression when HB looked at him.

Without being asked, one of the FBI agents started to talk.

"Harley, or should I call you HB?"

HB told him he could call him by his nickname.

The agent nodded.

"Alright fine, HB."

"HB, we have been contacted by several people in the past few hours telling us that you had contacted them with an unbelievable story about someone who had captured a young male Bigfoot primate."

"Is this information true?"

"Just let me tell you before you answer that question."

"You are not in trouble for doing anything illegal."

"It is just that so many people are contacting us about this story that you are telling them, that we felt compelled to come and talk to you ourselves."

"It is also something that we would have to check out as a precautionary measure, just in case this story actually turned out to be true."

"Do you understand what I have said to you HB?"

HB looked at his boss momentarily before answering because he had not told his boss about this story at all.

His boss was finding out about this story at the same time as these FBI agents were.

His boss had a slight frown on his face, but remained silent.

He would talk to HB later after these FBI agents had left.

HB started talking to the FBI agent who had just finished talking.

"It is true, I have been sending out e-mails to many media outlets around the world about a person who hired me who claims that he has captured a real life, living breathing young male primate that we call a Bigfoot."

HB looked over at his boss quickly, and told him that he was going to tell him about this story today, but got to caught up in all of the people that were contacting him about this story.

His boss told him to finish talking to the FBI agent's and they would talk later after they left.

HB shrugged his shoulders meekly, and turned back to the FBI agents who sat across the room in postures that suggested that they were about to physically pounce on him.

They both leaned forward waiting for him to continue to talk.

HB obliged them.

"I cannot give you the name of this person who hired me yet, or his location, but I can tell you that he does in fact live here in Humboldt County California."

"I cannot verify the information that he is claiming, but I have been given an exclusive on this story, whether it turns out to be true or not."

"As you yourself have already said, I have not broken any laws by doing what I have been doing today in relations to this story."

"So I would simply like to finish up with you two agents in saying, that I will contact you and let you know, as I have promised a whole lot of other people already, the date and time when this person who hired me is supposedly going to show to the world, the first living Bigfoot ever captured."

Upon hearing this, the two FBI agents rose to their feet and gave HB their respective contact cards from their wallets.

They left quickly, and silently.

HB turned to his boss after the agents left.

For about another hour, he and his boss talked things over about this story, and ironed out all of the details how the story would be handled by the newspaper.

His boss left, and HB got back to answering more e-mails that had come to his e-mail account while he was talking to the FBI agents, and his boss.

There were over sixty new e-mails.

This story was already snowballing into something as large as any story that HB had ever been involved with.

HB went to the break room and filled his coffee thermos up, it was going to be a long shift.

Chapter Forty Six

HB WORKED FOR A solid week talking to people about this possible bombshell story.

Samuel had inquired the day before to see how things were going, and HB had told him about how massive this story was growing.

This pleased Samuel immensely.

Samuel was going to call HB at the end of the day after HB came home from work, and let him know when and where he planned to show Esher to the world.

HB was so excited that he could hardly concentrate throughout the day.

The story had grown so big now, that it had predictably leaked out to an unbelievable amount of news media outlets around the world.

If you were to turn on the television at any give hour of the day, no doubt, you would eventually get tidbits of the Bigfoot story.

It seemed as if everyone was talking about this story.

There was an anxiousness throughout the world about this story that rivaled a story like Jesus returning to Earth on a specific date.

Shamieka and Sleeping Beaver were more nervous than anyone else because they knew that this was indeed a true story, and not a hoax.

Most of the people that were anticipating the showing of Esher were people that thought this event with Esher would certainly turn out to be a hoax, or very weak evidence not proving anything near the fact that a Bigfoot does really exist.

Augy had no idea at all what his Father was preparing to do.

He just went about his daily routine at home.

Augy did have one thing deep within him though that he was planning secretly without his Father's knowledge.

This was a plan to help his friend Esher escape from the little house in the backyard.

Augy also, without his Father's knowledge, paid a visit to his friend Esher every chance that he could get.

Most of these visit's were only very short visit's, but at least Esher was getting a chance to communicate with Augy and let Augy know how he felt.

Augy told Esher that he was going to help Esher escape when he had a chance.

Augy told Esher that when his Father left the house without him, as he sometimes did for a short period of time, maybe an hour or slightly less, he would come and let Esher out of the little house.

He told Esher that he knew how to do it, but he would need enough time to be able to do it without his Father catching him, and have enough time to get Esher out of the area and back into the forest area less than a hundred yards away from the house.

So Esher waited for his human friend to help him escape when the time was right.

He trusted that Augy would be able to do this for him.

So, in the meantime, Esher ate the food given to him by Samuel, and drank the water as well so he would not grow weak and slow when the time came to escape.

He needed to be as strong and fast as possible when that time came.

Shamieka, Sleeping Beaver, and Crazy Mylo were also hatching a plan of their own.

If they could somehow figure out where Esher was being held captive, they would attempt to help Esher escape too.

Unfortunately, they did not know where Esher was being held, so the next best thing that they could do was to secretly watch Samuel from the forested area near his home.

Because of the fence and tree's near the house, they were not able to see too much of what he was doing.

Crazy Mylo had the idea that when Samuel left the house with Augy, they could break into the house and see what they could find that might help them with their plan.

Everybody was busy with their agendas, all centered around Esher.

Esher's family and friends were absolutely in a state of extreme anger and sadness.

They felt helpless about what to do to try and get Esher back with them.

They also had no idea where Esher was located.

It seemed as if the whole world was thinking about Esher, in one way or the other.

Samuel had finally decided that the time had come to let HB know what date and where he would let the world see Esher for the first time.

He finished the last of his own preparations, and sat down with his cellphone.

Chapter Forty Seven

HB ALMOST JUMPED OUT of his chair in his kitchen as he ate a snack of cheese and crackers.

He had been unwinding from a long tiring day at work where his concentration level had been very low because of the thought that today, he would finally find out from Samuel, the date, and location where the young male Bigfoot would be shown to the world by a massive amount of media.

HB answered the phone on the second ring and greeted Samuel on the other end.

Samuel spoke very casually to HB.

"Well my friend, I am finally ready to tell you the time and location where we are going to show the world that the Bigfoot's do indeed exist."

HB waited patiently for this special moment in his lifetime.

Samuel paused slightly before continuing to speak.

"You can go ahead and let everyone know that your anonymous person who has the young Bigfoot in captivity has decided to do this on this weekend, three days from now, on Saturday."

"Tell them that the location will be announced on this same Saturday a few hours before showing Esher."

"The reason that the location is being delayed is because I want to be able to not be bothered by anyone until the time has come."

"Lastly, I did promised you that you would have an exclusive on this story, and I also have decided that since you did such a wonderful job in setting everything up for me and keeping my identity a secret, I am going to let you walk with me and be at my side when I let people see Esher for the first time."

"Your eyes will see Esher before any camera has a chance to start filming him."

"Even though it will only be a few moments before, you will be able to say afterwards that you did get to see the Bigfoot first, before the rest of the world."

"In doing this, you will be the first person to know that this is all true, and not a hoax."

"You will be the first person let into the location where I have Esher as you stand at my side."

"You and I will lead the crowd of media behind us to where I have Esher.

"Once the media has had a chance to see Esher, I am sure that there will be a media frenzy."

"At that time, I will talk directly to the media and tell them that I have given you… HB… the exclusive first rights to the story, and all initial questions on this day."

"I will also let them know that I will give them one full hour to film Esher."

"No interviews, just filming."

"Now, what do you think HB?"

"Does this plan make you happy?"

HB was overjoyed.

HB answered Samuel with obvious excitement.

"Samuel, I am so pleased right now, you could not even imagine how happy I am feeling at this moment."

"I will immediately start contacting everyone and let them know what you have just told me."

Samuel ended the conversation so HB could get to work with this new information.

As soon as the phone connection went dead with Samuel, HB dialed the FBI agents that had visited him in his office the week before, and immediately called his boss into his office.

Once his boss was in his office, he told him everything that Samuel had told him on the phone.

He let his boss know that he had contacted the FBI agents as well.

The FBI agents thanked HB and said that they would see him on Saturday along with everyone else.

HB and his boss talked for almost an hour about how they should go about this story now that the time was so close for a possible world shattering piece of news.

It was decided that they would put into tonight's paper a short story explaining that HB was the first reporter to have access to this story, and also have the exclusive rights to tell the entire story after Saturday in regards to the young male Bigfoot that everyone has been waiting to see.

They would have a slight jump on the rest of the media outlets by contacting their local television news for the announcement about Saturday.

But besides that, the whole world would know about Saturday very quickly after HB started to make his contacts.

HB would start contacting the media outlets after he was able to get this news to their local television station first.

Within a few hour's, HB had made enough contacts to get the ball rolling very fast in the media world.

The local news station made the special announcement during a commercial to pass on the news about Saturday as being the day that here in Humboldt County, a Bigfoot would be unveiled to the world to see.

Shamieka and Sleeping Beaver, along with a large number of Humboldt County residents, watched this special news announcement with interest.

Crazy Mylo went into a frenzy of anger upon seeing the commercial.

The three of them still had not been able to figure out a good plan in being able to find Esher before Saturday.

They felt helpless and very upset about this most current development.

Of course, little Augy still did not have an understanding as to what now was going to happen on Saturday.

But... he still had his own secret plan to help his friend Esher.

If only his Father would leave the house for awhile, then he would be able to help Esher escape from the little house in the backyard.

His Father had not left the house without bringing him along with him since Esher was locked up in the little house.

Within a few hours, and into the next day, hotels and motels throughout Humboldt County started to get rooms filled or reserved for people, mostly media types, for a few days leading up to Saturday.

Media satellite mobile trucks began arriving in droves as well throughout the County.

Humboldt County would experience a slight rise of unexpected capital over the next three days.

Businesses, and local restaurants were pleased by this unexpected surprise.

T-shirt shops started to make T-shirts for Saturday's event.

Vendors were stocking up on extra supplies.

Everyone, it seemed like, was talking about Saturday with many different opinions as to how it would turn out, true, or hoax.

More people leaned towards the event turning out as a hoax, than actually being true.

Every station on television, local, cable, satellite, National, and Worldwide, seemed to also be talking about what would actually happen on Saturday.

Samuel tried his best in the next few days to relax until the actual moment came for him to show Esher to the world, and also become the most famous person in the news cycle for who knows how long.

Samuel declined to answer any calls or communicate in any manner with anyone during this time.

He would basically become a hermit until Saturday, just stay home with Augy.

Chapter Forty Eight

SATURDAY FINALLY ARRIVED.

The whole world was waiting for a chance to see if in fact Bigfoot's actually existed.

Samuel woke up and started his day with his normal routine with Augy.

One thing about Augy in the morning, he had to stick very close to his routine, and especially when it came to eating.

If his routine was broken, he would go into a screaming fit that was totally unbearable for Samuel to deal with.

So Samuel always had made sure that his son had the food that he was used to eating in the morning… except today.

Flaked cereal with raisins were an absolute must for Augy in the morning.

Even when they traveled abroad together, Samuel had always made sure that Augy had this cereal.

But today, of all days, when Samuel went to the cupboard to get his son's special cereal, the box did not have enough cereal in it for even a few bites.

He went up stairs quickly and peaked in on Augy, his son was still asleep.

Samuel grabbed his keys quickly, and decided that he still had time to go to a store over in Fortuna, which was only fifteen minutes away, and get the cereal and be back home before Augy woke up.

He should only be gone for about forty five minutes at the most.

He left his house and sped off on his quest to prevent a screaming fit from his sleeping son if he awoke to find he did not have his special cereal for breakfast.

As Samuel drove away from the house, Augy heard the exhaust of his Father's vehicle, and the tires rolling over the gravel in the driveway to the nearby street.

Augy got out of bed and quickly dressed.

This was what he had been waiting for with his Father.

Augy grabbed his jacket and put it on.

He made sure that he had his good hiking boots on his feet.

He went down stairs very quickly and went into the backyard, making sure to close the door behind him.

Augy went around the corner of the backyard where the little house was located.

Esher sat inside, not knowing what was about to happen.

The young autistic boy walked over to the box that had the keypad underneath and lifted the flap that concealed the numbered keys.

Esher heard the sounds of what Augy was doing just outside the door.

Esher stood up, not knowing what might be happening.

Augy quickly pressed the buttons of the code numbers on the keypad.

After doing this, a green light came on and there was a short buzz on the area of where the door lock was located.

The door was now unlocked.

Augy grabbed the door handle and turned the knob.

He pulled the door open, and standing there a few feet away was his friend Esher.

Esher was very surprised to see Augy and started to talk to Augy rapidly in the Bigfoot language.

Augy quickly told Esher that it was time for them to leave this place and go.

Esher bolted towards the door and stepped outside.

Augy now stood next to his friend who was now seeing the sky for the first time since Samuel had kidnapped him from his home in the mountains.

Esher looked around the yard with caution, not really knowing where to go.

As Esher looked around, Augy shut the door to the little house, and opened the flap to the keypad.

The locked automatically engaged and a red light came on the keypad.

Augy shut the flap to the keypad box.

He looked away from the house towards the far backyard fence, and now he could see something that made him feel happy... the forest!!

He could see a vast forest of tall redwoods timbers.

Esher started towards the backyard fence in the direction of this forest that was less than a hundred yards away.

Augy followed Esher, and when they arrived at the backyard fence that stood eight feet high, Esher was about to climb over it, but Augy showed him the gate that he usually went out when he went hiking in these same woods.

Esher watched Augy as he opened the gate to the fence, it swung open with a loud creaking sound that indicated the hinges needed to be oiled.

Esher walked through the gate and stopped, waiting to see what his human friend was going to do next.

Was he going to continue on with Esher into the forest? . . . or would Augy go back to the human dwelling?

Esher did not have to wait very long, only a few moments before he got the answer to what he was wondering about.

Augy shut the gate door and stood next to Esher.

They did not have to worry about being seen because there were no houses near enough to them in this area for anyone to be able to see them.

Augy started to quickly walk towards the forest, Esher was right at his side.

They arrived at the edge of the forest in about thirty seconds.

Both of them stepped into the shadows of the tree's together, already blending in enough to avoid being seen by anyone if there did happen to be someone actually watching that particular spot of land.

Which there was not.

As they walked together deeper into the forest, Augy asked Esher if he knew how to get back to his home at the waterfall.

Esher told Augy that he can always find his way home when he is in the forest.

All he had to do was get to the top of any mountain, and he would be able to know which mountain to go to next.

He also told Augy that once they found a river, then he would follow that river in the direction leading him back to his home.

They both hiked to the top of this first mountain, and instantly, after looking at a neighboring mountain, without hesitation, Esher started off towards that mountain.

After getting to the other mountain top, Esher spotted a river down below.

This winding water flow was called the Eel river.

They arrived near the Eel river, parallel to it's banks at a distance of about fifty feet, still inside of the forest.

Esher explained to Augy that they had to stay inside the forest but also follow the river.

This was so that there would be less of a chance that they would be seen by anyone if there happened to be someone in the area.

Which there was not.

They followed the Eel river at a distance inside of the forest for almost three miles, Esher stopped.

Esher looked at a mountain range in the distance.

He told Augy that he recognized those mountains as a place that he had been with his Father.

The mention of the word Father made Augy think for a moment about his own Father.

Augy knew that his Father would be upset at him when he came back home and realized that Augy was not at home.

Unknown to Augy as he stood there with Esher, his Father Samuel had already came home.

Samuel had not even known that his son, or Esher were gone yet.

Samuel decided to let his son sleep and wake-up on his own.

When his son woke up, he would have his raisin and flakes cereal for him as usual.

Samuel went to the living room and opened his laptop computer.

He wanted to check out how the media was acting on this special day.

Samuel spent the next hour and a half reading all of the many media sites.

There was a lot of excitement brewing in anticipation of what was going to happen today.

It was not unusual for Augy to sleep in very late, so Samuel did not think anything of it when his son had still not woken up.

It was now time to contact HB and tell him that he could come over to his house to get ready for the big event.

Samuel called HB, and his friend answered on the first ring.

HB had been camped out near his phone, waiting for this call from Samuel.

Samuel told HB to start telling the media that they could come to his home.

This is where the event would take place.

He told HB to get here before the media trucks started to arrive.

He wanted HB to be the person that controlled the media outside of his house until the time came to show Esher to the world.

The conversation continued only for about another minute before their phones hung up from each other, and HB could get the ball rolling for today.

Samuel went back to his laptop to monitor the media sites as they received the news from HB.

Samuel decided that even if Augy was still asleep when everything was about to happen, he would let him sleep through it all.

Besides, he had already made the decision to keep Augy away from the media anyway, and have his son remain inside of the house while all of this was happening outside.

He did not want to have his son become frightened and freakout about all the crowds of people that will surely be just outside of the house.

Samuel sat at his computer, mesmerized by how quickly the word was getting around about the location where supposedly, the Bigfoot would be seen for the first time.

Within the hour, HB arrived, and was already controlling the media trucks that had also started to arrive.

It was becoming very crowded outside in the front of the house.

Samuel still did not even have the faintest thought that his son, and Esher were actually many miles away from his home.

It was almost time to bring in HB, and have the media follow close behind them into the backyard to the little house.

Samuel was feeling extremely excited.

Samuel's phone rang, it was HB on his cellphone in the front yard.

HB wanted to know how much longer before the event started.

Samuel shut down his laptop, and told HB… "It's time my friend, meet me at the side gate to the backyard and let's show the world what they want to see!!"

HB started to giggle in an immature voice because of his extreme excitement of the moment.

He turned to the crowd of media and started to talk to them with obvious excitement.

"The time has come people."

"I have just received word from the person inside, my friend Samuel Goodson, that it is time for the world to see and finally know that the Bigfoot primates actually do exist on this Earth."

"I am going to meet him at the side gate to the backyard, and you can all follow us from a distance where we still feel comfortable.'

"If anyone gets to close to us, then Samuel might not feel comfortable enough to show this Bigfoot to you today."

"Do we all understand this simple request?"

"I know you are all just as excited as I am, but please just stay back and let Samuel do this comfortably."

"You will all have a chance to get a look and film the Bigfoot, so don't blow it for everyone else!!"

There were many voices that answered back to HB promising to be civil, and keep a comfortable distance for Samuel.

HB started his walk to the side gate, the crowd of media slowly followed him as he had just asked… at a comfortable distance.

Chapter Forty Nine

SAMUEL OPENED THE GATE cautiously for HB, looking at the massive crowd of media behind his friend.

Nervousness shot throughout his body as he let his friend into the yard.

They stood side by side and walked towards the backyard to where the little house was located.

The media crowd followed them exactly how they were asked to do.

They all walked around the backside of the main house and over to the little house.

Samuel stopped for a second to address the media.

"This is where I have the young male Bigfoot, inside of this little house."

Sleeping Beaver, Shamieka, and Crazy Mylo watched their television as this event unfolded LIVE, in real time.

They were now feeling very disappointed that they had not figured out that Esher had been kept inside of that little house all of this time.

They had been watching Samuel's movements as much as they could up until today in order to try and find out where Esher might be so they could rescue him.

They continued to watch the television, and felt utterly helpless, and sad about what was about to happen to Esher.

Samuel continued to speak to the media.

"My friend, HB has already told all of you to stay back at a comfortable distance as I open the door to show the young male Bigfoot to all of you."

The crowd of media were only about five feet from Samuel and HB.

Samuel felt comfortable that this was enough distance, so he proceeded to open the cover to the keypad.

HB stood next to him, and Samuel whispered to him that he would crack the door open at first so he could get the first peak at Esher, and then he would open the first security door wide open for the media to see the young Bigfoot.

Samuel entered the code that opened both doors, and quickly pushed additional buttons that would allow only the outer security door to open, leaving the inner iron bar security door locked.

The keypad buzzed as he went through this process.

Samuel grabbed the door handle once he knew that only the outer security door was unlocked.

He turned the handle and pulled the door slightly open for HB.

HB leaned over to the small opening and looked inside.

He saw nothing.

Samuel asked him what did he think because HB did not say anything.

He thought that HB must be shocked at what he saw, and was momentarily speechless.

HB finally answered Samuel.

"Look for yourself Samuel"

Samuel, with a broad smile upon his face spoke to the crowd just behind him now, they had crept closer to the door opening.

"Well here we are… Bigfoot lives!!"

He started to swing the door wide open, and HB tried to grab his arm, but he could not stop Samuel.

Samuel was too caught up in the moment, and did not realize that HB was trying to stop him to prevent the media from finding out that Esher was not inside of the room.

The door swung wide open, and Samuel turned around to face the crowd of media that were now trying to position themselves to get the best camera shots.

Samuel still did not realize that the room was in fact empty… no Bigfoot inside.

Instantly, many voices hollered at Samuel asking where the Bigfoot was.

Confused, and shocked by that question, Samuel quickly turned around to face the room.

As he did this, several camera's now panned the entire room to show that there was not a Bigfoot inside of the room.

Samuel started to holler at everyone around him, now in a frenzy, and out of control.

The media caught all of this on video as well.

"I don't understand!!"

"He is supposed to be here!!"

"I seen him this morning when I fed him!!"

"Where is he?"

"How could he not be here?"

Samuel did the code again, and opened the other door to the room and stepped inside of the room.

HB also stepped inside and stood next to Samuel feeling totally embarrassed and speechless.

The media started to say with many voices the word… Hoax.

This upset Samuel.

Samuel started to scream at the media people to leave his property, and began to push several individuals away from the door.

Samuel never shut the security doors, they both remained open.

He pushed and screamed in a crazy uncontrollable fit now as he pushed and herded all of the media people out of his backyard.

HB had already made a quick exit before the first of the media people started to leave the backyard.

HB got into his vehicle and drove off… mad and embarrassed.

The crowd of media continued to say the word hoax now, almost in unison.

There was already reporters in the front of Samuel's house telling the whole world that this was once again another instance of someone creating a hoax about the existence of a Bigfoot.

Samuel was indeed now getting his fifteen minutes of fame, but not in the way that he had wanted.

It was a great moment of humiliation for Samuel.

Samuel never went back to the little house to shut the two security door's, what did it matter anyway? . . . Esher was not inside.

Samuel went back into his house and ran upstairs to find Augy.

He wanted to make sure that Augy was not awake and upset by what was now happening outside in the front of the house.

Samuel opened the door to his son's room.

Augy was not in his bed!!

Confused, now thinking that Augy must be somewhere else in the house, Samuel started calling out his name as he started to check all of the rest of the rooms in the house.

"Augy!!"

"Augy!!"

"Come out son, it is alright, Dad is here."

Samuel started to feel very nervous, and scared as he went through the house and not finding Augy.

Samuel double checked the entire house, now very meticulously.

Closet's, underneath beds, almost comparable to a search during a child's game of "hide and seek."

After exhausting himself with an unsuccessful search to find his son, Samuel collapsed on the living room couch.

Where was his son?

Where was the young male Bigfoot?

How did the Bigfoot escape from the little house in the backyard?

Samuel's first thought was that Sleeping Beaver, and Shamieka must have come and taken his son, and let the Bigfoot out of the little house.

But how could they do that?

They did not know the code, and there was not any damage to the security door's.

Samuel was now frustrated and clueless, but still now thinking that his suspicions about Sleeping Beaver and Shamieka must be correct.

What else could it possibly be?

They had all of the reasons in the world to do something like that.

As Samuel sat there on his couch trying to get himself composed somewhat, Sleeping Beaver, Shamieka, and Crazy Mylo had just witnessed everything that just happened in Samuel's backyard on the television.

They were all happy for the moment because they now knew that somehow, Esher had escaped, and was now probably on his way back to his home to the other Bigfoot's.

They did not have the slightest clue that Augy was now with Esher.

The media had not become aware of the fact that Augy was now with Esher somewhere in the mountains.

Nobody had this knowledge . . . yet.

The phone rang on the table near Sleeping Beaver.

Sleeping Beaver answered the phone.

On the other end was none other than Samuel Goodson.

Samuel started to scream into the phone at Sleeping Beaver.

"Where is my son?"

"You better return him to me right away, or I will call the Sheriff's and have them come and arrest all of you for kidnapping Augy!!"

Samuel then screamed out another question to Sleeping Beaver.

"Also… how did you help the Bigfoot escape?"

"Those doors were coded, there is no way that you could have the codes to open those doors!!"

"Unless… you broke into my home, and found the codes, but I cannot believe that you even did that because the codes were stored away in an unnamed file on my laptop."

Sleeping Beaver switched his phone onto the speaker phone mode so everyone in the room could also hear what Samuel was now saying.

In doing this, it gave Shamieka and Crazy Mylo the opportunity to speak to Samuel if they wanted too.

Shamieka took her opportunity to speak to Samuel.

"Samuel, this is Shamieka."

"Let me quickly tell you the answers to your questions."

"First of all, we do not know where Augy is located."

"You can go ahead and call the Sheriff's if you want, and have them come and check everything out with us."

"They would not be able to find out anything, because we absolutely do not have a clue about where your son might be."

"As for your question about the Bigfoot having had help escaping, well, let me tell you first off, I am glad that he has escaped, but unfortunately, you are wrong about thinking that we had anything to do with that as well."

"Honestly? . . . if we did have a chance to rescue Esher, we would have."

"The problem for us was that we did not have any idea where you had him captive."

Sleeping Beaver started to talk in the same manner as Shamieka, basically saying the same things about Augy and Esher.

Even Crazy Mylo spoke up to put his two cents in, and saying much of the same things to Samuel.

Samuel started to weep and sob, obviously not an acting performance.

It was obvious to the three people that now listened to Samuel, that he was indeed crying like a little baby.

Finally, the crying stopped.

Samuel began to speak again.

"I do not believe what you are all saying, I am calling the Sheriff's and have them come out to where you are now, and interview the three of you about where my son might be."

"So you better not take off and hide my son!!"

"Stay right where you are until the Sheriff's arrive to talk to you."

The phone line went dead.

The three of them were not paranoid that the Sheriffs would now come to interview them, in fact they wanted to clear themselves of these accusations by Samuel as quickly as possible so the proper authorities could begin looking for, and try to find Augy as quick as possible.

Chapter Fifty

S AMUEL CALLED THE SHERIFF'S Department located in Eureka, and spoke with a dispatch person.

He told the dispatch that his son was missing, and that he was sure that he had been taken by Sleeping Beaver, Shamieka, and Crazy Mylo.

He told the dispatch where they were now located.

The dispatch told Samuel that the Sheriff's Department would have to send out a deputy to interview him also, while they interviewed the people that he was now accusing of taking his son.

Samuel gave the dispatch his address, and said that he would be waiting for a deputy to arrive at his house.

Within the hour, there was deputy sheriff's at both locations, interviewing all parties.

The residents of both parties were also thoroughly searched to make sure that Augy was in fact no where to be found.

After interviewing all parties, and doing their searches, the sheriff's contacted the FBI to get involved.

Unknown to the Sheriff's Department, the FBI was already, in a way, involved.

They had been at Samuel's house when the media crowd was there for the filming of the event.

They had not contacted Samuel yet, but now that the Sheriff's were contacting them in an official capacity, they were now going to have an official interview with everyone that had already been interviewed by the deputy sheriff's.

The two FBI agents that had spoken to HB in his office recently, were assigned the case.

One agent went to speak with Sleeping Beaver, Shamieka, and Crazy Mylo, while the other agent went to talk to Samuel.

The interview with Sleeping Beaver, Shamieka, and Crazy Mylo was fairly quick.

There did not appear to be any type of evidence in any way that would indicate that the three people had kidnapped Augy.

So the agent went out to where his partner was at Samuel's home.

The first agent had already began his interview with Samuel's for about twenty minutes before his partner arrived.

The two agents excused themselves for a few minutes to compare their notes with each other.

After they did this, they went back to where Samuel sat in his living room.

He looked very distraught.

The agent who had been talking to Samuel started to talk once again.

"So… my partner has interviewed the people that you have accused of kidnapping your son Augy."

"There does not appear to be any kind of evidence to suggest that they have perpetrated the crime that you accuse them of."

"Me and my partner also witnessed the media circus that was here earlier about the Bigfoot."

"Now you are telling me that these three people that my partner just finished interviewing, kidnapped your son, and helped a Bigfoot creature escape from a little house located in your backyard?"

"This story is starting to sound like something else."

"Let me ask you Mr. Goodson, it is true that your son is autistic… correct?"

Samuel shook his head to indicate this was a correct statement.

The agent continued to talk.

"Maybe, Mr. Goodson, this is all a well thought out plan to have your son disappear because you are getting tired of the extra responsibility and hardships in taking care of a mentally challenged son who is autistic."

"It is a well known fact that you have spent many years traversing the world in search of the elusive primate with many nicknames, here in this area of the world the creature is called "Bigfoot.""

"It must be hard for you to have to take your handicapped son everywhere with you as you try to succeed in this quest to try and prove that this primate does indeed exist."

"He must be a heavy burden for you."

"With the whole world watching, your son conveniently disappears at the same exact time that this supposed Bigfoot escapes from a little house in your backyard."

Samuel did not like what this agent was suggesting, and started to speak with passion.

"Everything that you are saying to me is absolutely ludicrous."

"I love my son dearly."

"Augy is not a burden for me at all."

"I just want to find my son and get him back home where he belongs."

Samuel went silent for a few moments before resuming.

"Maybe, as crazy as this sounds, maybe Augy helped the Bigfoot escape."

"They were very close friends."

"The Bigfoot even had a name… it was "Esher.""

"They were able to talk to each other in the Bigfoot language, and also when my son was in close proximity to the Bigfoot, he was able to communicate with me in English."

"If you do not believe me when I tell you, as fantastic as it may sound, then why do you not go back and ask the three people that your partner just interviewed, and they will verify what I am saying."

The two FBI agents looked at each other.

They stood up, and one of the agents told Samuel to turn around.

They read him his rights, and handcuffed him.

They told him that they were going to detain him for more questioning at their office.

As they left Samuel's house with Samuel between them handcuffed, there was still a media truck outside, still filming the area.

Right away, they noticed Samuel walking with the agents to their vehicle in handcuff's.

A reporter ran over and tried to ask a few questions, but all three men remained silent as they entered the vehicle and quickly drove away.

This happened to be the station that was still filming LIVE on air, and had not left the area as the other media crews had.

Sleeping Beaver, Shamieka, and Crazy Mylo just happened to still be watching the television.

They were exhausted from the interview by the FBI agent who had left a little while ago.

To their surprise, they watched how Samuel had been led away in handcuff's by the two FBI agents.

They all looked at each other silently.

Crazy Mylo was the first to speak.

"Hey… lets go over to Samuel's place before he gets back and see if we can find anything in his house that can tell us what happened to Augy."

"We can also get all the evidence that we can that would show that the Bigfoot's exist."

"This is probably our only chance."

"I know it is illegal, but we have a small window of opportunity to get rid of all the evidence that would prove the existence of the Bigfoot's, and hopefully figure out what has happened to Augy too."

Shamieka and Sleeping Beaver at first told Crazy Mylo that this was a crazy idea, but then they realized that what Crazy Mylo was saying was in fact true.

This very well might be the only chance that they would ever have to get rid of any evidence that Samuel has that the Bigfoot's exist.

So they decided to immediately go over to Samuel's place and sneak into his house with the intent of trying to find all of the evidence that he has that would prove that the Bigfoot's exist.

They were willing to take this risk for a few reasons.

One… hopefully attain all of the evidence about the Bigfoot's that Samuel might have, and thus protecting them in the future, and two… maybe find something that would help them figure out where Augy might be located.

They were near the area where Samuel's house was located within the hour.

They hiked up into the forest behind his house.

This was the same area that they had been secretly monitoring Samuel in recent day's.

Chapter Fifty One

AS SAMUEL SAT IN a holding cell waiting for the FBI agents to talk to him again, over at his home Crazy Mylo and Sleeping Beaver were entering the backside of Samuel's house through the backyard where nobody could see them.

Shamieka stayed at the edge of the forest as a lookout.

They had brought along three radios to communicate with each other.

With total luck, Sleeping Beaver and Crazy Mylo were able to enter the house without damaging a window or a door.

A side door in the backyard was unlocked.

Samuel never had a chance to lock the door before he was taken away by the two FBI agents.

They spread out throughout the house, searching for anything that they thought might be evidence about the Bigfoot's or where Augy might be.

Samuel spotted Samuel's laptop.

He grabbed it right away.

Upstairs, Crazy Mylo found the GPS bracelet, and all of the software that went with it.

He also found two DVD's labeled Bigfoot in a desk drawer.

He grabbed those along with the GPS items.

As he was about to leave the room, he also noticed a small digital camera, he did not bother to check to see what photo's might be on it, he just simply put the camera in his vest pocket.

After searching as fast as they could for about fifteen minutes, they were convinced that they probably had all of the Bigfoot evidence.

Hopefully they were right in this assessment.

Unfortunately, they were not able to find anything that would give them a clue as to where Augy might be located.

The two men wore elastic surgical gloves in order not to leave any fingerprints behind.

They shut, and now locked the side door as they exited into the backyard.

They went back around to where the little house was located.

Crazy Mylo had brought along a small bundle of rags, some bleach in two one gallon jugs, and a small can of drain cleaner that dissolved virtually everything it came in contact with.

They went inside of the little house.

They soaked the rags with the bleach, donned painters mask's and goggles, and quickly wiped down the entire room from ceiling to floor.

As they wiped with the bleach soaked rags, the rags picked up all of the hairs that Esher had shed inside of the room.

Esher had not bothered to used the set-up that Samuel had mad for his bodily discharges, so the bleached rags picked this up as well.

Finally, they poured the drain cleaner down the drain that Esher had not used, and then poured the bleach into the water supply that Esher had used for drinking.

As far as they were now concerned, this room was 100% clean from any evidence that Esher had ever been housed here.

They left the little house, and shut the door behind them.

They left the backyard and made their way back to Shamieka after she gave an "all clear" over their radio's that there was not anyone in the area that would see them as they came back to the area where she was hidden.

Shamieka was pleased and not pleased at the same time when the two men got back to her and they started to go back to their vehicle.

On the one hand, she was not satisfied that the men had not found anything that might help them figure out where Augy might be, and on the other hand, she was very happy to hear how thorough the two men had been in gathering and getting rid of all the evidence about what Samuel had about the Bigfoots.

She could only hope that their thoroughness had been good enough to protect the Bigfoot's.

They got into the vehicle and drove away back to Shamieka's place.

The plan was to go to her place and get all of the video evidence that she had on her computer and get rid of that along with everything they had got from Samuel's place.

As a precaution, when Shamieka went inside of her place to get the video evidence on her computer, instead of getting the DVD's, and deleting the file on her computer, she took the entire computer tower, and her laptop with her back to the vehicle.

They drove over thirty miles to a place that Sleeping Beaver was sure would be a perfect place to get rid of all of this evidence.

Once they were at this location, they destroyed all of this evidence inside of an old abandoned mine, and threw it all down a shaft that was several hundred feet deep, and almost impossible to ever again explore because of a high chance of danger of a cave-in.

With this complete, they went back into Eureka and rented a couple of motel rooms for the night because they did not want to be bothered by law enforcement, or anyone else for now.

They would now concentrate all of their efforts in finding Augy.

Samuel was now just being released from the FBI office after extensive questioning.

They paid for a taxi to drive him back home.

Samuel was very traumatized by the events that had occurred today.

Nothing had gone the way he had planned, and now his son was still missing, and he was a prime suspect in his disappearance.

The FBI released him because they did not have any evidence that pointed to Samuel as being guilty of his son's disappearance.

On top of everything else, Samuel also suffered from extreme humiliation about not being able to show the world that the Bigfoot's exist.

The whole world now thought that he had pulled off a large hoax.

HB had immediately went back to his office and along with his boss, had started to write a story for the newspaper's next day special edition.

He would still go back and interview Samuel, who he now considered someone who was not his friend anymore.

But for now, he had to try and clear his name and reputation with a story that suggested that Samuel had fooled him as much as the whole world about Esher.

As Samuel traveled back to his home, he now had a plan that would hopefully eliminate the embarrassment and humiliation that now coursed through his body.

He would gather up all of the evidence that he still had about Esher and show that to the authorities, and to HB.

He would show the GPS evidence that showed exactly where the Bigfoot population was located.

He would show the video's that he had shot of Esher.

He would show the pictures that he still had on his digital camera and laptop computer.

Finally, he would show real physical evidence.

Surely there would be plenty of DNA evidence throughout the whole room of the little house in his backyard.

He had noticed that Esher had shed hair in many area's of the room.

There was also urine and feces as well that could be tested for DNA evidence.

But even though Samuel felt confident that he would still be able to show some type of evidence that he did in fact have an unknown primate in the little house, with claims that it was indeed a Bigfoot, he was still very troubled as to the where his son Augy was located.

He was worried sick for his son.

How would Samuel react when he got back home and found that all of the evidence about Esher was completely and very thoroughly gone?

How would Samuel be able to figure out where his son might be?

When he got home and exited the taxi, he noticed right away that the one remaining news truck was still parked in front of his house.

This irritated him immensely.

He walked over to where a female reporter stood and confronted her.

A camera panned in his direction as he approached.

He screamed at the reporter to leave his property immediately.

She tried to ask him a few questions, but he ignored her, and went directly into his house, slamming the door behind him.

Within a few minutes, the news truck started it's engine and drove away.

Samuel went directly to his kitchen, ignoring everything around him, and got out a bottle of whiskey from a cupboard.

He did not bother getting a glass, he took off the cap from the top of the bottle and took three very long swigs as he walked back into the front room.

The house was as quiet as a soundproof room as Samuel sat down on a couch… still oblivious that some people had entered his home while he had been detained by the FBI.

Samuel drank the bottle of whiskey, and passed out on the couch.

Chapter Fifty Two

SAMUEL WOKE UP FROM his drunken slumber in the early hours of the morning… around five a.m.

His head felt like it was going to explode from the whiskey hangover.

He felt depressed and helpless about his son Augy.

Where was he?

If it was true that Sleeping Beaver, and Shamieka had not been involved in his son's disappearance, then how and why did Augy leave.

The disappearance of the young Bigfoot also puzzled Samuel.

How did he escape?

Somehow the code was pressed in the keypad box to unlock the doors to the little house.

But how?

Samuel decided that finding Augy was the most important thing in the world right now for him to do.

Samuel made some toast, and drank two large cups of coffee to clear his head.

After doing this, he was able to start thinking more rationally about what he could do to find Augy.

He thought about the fact that the Bigfoot had disappeared at the same time as Augy.

This surely was not a coincidence.

Samuel came to the conclusion that they must have both left together… with each other.

So thinking along these lines, Samuel next concluded that somehow, Augy must have been able to get the code to the security door's, and helped Esher escape.

Then… if that was the case, and they both left together… where did they go?

It had to be back to where the rest of the Bigfoot's were located.

The young Bigfoot would want to go back home to the rest of the Bigfoot's.

If this was in fact true, then Samuel had the answer.

He would simply go back to his computer and get the GPS coordinates to the Bigfoot's location as he had done before when he went to capture Esher.

Samuel had these GPS coordinates written down, but had destroyed them when he got home with Esher so that there would not be any evidence just laying around his house.

But that was no problem, he had the coordinates on his laptop computer.

Samuel walked into the other room to retrieve his laptop.

Samuel's eye's widened when he seen that the laptop was not where he had last left it.

He shrugged his shoulders.

Maybe he moved it somewhere else when he got drunk the night before.

Samuel started to walk around the house, looking very meticulously in every room.

After several minutes of doing this, a panic started to rise inside of his head.

He could not find his laptop anywhere.

Did someone burglarize his home?

He looked around even more carefully and noticed that his digital camera was also missing.

What?

Samuel started to think about the fact that nothing else of value was actually missing.

Only objects connected with the Bigfoot's.

He looked for other objects of proof that he had about Esher.

The photo's, and DVD's were also missing.

This caused Samuel to scream in anger once again.

He ran out of the house into the backyard to the little house.

He quickly did the code on the keypad that would open both of the security door's.

He opened both doors wide, and entered inside of the room where Esher had been held captive.

Instantly, Samuel's eye's started to burn very bad.

He started to choke as well.

The toxic smell in the room was so powerful that he could hardly breathe any air into his lungs, or open his eye's to see anything in the room.

He backed out of the room to the outside fresh air and cleared his lungs.

He blinked his eye's until his vision came back into focus.

Samuel left the two door's wide open in order to air the room out.

He now realized that the toxic smell in the room was bleach.

He could not smell the other toxic smell of drain cleaner that was also present in the air of the room along with the bleach.

Samuel was now officially freaked-out about everything.

It now appeared very clear to him that someone had taken the time to get rid of all of the evidence that was related to Samuel ever having Esher here at his home.

He thought of two possibilities.

The first possibility was maybe the FBI had come to his house while he was detained at their office and got rid of all of the evidence.

He knew, as everyone else in the world that the FBI was capable of doing such a thing.

It had been documented many times over the years that the FBI was good at covering up evidence.

The other possibility that came to Samuel was that maybe Shamieka, and Sleeping Beaver had been involved.

As Samuel thought about these two possibilities, he started to lean more towards the probability that the FBI was not involved because it was not like this was a National security issue.

It seemed like it was more probable that Shamieka and Sleeping Beaver was involved in this cover-up.

He thought that Crazy Mylo was probably involved as well.

Those were the people that had reason's to do something like this.

It had to be them.

After letting the room of the little house air out for a few hour's, Samuel was able to go inside and see that the room had been cleaned very thoroughly.

He could even tell that the drain had been cleaned because the lid of the drain had been taken off, and the rim was shiny from a chemical that had obviously cleaned it's surface.

Even the ceiling had been cleaned.

Samuel now realized that he did not have any evidence of any kind that could prove to anyone that he had ever had a Bigfoot at this location.

Samuel also realized that he would not be able to remember the exact route that he had taken when he went and captured Esher in the mountains.

He also realized that even if he could get to the location where he had actually captured Esher, he knew that the spot where he had tranquilized the young Bigfoot was not where the rest of the Bigfoot's could be found.

Their location could be far from where he captured Esher.

Samuel now felt frustrated as he realized that he was basically helpless in his current situation.

The FBI now surely had him as a suspect in the disappearance of his son Augy.

All evidence that he had ever captured a Bigfoot was non-existent, and he did not even know where the Bigfoot's were located.

He knew in his gut, that Augy must surely be with Esher, and that they were on their way to where the Bigfoot's were located.

Desperation was now consuming his heart and soul.

The only thing that was important to Samuel at this point was to find his son Augy.

For a few more hours, Samuel contemplated what course of action he might, or should pursue.

Finally, he thought of the only solution that could possibly result in finding his son.

He had to get help.

Who would be the people that he needed to help him?

His only answer to that question was Shamieka and Sleeping Beaver.

He would have to beg them, if need be, to help him locate Augy.

He knew that they had traveled to the Bigfoot location several times over the past few month's with his son, and they could get there without the help of using GPS coordinates.

Samuel sighed, and exhaled.

He then picked up the phone to call them.

Chapter Fifty Three

SHAMIEKA, SLEEPING BEAVER, AND Crazy Mylo had already figured out that Augy and Esher had to be together.

They also figured out that the two youngster's would most probably be making their way's to Esher's home with the other Bigfoot's.

They decided that they should travel to the area where the Bigfoot's could be found, and try to find Augy.

Hopefully their theory about Esher and Augy being together was correct.

They started to pack the items they would need for their hike to the area.

The phone rang across the room.

Sleeping Beaver walked over and answered it.

Samuel was on the other end, not sounding angry as he had the last time that they talked on the phone.

Sleeping Beaver asked Samuel why he was calling him after all that has happened.

Samuel answered in a very civil manner.

"Sleeping Beaver… I cannot prove that it was you and Shamieka that came to my home and got rid of all the evidence that would prove that I ever had a Bigfoot here, but right now, I do not care about that."

"All I care about right now is that I find my son Augy."

Sleeping Beaver could not help himself when he answered back to Samuel… very rudely… "Now you might be able to understand how the Bigfoot's felt when you took their youngster from them."

"Do you not think that they were stressed out... sad... angry... and feeling very helpless about what they could do to get Esher back with them?"

"It's not like they could have simply walked out of the forest and approached the human's and asked for them to give Esher back to them... right Samuel?"

Samuel started to sob openly, understanding that what Sleeping Beaver had just said to him was absolutely true.

Samuel started to grovel at Sleeping Beaver.

He sounded so pitiful as he spoke.

He told Sleeping Beaver that he was very selfish and non-caring about what he had done with Esher.

He agreed with what Sleeping Beaver had just said.

He now did have an understanding as to how the Bigfoot's must have felt when he took Esher from them.

He apologized to Sleeping Beaver, and asked him to pass that same apology to Shamieka and Crazy Mylo as well.

Sleeping Beaver told Samuel that he could do that himself, whenever he seen them in person in the future.

Samuel now openly begged Sleeping Beaver to help him get Augy back to him.

He explained to Sleeping Beaver that he figured out that Augy and Esher must surely be together and must have gone back to where the Bigfoot's lived.

Sleeping Beaver relented to Samuel's plea's.

He told Samuel that he and Shamieka had come to the same conclusion, and that they were now actually planning to travel to the Bigfoot location today and see if they could find Augy.

Samuel started to thank Sleeping Beaver over and over.

Sleeping Beaver cut Samuel short and spoke one last time before hanging up the phone.

"Samuel, we do not forgive you for what you have done, but we also realize that Augy does need to be back home with you as soon as possible."

"We are now going to leave and see if we can find Augy, and get him back home too you."

Just as Sleeping Beaver was about to hang-up the phone, the door bell rang at Samuel's home.

Samuel asked Sleeping Beaver to please hold on for a minute because he wanted to say a few more thing's to him, but he needed to answer the door first and see who it was.

Sleeping Beaver said he would wait for Samuel to come back to the phone to finish their conversation.

Samuel put the phone down and walked to the door and opened it.

Standing on the other side of the security screen was two sheriff's deputies.

They asked Samuel if they could come inside his home.

Samuel let them into his house with no hesitation.

They walked into the front room and stood a few feet from each other.

Sleeping Beaver could hear everything that was being said.

He could hear the deputies tell Samuel that they were going to have to bring him to the Sheriff's Office for further questioning about the disappearance of his son Augy.

Samuel did not pick up the phone because what he wanted to say to Sleeping Beaver involved mentioning his son and the Bigfoot's.

So he left the phone on the table with Sleeping Beaver still on the other end listening.

The Sheriff's deputies did not notice the phone on the coffee table, and even if they did, it was not uncommon to see a phone laying around somewhere in a house, and as long as Sleeping Beaver remained silent, there would not be any sound coming from the earpiece of the phone to hear.

Sleeping Beaver heard Samuel tell the deputies that he had no problem in going with them to the Sheriff's Office.

He told them that as long as it would hopefully help to get his son home as quickly as possible, he would cooperate as much as the authorities wanted him too.

Sleeping Beaver listened on the phone for several more minutes before he heard what appeared to be all of them leaving… the Sheriff's deputies, and Samuel.

Sleeping Beaver hung-up the phone when he heard the front door shut.

Samuel followed the Sheriff's deputies back to Eureka to where the Sheriff's Office was located.

Samuel's phone started to beep loudly because it had never been hung-up.

Shamieka, and Crazy Mylo told Sleeping Beaver that they were ready to leave for the Bigfoot area to hopefully find Augy.

Sleeping Beaver told them everything that Samuel had said to them, even though they had been there a few feet away as he talked to Samuel.

He also told them about how Samuel had left with the Sheriff's deputies to go to the Sheriff's Office in Eureka.

They exited Sleeping Beaver's home, and got into Shamieka's vehicle, and drove away… wondering if they would succeed in finding Augy today.

Chapter Fifty Four

A FTER SAMUEL HAD SPENT a few hours being questioned by detectives at the Sheriff's office, it was decided that Samuel would stay for a while longer then he had anticipated.

They decided to lock him up in the County jail while they further investigated the disappearance of Augy Goodson.

They were also contacted by the FBI on the same day, and asked to detain Samuel until further notice.

So… Samuel sat in jail now, wondering if his son would ever be found, and was now a prime suspect in his disappearance.

Elsewhere, quite a distance from Samuel's location, Sleeping Beaver, Crazy Mylo, and Shamieka were busy hiking to the waterfall area where they knew they would find the Bigfoot's.

But… would they also find Augy?

They also knew that the Bigfoot's were angry with the human's right now, even if Esher had already made his way home with or without Augy.

All three of them carried a large can of Bear spray for protection against attack.

All they had to do was to look at their friend Crazy Mylo as he gingerly limped his way with them during their hike.

Once they arrived at an area that was fairly close to the waterfall area… less than half a mile they stopped.

The plan now was for Shamieka to travel the rest of the way to the waterfall area and make contact with the Bigfoot's.

Sleeping Beaver argued with his girlfriend about her doing this alone, but as normal, she was very stubborn, and would do it with or without his blessing.

Sleeping Beaver and Crazy Mylo would stay in this area until Shamieka returned… hopefully with Augy with her.

Shamieka reassured both men that she was confident that the Bigfoot's would not harm her when she came in contact with them.

Especially if Augy was in fact with Esher.

So off she went, leaving both men behind, and both wondering how long she would be gone.

The Sheriff's Department, and the FBI both attained warrant's to do a very thorough search of Samuel's home.

They spent the later part of the day going through every inch of Samuel's home.

They thought that it was odd that they did not find a computer in the house, and even more odd that the room of the little house in the backyard had been chemically cleaned of any type of evidence that might have been found.

Through past experiences, they had seen this same thing done in crime scenes involving homicide.

They would have to ask Samuel why the room had been chemically cleaned, and they also noticed the drain had been cleaned as well.

As far as not finding a computer in his home, it was possible that Samuel did not own a computer, but not likely.

So they would question him about this too.

Both law enforcement agencies were now very suspicious that Samuel was definitely not telling them everything, and that he might be guilty of perpetrating his son's disappearance.

Chapter Fifty Five

AUGY AND ESHER HAD finally made it back to the area where the rest of the Bigfoot's could be found.

They had actually been found by two adult Bigfoot's about two miles from the waterfall area when Esher had screamed out a call that would be recognized by any Bigfoot's that might be in the area.

These two Bigfoot's had heard Esher's loud call, and answered him back with their own call's.

At first, they did not realize who they were calling to, but they were sure that it was another Bigfoot.

Still, even though they were sure that the call from Esher was from a Bigfoot, they cautiously approached the area where the call came from.

When they seen Esher, they were overjoyed to find him.

They did not show the same reaction to Augy, but they knew him, and still had a trust towards him even though he was a human.

Quickly, the three Bigfoot's and the young human, traveled back to the waterfall area to the other Bigfoot's.

It only took a few minutes before Esher was re-united back with his parents.

They too were reluctant to show any hospitality towards Augy.

They did not talk to Augy when he spoke to them… they simply ignored the young human.

It was after several minutes of Esher explaining everything that had happened to him, and how Augy had helped him escape when the Bigfoot's finally softened how they were treating Augy, and started to make him feel more comfortable and very welcome in their presence.

Augy talked with them, and told them as much as he could in relations to Esher's kidnapping by his own Father.

They invited Augy into the cave system, for the very first time.

They had never allowed him to do this in the past when he had visited.

But now, they wanted to stay out of sight, and they trusted the young human enough to allow him to enter where no other human had ever stepped foot.

Shamieka cautiously made her way over the final mountain ridgeline that overlooked the area where the waterfall cascaded down the mountainside.

She had her can of Bear spray in one hand, ready for a possible attack, even though she felt confident that an attack from a Bigfoot would not happen.

But she had the can of Bear spray in her hand… just in case she was wrong in her line of thinking.

She stopped and looked very carefully around the area below her in the small valley.

She could not detect any movement, but this was not unusual because how stealthily the Bigfoot's normally traveled.

So she started to walk slowly down the mountainside to the valley down below.

Just as she was halfway down the mountainside, a Bigfoot happened to be leaving the cave system that was well hidden behind the waterfall.

As the large male Bigfoot stepped out into the open, he instantly detected movement on the mountainside.

Shamieka did not notice him because she was concentrating on not tripping as she made her way down the side of this steep mountain.

She had her eye's looking down at the ground for every careful step that she had to take in order to make it to the bottom safely.

The Bigfoot quickly stepped aside into the treeline, disappearing instantly from view if Shamieka happened to look down towards him.

He watched her as she made it all the way down to the valley floor to level ground.

Shamieka walked towards the waterfall area and came to within fifty feet of the male Bigfoot who stood motionless within the thick forest watching her carefully.

He had an urge to attack her, but decided that he would wait and see what Big Arch wanted to do with her.

He would not attack her, but he would not let her leave this area without Big Arch having a chance to see and communicate with her.

This Bigfoot knew that this female human was able to communicate with the Bigfoot's because she knew the silent hand language.

She had been the human that had implemented this special silent language into the Bigfoot population which was a very popular device for them to use stealthily during the daytime to communicate with each other.

A few minutes later, another Bigfoot exited the cave system.

This time it was a female Bigfoot.

She also instantly caught sight of Shamieka, and froze for a second because Shamieka had spotted her as well.

This female Bigfoot right away went back into the cave system and sounded the alarm to the rest of the Bigfoot's.

Shamieka had thought's of running, but knew that it would be a waste of time to try and get away.

She knew that the Bigfoot's would easily catch her if she tried to flee the area.

Anyway… why run?

She was here for a reason, and that was to see if Augy was somewhere nearby.

The male Bigfoot who had been watching her jumped out of the cover of the forest, and approached Shamieka rapidly.

Shamieka froze, holding the can of Bear spray in her hand at her side, ready to use it if she felt threatened.

The way he was now approaching her, she did have a feeling that harm might come to her.

As he got within range of the Bear spray, she raised it up and showed him the can.

She started to do sign language to him with only one hand to try to warn him to stop, and make him understand that she did not want to hurt him with the can of spray that she was now aiming at his face.

He stopped about twenty feet from her, and signed back to her to stop pointing the can of spray at him, and that he was not going to harm her.

Shamieka put the can back into her vest pocket.

Within a minute, the cave system started to empty out with a large number of Bigfoot's.

They all started to surround her in a large circle that would prevent any type of possible escape if she chose to try to do so.

The Bigfoot's told Augy that Shamieka was outside, and asked him to remain inside of the cave system with Esher and some other Bigfoot's.

Esher's father, Big Arch, would go outside and talk to Shamieka.

Chapter Fifty Six

BIG ARCH WALKED OUT from behind the waterfall and right away looked over in the direction where Shamieka stood with the Bigfoot created circle.

He did not show on his face anything that could be deciphered as mad, or glad to see her.

He stared into her eyes as he walked towards her.

Shamieka started to feel slightly uneasy as he came closer to her.

The circle of Bigfoot bodies opened up enough to let the giant Bigfoot through to the inside where the female human waited, not knowing whether she was going to be harmed or not.

Big Arch waded through the crowd of Bigfoot's.

Shamieka stood in the center of this large circle waiting for him, slightly scared for her life.

Big Arch walked to within a few feet of Shamieka and stopped.

He started to do the silent sign language to her.

He asked her why she was here, and were there any other humans with her.

Shamieka did not want to lie to Big Arch, so she told him about Sleeping Beaver and Crazy Mylo.

She told Big Arch that they were waiting for her to come back with Augy.

Big Arch asked Shamieka where exactly were the other two humans located.

Shamieka told him exactly where they were and asked him to please not to go and harm them.

She explained that they had not come to start any trouble with the Bigfoot's, and that they just wanted to find Augy and bring him back home to his Father.

Big Arch frowned when she said this to him.

Big Arch then looked over to a few of the male Bigfoot's in the circle and spoke to them in the Bigfoot language so Shamieka did not know what he had just told them.

Five of these male Bigfoot's left the circle and started to go in the direction where Shamieka had told Big Arch moments before where Sleeping Beaver and Crazy Mylo were located.

Shamieka pleaded with Big Arch when she noticed the five Bigfoot's leave the circle.

Big Arch signed back to her that he would not harm the adult humans unless they tried to harm a Bigfoot.

He also told Shamieka that Augy was safe, and inside of the cave behind where the water falls from the mountain.

Shamieka asked Big Arch to have Augy come out to see her.

She wanted to see for herself that the little boy was in fact safe and unharmed.

Big Arch replied that he would not have Augy come out from cave.

Augy would stay inside of the cave for now.

This worried Shamieka.

Big Arch asked Shamieka to sit down on the ground.

He told her that he wanted her to sit on the ground until the other humans came back with the other male Bigfoots that went to get them.

Meanwhile, not too far away, Sleeping Beaver heard some crackling of leaves being crushed on the ground.

He alerted Crazy Mylo without talking, and motioned in the direction where he heard the sounds.

Both men froze… listening.

All of a sudden, before either man could react, five male Bigfoot's appeared from behind the tree's that surrounded them.

The Bigfoot's quickly stepped forward and surrounded the two surprised men.

Both men stood perfectly still, not wanting to provoke any of these huge giants to violence towards them.

Both men felt extreme fear race through their bodies.

The Bigfoot's stood completely around them for a few moments before one of them started to do sign language to the two men.

He told the two men that they were to come with them back to where the female human was.

Sleeping Beaver signed back to the Bigfoot asking him if the female human was safe and unharmed.

The Bigfoot did not sign back to Sleeping Beaver.

He motioned Sleeping Beaver and Crazy Mylo to start walking.

The two men started to walk, still completely surrounded by the five male Bigfoot's.

It took less than twenty minutes to arrive back to where Shamieka was still sitting inside of the Bigfoot circle.

As they approached the circle, Sleeping Beaver could not see Shamieka, because of all the giant bodies that surrounded her, and also because she sat on the ground.

The circled opened a gap just big enough for the two men to enter inside.

As they stepped into the circle, they instantly seen Shamieka sitting on the ground, and Big Arch standing nearby looking over at them as they slowly walked towards him.

They walked to within a few feet of Big Arch and stopped.

Big Arch motioned them to sit down on the ground next to Shamieka.

With no hesitation, the two men sat down next to Shamieka.

Sleeping Beaver gave Shamieka a hug as soon as he sat down next to her.

He could feel her body shake slightly during their embrace.

He patted her on the back and rubbed the back of her head to help calm her nervousness.

Crazy Mylo sat nervously by with his friends… wishing that he had someone to hug for his own nervousness that he was also feeling from his head to his feet.

The three people feared for their lives as time seemed to stand still for them.

Finally, Shamieka was settled down enough to once again start doing sign language with Big Arch.

She asked him once again if she could see Augy.

Big Arch told Shamieka that he would let her see Augy, but only she would be able to see him, the other two humans would have to wait here inside of the circle while she visited the little boy.

Shamieka had no choice in the matter, all she could do for now was to agree with Big Arch so she could have the opportunity to see little Augy.

Big Arch motioned her to stand up to her feet, and to follow him.

He was going to take her to see Augy.

Shamieka followed Big Arch to the waterfall near the side of the mountain.

Big Arch motioned her to go in front of him towards the wall of the mountain where the water cascaded down it's side.

Shamieka hesitated because she did not see anything but water falling from the side of the mountain.

Big Arch signed her that there was an opening just beyond the falling water.

Shamieka crept closer to the waterfall, now only inches away.

Close enough now, to where the spray of the falling water made contact with her skin and clothing, making her slightly wet.

As she looked carefully at the small gap between the mountain and the falling water, Shamieka could see a dark void.

She could now see what looked like a cave behind the falling water.

Big Arch told her to go past the falling water to the cave on the other side.

Shamieka stepped forward, and past the falling water, and into a cave on the other side.

She got wet, but not as much as she had expected.

Shamieka now stood at the beginning of the cave system.

Nearby, there were several Bigfoot's standing, looking at her silently.

Big Arch entered inside of the cave system right behind Shamieka moments after she had stepped inside the large hollow void.

The visibility was surprisingly good.

She did not try to understand why this was the case, all she cared about at this moment was to find Augy.

Big Arch spoke the Bigfoot language to a few other Bigfoot's.

They quickly disappeared deeper into the cave system.

A few minutes later, Augy appeared with Esher at his side.

Augy greeted Shamieka in the English language.

Shamieka started to talk to Augy right away after he greeted her.

"Augy, are you alright?"

Augy told her that he was alright and happy.

Shamieka continued to talk.

"Augy, you need to come with me to go back home to your Father."

"Your Father is very worried about you."

Augy answered back to Smamieka… was his Father feeling the same type of worry as Esher's family felt when he was not at home with them?

Shamieka told Augy that it was the exact same feeling.

Augy frowned at Shamieka, and stood silent.

Shamieka once again asked the little boy to leave this cave, and come with her so she could take him back to his Father back home.

Instead of answering Shamieka, Augy started to talk in the Bigfoot language to Big Arch, and Esher.

Shamieka felt alienated as she stood by, not understanding any of the Bigfoot language that came from Augy's mouth.

Big Arch spoke back to Augy.

Esher spoke to Augy after his Father had stopped talking.

Augy answered back to them.

This conversation between Augy and the two Bigfoot's went on for several minutes before Augy turned to Shamieka and told her that he did not want to go back home to his Father.

This startled Shamieka.

She told Augy that he had to go with her back to his Father, and that he really did not have a choice to stay here with the Bigfoot's.

Augy screamed at Shamieka to leave.

Big Arch motioned Shamieka to walk back to the entrance of the cave system, and to walk outside past the waterfall.

Shamieka pleaded with Augy to come with her, but he ignored her.

Big Arch walked towards Shamieka and made it obvious by his body movements that he wanted her leave the cave . . . now.

Shamieka looked back at Augy as she started to depart the cave, and the last thing that she could see was Augy and Esher disappearing into the depth's of the cave.

Shamieka stepped through the waterfall with Big Arch quickly right behind her out into the open air.

She walked back to the circle and sat back down with Sleeping Beaver and Crazy Mylo.

Big Arch now stood near them, towering above them silently.

Shamieka told Sleeping Beaver what had happened with Augy inside of the cave.

Sleeping Beaver was shocked, but actually not very surprised.

He told Shamieka that he was not surprised that Augy had made a choice to stay here with the Bigfoot's

He told her that there was not anything more that they could do today, and that they should try to get back home safe, and then try to figure out another way to get Augy back home to his Father.

Crazy Mylo agreed with Sleeping Beaver and said the same thing to Shamieka.

Shamieka realized that what the two men were saying was the most logical thing for them to do at this time.

Hopefully they would be able to make it out of this place safely, and go back home.

Shamieka told Big Arch that they wanted to leave and go back home.

She also told Big Arch that they would not ever come back to this area, and not tell any other humans about this place.

They would leave the Bigfoot's forever so that the Bigfoot's could live a peaceful life without interruption from the humans.

She finished in saying that if Augy ever wanted to come back home, he would make that decision and come back on his own, however he wanted to do so.

She pleaded with Big Arch with promises that she would abide by what she was saying to him.

Big Arch asked about Augy's Father, did he know how to get to this place?

Shamieka told Big Arch that Augy's Father did not know how to get to this place.

She also admitted her fear of being harmed by the many Bigfoot's that surrounded her and her other two human friends that sat beside her.

Big Arch told Shamieka that he would trust what she had just told him, but also warned her that if she broke her promises, that harm would happen to them.

If any of them ever came back to this area, they would be harmed.

He also agreed that it would be Augy's choice to leave when he wanted, or never to leave at all.

Upon saying this, Big Arch hollered out in a deep booming voice to the other Bigfoot's in the circle.

The circle of Bigfoot's quickly turned into a crowd of giants walking back to the cave system

Within a few minutes, the area was clear with the exception of Big Arch and the three humans.

Big Arch told them to leave immediately.

They got to their feet and left, not knowing if they would ever see Augy ever again.

Big Arch had two large male Bigfoot's follow the three humans until they had left the area and traveled several miles further away.

Chapter Fifty Seven

SLEEPING BEAVER, SHAMIEKA, AND Crazy Mylo got back to Sleeping Beaver's home and settled in for the night.

They would go and talk to Samuel on the next day, no matter where he was.

When they woke the next morning, they called the Sheriff's office, and quickly discovered that Samuel was still being detained at the Humboldt County jail.

Because there was no evidence against Samuel in the disappearance of his son, he would only be detained for forty eight hours.

But the investigation would continue with a cooperation between the FBI and the Humboldt County Sheriff's Department.

So... the trio would have to wait until Samuel was released before they could have another opportunity to talk with him.

The forty eight hours went by at a snail's pace, but finally Samuel was released from jail.

He immediately contacted Sleeping Beaver and asked him if he, and Shamieka would be able to come to his home and see him.

Sleeping Beaver told Samuel that it would probably be better if they met in Eureka because Samuel was already close by, and why should they travel all the way down south to Rio Dell for what would amount to a short conversation.

Samuel agreed to meet in Eureka.

They decided to meet at a popular Chinese food restaurant.

Within the hour, everyone had arrived except Crazy Mylo.

He declined to go to the meeting for unknown reasons.

They sat at a booth in the far corner of the restaurant far enough away from other patrons so their conversation would not be heard.

Samuel got right to the point.

"Well? . . . where is Augy?"

"Did you find my son?"

"Is he safe and unharmed?"

"I am so worried about him… talk to me."

Shamieka explained everything that had happened when they went to the Bigfoot area and that Shamieka was able to actually see and talk to Augy.

After she explained that Augy decided not to come back with them, Samuel looked crushed.

All of the color from his face disappeared, and now was very pale with utter shock.

Shamieka made it perfectly clear to Samuel that they did not have any kind of a choice in the matter of Augy coming home.

Their lives were in danger, and they could not force Augy to come home, especially when they were surrounded by a large crowd of Bigfoot's that were on the verge of committing physical violence upon them.

When they were asked to leave, and to never come back, they had no choice but to relent to the command from Big Arch.

Shamieka explained that Big Arch was the Father of Esher.

Samuel asked them what they thought they should now do to get Augy back.

Sleeping Beaver answered the question calmly.

"Samuel, there is really nothing we can do for now, and maybe never."

"If we tell the authorities our story, you already know how they will react, and treat us."

"Also, you have to give-up any thoughts that you might have to ever pursue the Bigfoot's anymore."

"You have already embarrassed yourself throughout the world."

"Your credibility has been destroyed, and it is time for you to realize that if you continue to try and pursue the Bigfoot's, nothing good will ever come of it."

"As far as Augy is concerned, we can only hope that he will decide that he wants to come back home."

"For now, he feels better about being with the Bigfoot's, and you have to accept that, whether you like it or not."

Samuel felt a full range of emotion's racing throughout his body as he listened to Sleeping Beaver.

He did not want to accept what Sleeping Beaver was saying, but he realized that Sleeping Beaver was right about all that he had said, and he would now have to basically continue on with his life, and hope that his son decides to come back home.

Samuel also realized that his Bigfoot hunting days were officially over, and he told Shamieka and Sleeping Beaver that he would never again make any type of an attempt to find or prove that the Bigfoot's exist.

The conversation ended, and they all left the restaurant.

Samuel went home with only hope left for his son, and also the feeling that he was being watched by the authorities because they still suspected that he made his son disappear.

Samuel did not feel any fear that he would ever be locked up in jail again, because he knew that there was absolutely no proof that he was responsible for his son's disappearance.

So life went on… with only a slither of hope from all involved and concerned parties that Augy would ever be seen again.

Chapter Fifty Eight

FOR THE NEXT SEVERAL weeks, Augy and Esher spent time with each other like brother's.

Esher showed Augy many area's of the cave system that went on for many miles.

Esher showed Augy the area where the Bigfoot's were taken when they died.

It was a deep dark abyss where the bottom could not be seen.

Basically an underground cliff.

Esher explained to Augy that the dead Bigfoot's were taken to the edge of this cliff and rolled over into it's deep darkness.

Esher also explained that if a Bigfoot died outside of the cave system they were retrieved and taken to this place as quickly as possible.

As far as eating was concerned, that was not a problem at all for Augy.

Augy came to realize that not only could he talk with the Bigfoot's when he was in their presence, he was also a completely different type of person as compared to the way he was back home.

He did not show any signs at all of being someone who was autistic.

He was a completely normal person, with no signs of autism whatsoever.

The adult humans had not noticed this when he had been around them and the Bigfoot's at the same time.

They had only noticed that he was able to talk with the Bigfoot's.

What they never were able to realize, as Augy now was able to do, was that when Augy was around the Bigfoot's, he was a completely normal person.

So... instead of his ritualistic raisin and flakes cereal that he had always insisted upon having in the morning, Augy ate what the Bigfoot's offered him.

He actually liked most of what they gave him to eat, with the exception of raw meat from the wildlife kills that they made.

The Bigfoot's did not know how to make fire, so they never heated their food.

Everything was ate in raw form.

The Bigfoot's certainly knew about fire because of the many forest fires that they had witnessed, but they never were able to make a connection that the fire could cook the meat for a different taste.

They feared fire, as all of the other animals who lived in the forest's of the mountains.

The cave system was also a place that they could also feel safe in the event of a forest fire.

When Augy wanted to sleep, and appeared to be cold, there was always a Bigfoot nearby that would offer to cuddle with the young human with their long fur of their body acting as a warm blanket.

The Bigfoot's liked Augy, he was becoming special to them.

After two and a half month's went by, Big Arch, and some of the other Bigfoot's started to talk about Augy's future with them.

They came to the conclusion that it would probably be better for the young human boy to go back to his human world.

They decided that it was time to sit with Augy and tell him their opinion.

Big Arch asked Esher to bring Augy to speak with him the next morning when he woke from his sleep.

The morning arrived, and Augy started to walk around the cave looking for Esher.

It was not long before he found his friend with a group of other young Bigfoot's.

When Esher seen Augy, he told him that his Father wanted to speak with him.

He asked Augy to come with him to where he knew his Father was located.

They went to an area of the cave that Big Arch liked to be whenever he wanted to be alone.

Augy approached Big Arch respectfully, and sat down near the giant.

Augy asked Big Arch why he wanted to see him.

Big Arch told Augy what he and the other Bigfoot's had talked about.

Augy did not like what he was hearing, he was happy with the way he was now living his life.

He was still very mad at his father about what he had done to his friend Esher.

Big Arch explained to Augy that he understood how he felt about his Father.

He explained to the young boy that his Father needed Augy to be home with him.

He told Augy how he himself had felt when Esher was not at home with him, and compared that feeling with how he thought Augy's father probably felt right now.

He told Augy that he belonged in the human world, but he could always come and visit with the Bigfoot's anytime he wanted too.

Augy was sad to hear what Big Arch was saying to him, but he realized that what he was hearing was indeed correct.

So, it was decided that Augy would return to the human world the next day.

Big Arch, and his son Esher would guide Augy back to his home to his Father Samuel.

Big Arch did not know how to get to Augy's home, but his son Esher knew the way.

Augy's sadness went away fairly quickly because of the realization that he would be able to visit the Bigfoot's sometime again in the future.

Chapter Fifty Nine

THE AUTHORITIES STILL SUSPECTED that Samuel had caused Augy's disappearance, but they still did not have a shred of evidence pointing to that possibility.

They came out to visit Samuel about once a month for further interview's in the hope that they might get lucky, and finally detect some type of evidence about the Augy Goodson case.

This happened to be one of those days.

These visits were always unannounced, but not surprising to Samuel when they appeared at his driveway in front of his house.

During the time that Augy had been gone, Samuel had made it a point to deliver his promise that he had made to himself after his last conversation with Shamieka and Sleeping Beaver at the Chinese restaurant a few month's earlier.

He decided that he would now present himself to the world as a complete critic that the Bigfoot's ever existed, and that he had been a fool for all those years in thinking that they actually existed in these modern times with the human race.

He did several interviews with various media's admitting that the event that he had at his home had been a complete hoax for publicity.

He apologized for what he had done, and when asked about his son, he could only answer that he did not have a clue as to where his son was located.

No matter how many times Samuel said to the authorities or to any media types that he did not know anything about where his son might be, there was still doubt and suspicion that he was not telling the truth.

The Bigfoot's found where Crazy Mylo was located before Big Arch and Esher took Augy back home.

They brought Crazy Mylo to a location where Big Arch, Esher, and Augy waited.

Once Crazy Mylo was in contact with Big Arch, the giant explained to him that they wanted him to contact Sleeping Beaver, and Shamieka to tell them that they were taking Augy back to his home to his Father.

Big Arch also explained that they would stay in the forest near Augy's home until they were able to see Shamieka and Sleeping Beaver.

Once they were able to see Shamieka, and Sleeping Beaver, Augy would come out of the forest to meet them near his home to be re-united with his Father.

Big Arch also told Crazy Mylo to not tell Augy's Father that his son was about to come home.

He also told Crazy Mylo to ask Shamieka and Sleeping Beaver to also not tell Samuel about his son's homecoming.

Crazy Mylo hugged Augy and made sure that he was unharmed.

He did not notice any outwards signs that the young boy had any injuries.

Surprisingly, Augy hugged him back… he had never done that before… the boy was different now… normal?

Crazy Mylo told Big Arch that he would immediately go and tell his friends that Augy was on his way home.

Crazy Mylo left the area and traveled out of the forested mountains to contact his friends Shamieka and Sleeping Beaver.

Big Arch, Esher, and Augy left awhile later on their journey to the human world.

Several hours later, Crazy Mylo was able to contact his two friends and pass on to them what Big Arch had told him to tell them.

They were very excited to hear the news.

They felt very tempted to disregard what Big Arch had asked in regards to telling Samuel about Augy coming home, but they decided to honor Big Arch's request.

As quick as they could, they got into Shamieka's vehicle and drove straight to Samuel Goodson's house on the outskirts of Rio Dell.

At the same time that they were driving on Highway 101 South to Samuel's home, the FBI was also traveling the same route to the same location for their monthly unannounced interview with their prime suspect in the Augy Goodson case.

The FBI agents were actually only a few minutes behind Shamieka and Sleeping Beaver on the highway.

Within forty minutes, Shamieka and Sleeping Beaver pulled into Samuel's driveway.

They would tell Samuel that they were just out for the day, and had decided to come visit him and see how he was doing.

Samuel seen them drive into his driveway, and decided right away to invite them into his home.

Maybe they had some news about Augy!!

Whatever the reason, he felt comfortable to have them here at his home for a visit.

They all went into his living room and sat down.

Right away, Samuel asked if they were there to give him any news about his son.

Shamieka told Samuel that they were just there for a visit with him to see how he was doing.

Shamieka knew that somehow, without Samuel figuring anything out, needed to go into the backyard so that Big Arch and Esher would be able to see them.

Shamieka and Sleeping Beaver had discussed this as they had drove to Samuel's home.

They decided that they would ask Samuel if they could see the little house in the backyard.

If asked why, they would tell Samuel that they were just curious, and if it was alright with him, maybe he could show the little house to them.

Moments after Shamieka asked Samuel about seeing the little house in the backyard, the doorbell rang.

Samuel was not expecting to see anyone today, and a look of surprise came to his face.

He went and answered the door.

It was the two FBI agents.

Samuel let them in the house right away without them requesting to enter.

As the FBI agents entered the house, they noticed Shamieka and Sleeping Beaver sitting in the living room.

They already knew them, so they did not introduce themselves, instead, one of the agents made a generic comment that it was surprising to see them here today.

Shamieka answered back that they had decided to visit with Samuel to see how he was doing.

Samuel told Shamieka that she and Sleeping Beaver could go out to the backyard to see the little house.

This intrigued the FBI agents.

They asked Shamieka why she wanted to see the little house.

Shamieka gave a simple answer that she was just curious about the little house that had been the place of a great worldwide hoax.

She simply just wanted to see the little house that had become so famous for a single day throughout the world with a huge audience witnessing one of the biggest hoaxes in modern times.

Samuel started to walk to the back door to the backyard.

Everyone followed Samuel silently, as if this might be an important moment, even though Shamieka claimed otherwise.

They went to the backyard to where the little house still stood.

Sleeping Beaver stood out in the open, several feet from the side of the little house as Shamieka acted like she was looking at the little structure with curiosity.

The FBI agents watched Shamieka silently with their own curiosity.

Finally, after several minutes of looking at the little house, and making no comments, Shamieka walked back over to Sleeping Beaver and stood next to him.

An FBI agent asked her if she was satisfied with what she had seen.

She answered calmly that she was in fact satisfied.

Shamieka hoped that Big Arch was nearby in the forest watching her and the other's in the yard.

Her hope turned out to be a reality.

Big Arch, Esher, and Augy had been waiting inside of the forest for almost two hours, hidden among the many giant redwood tree's... watching the backyard of Samuel's home.

After observing the humans from a distance, and seeing Shamieka and Sleeping Beaver in the backyard for several minutes, Big Arch told Augy that it was now time to return to his home to his Father.

Augy hugged Big Arch, and did the same to his best friend Esher.

He told his two Bigfoot friends that he would someday travel back to the mountains and visit them.

Both Bigfoot's cocked their heads from side to side in recognition of this friendly statement, and they actually had smiles upon their faces.

Yes... Bigfoot's could smile just like any human could, the only difference was that their smiles were much larger than any human could ever make on their face.

It was time.

Augy turned around and started to walk out of the forest towards the backyard of his house where the human adults still stood.

Chapter Sixty

S HAMIEKA WAS THE FIRST person to notice a movement at the edge of the forest.

She did not at first show any signs that she had noticed anything.

Moments later, Augy appeared out in the open outside of the towering redwood tree's.

Shamieka gasped openly.

Sleeping Beaver turned his head in the direction that Shamieka was looking.

He gasped as well at the sight of Augy walking towards the backyard fence to his home.

Seconds later Samuel and the FBI agents were also looking at the young boy walking towards them.

Samuel screamed out.

"Augy!! . . . my son!!"

Samuel started to run to the back gate of the yard.

Everyone followed behind the excited Father.

Samuel opened the gate to the backyard and ran towards his son.

He was openly sobbing with delight of this moment in once again seeing his son Augy.

He ran to the little boy and picked him up and held him in a loving embrace, crying into his son's shoulders.

Shamieka stood by a few feet away and simply watched in silence.

Sleeping Beaver and the FBI agents did the same.

Finally, Samuel let Augy down to the ground and held his hand and started to walk with his son back to the house.

As they walked back to the house, Big Arch and Esher witnessed the Father and son re-uniting with each other.

Big Arch put his arm around Esher's shoulder and pulled his son towards him and showed him some affection.

Big Arch understood how Samuel was feeling right now.

This was the same feeling that he himself had experienced when Esher had returned a few month's ago with the little human boy named Augy… forever a friend of the Bigfoot's of Humboldt County.

He turned away from the direction of the human house, and started to walk with Esher back to his own home.

Samuel, Augy, Shamieka, Sleeping Beaver, and the two FBI agents went back into Samuel's house.

One of the agents immediately contacted his boss and told him that Augy Goodson had returned, and they would question everyone present about this surprising development.

He told his boss that Augy appeared to be perfectly healthy as far as he could initially observe.

His boss told the agent to question everyone, and then return back to Eureka to inform the Sheriff's Department that Augy Goodson had returned home.

The FBI agents questioned all of the adults, but were not able to attain any new information about how, why, or where Augy had been all of this time.

They asked Shamieka to communicate with Augy by using the sign language, and when she did, Augy acted as if he did not understand what she was doing.

He was acting autistic again.

When they spoke to Augy, the only sound he made was garbled, and not understandable to the average person.

Finally, for the FBI agents, there was not anything else that they could do today.

They informed Samuel that they were going to contact the Sheriff's Department, and the local news media about Augy's safe return to his home.

After the FBI agents left, Sleeping Bear asked Samuel if he could try an experiment with Augy that was totally safe.

Samuel agreed to let Sleeping Beaver try his experiment.

Sleeping Beaver turned to Augy and pulled out of his pocket a baggy and a deer leather necklace with a medicine pouch on the end of it.

Sleeping Beaver knew that Augy could understand what he would say to him in English, even though the boy would not, at the moment be able to communicate back in the same language.

Sleeping Beaver spoke.

"Augy, in this baggy, I have some hair that I gathered from the Bigfoot's when we visited them one time in the past."

"I have a theory that there might be a chemical in this hair that is able to make you talk in English when you are exposed to it by smell."

"I want to put this hair in this medicine pouch and have you put it around your neck to see if my theory is correct."

"Would you do that for a friend?"

Augy surprised everyone and got up and left the room, he ran upstairs to his bedroom.

All the adults in the room were surprised by this.

Samuel asked Augy to come back to the living room.

Augy went to his bedroom to his dresser.

He opened a drawer and retrieved a ball of hair that he had stashed there when Esher had been here at his home in the little house in the backyard.

Augy put the ball of hair to his nose and whispered.

"I can talk."

He smiled very broadly.

He was happy.

Just as Samuel was about to go upstairs to bring Augy back to the living room, Augy appeared at the top of the stairs.

He ran down the stairs, and back to the living room.

He stopped in front of Sleeping Bear and opened his hand.

He showed the ball of hair to Sleeping Beaver and shocked all of the adults.

"He put the hair up near his nose and inhaled once… next?

He spoke.

"This is Esher's hair, I can talk!!"

Augy handed the ball of hair over to Sleeping Beaver.

Sleeping Beaver took the ball of hair, and along with the hair inside the baggy that he held in his own hands, he put both sets of hairs into the medicine pouch.

Once he did this, he handed the medicine pouch over to Augy.

Augy put the medicine pouch around his neck with a very large and obvious smile.

He started to talk up a storm for the next several minutes to the delight of his Father and the other two adults who were witnessing something very special.

To the delight of everyone that was witnessing this wonderful thing with Augy, It was now apparent that not only did the Bigfoot hair inside of the medicine pouch give Augy the ability to talk normally... English... but it also appeared that the little boy was completely normal as well.

He did not show anymore signs of withdrawing into an introverted state as he had always been.

Quiet? . . . not anymore.

He showed a focus of attention that had never been seen before by anyone.

This was comparable to that of a miracle.

But everyone who now watched the little boy in this transformation knew that it was definitely a scientific reason relating to the hair of the Bigfoot in the medicine pouch.

So the rest of the day was spent watching the young boy, and listening to him.

Shamieka and Sleeping Bear finally left Samuel's home, satisfied that everything had finally turned out well for everyone... humans, and the Bigfoot's.

Several days passed, and then it was finally decided by all of the authorities that had been investigating Samuel, that since there did not even appear to be any crime committed, they simply dropped the case and any further investigation officially ceased.

Life went back to normal for everyone.

As time passed into the future, Samuel settled into a different life.

He wrote a book on his exploit's concerning the pursuit of the Bigfoot primates, and in the book he told a story of a desperate man who was frustrated in not being able to prove that the Bigfoot's existed, so he had come up with a plan that ultimately turned out to be the infamous worldwide hoax.

After the book was completed, he spent many years thereafter concentrating on being a critic of the Bigfoot's existence.

Sleeping Beaver and Shamieka eventually parted ways and remained very close friends.

Sleeping Beaver eventually became a Shaman for his tribe and became a very well respected elder.

Shamieka eventually moved on from her cherished job in the Forestry Service, and moved out of Humboldt County to the Bay Area near San Francisco.

She went to work at a major International Airport doing Security screening.

She eventually moved up in the ranks and became a well recognized and respected supervisor.

She stuck to all her goals, and lived a happy life.

Crazy Mylo went back to the mountains and continued to do what he always did.

Finally… Augy Goodson grew up to become a well known figure in Humboldt County.

He eventually became a County Supervisor for the district that he grew up in.

The Bigfoot's… they continued to have a relationship with Augy as he grew into an adult.

Esher remained a very close friend to Augy and actually had a purpose that was very important for Augy.

It turned out that there was a chemical in the Bigfoot hair that when breathed in by Augy, it stimulated a part of his brain that made the Autism go away, and made Augy into a normal person.

This chemical only lasted for about a year inside of Augy's medicine pouch that he always wore around his neck.

A year after Augy started wearing the medicine pouch as a boy, the chemical finally evaporated and the Bigfoot hair did not stimulate Augy's brain anymore.

Samuel had quickly discovered this, and had asked Shamieka to bring Augy to the Bigfoot's and explain to them the importance of their hair that they would normally shed.

Big Arch understood what was explained to him, and asked his son Esher to always make sure that Augy had some hair so he could live a normal happy life.

So… Esher, a couple of times a year, would meet with Augy to spend time with him as a friend, and then give him a supply of fresh Bigfoot hairs to put into his medicine pouch.

Until Augy became a young adult, either Shamieka or Sleeping Beaver would take him to the Bigfoot area to meet with Esher.

Eventually, Augy started to make the trip's alone.

Life went on… as it always does… in Humboldt County, California… the most beautiful place on this planet we human's call Earth.